Borrowed Time

Authored by

Daryl Duwe

Robbie/
Thanks for
your friendship.

Enjoy

R Duwe

Published in the United States of America by Daryl Duwe

Available for purchase at www.lulu.com and through most on-line bookstores

Copyright © 2005 by Daryl Duwe

Cover design by Daryl Duwe using a photograph licensed by and purchased from www.shutterstock.com. Used with permission.

ISBN 1-4116-5475-7

For Yolanda

My editor
My wife
My life

1

Friday, September 5

He still wasn't used to it, this business of raining every day all summer long. After all, he grew up and spent most of his life in places where snow, not rain, was measured by the foot. Most people thought nothing of it. They jogged in the rain, walked their dogs in the rain, and even played golf in the rain. Not him. He stayed out of the rain.

And we're not talking a light drizzle here. No, sir. In Tallahassee, when it rains, it usually comes down with a vengeance.

So, of course, it was pouring like mad and Rip Snyder was getting antsy. It was Friday afternoon, five o'clock, and he wanted a beer. He had just put the finishing touches on this week's version of *The Ripper,* an Internet political newsletter that made him famous and infamous, loved and hated, admired and despised. He didn't really care what other people thought of him, as long as they thought of him at all.

Rip Snyder loved the limelight and the trench warfare aspects of modern politics. In fact, according to Rip, politics was nothing short of warfare. Us versus them, good against evil, Republicans versus Democrats, winner takes all. He was born a poor Iowa Democrat in all that cold and snow. But, by God, he was determined to die a rich Florida Republican.

The Ripper had started small, just a few hundred hard-core Republicans scattered across Florida with e-mail addresses. But Rip's ability to twist words into phrases that were funny to Republicans and mean-spirited to Democrats made *The Ripper* an instant hit. Just before lighting up a cigar and staring out the window at the rain, Rip had e-mailed the latest version to 78,203 subscribers, many of whom would gleefully forward it on to friends. He also posted it on his website, which is where most of the Democrats picked it up. They couldn't resist reading it, even though they hated it, or claimed to. They needed to know if they had been skewered by name or implication before hitting the bars. It was foolish for any high profile Democrat to show up at Klinger's, for instance, without knowing if he or she had been *Ripped*.

The Ripper was becoming so commonplace the major newspapers were even quoting it. *The Miami Herald, St. Petersburg Times, Orlando Sentinel* and *Suncoast Gazette* had all referred to items in *The Ripper* in political columns and editorials. Never kindly, of course, but that suited Rip just fine. They were all a bunch of worthless left-wing lug nuts as far as he was concerned and he often said so. Tit-for-tat.

Besides, the publicity had always been good for him. His subscriptions always went up after a good creaming by the mainstream press. Rip expected another smack from the *Gazette* soon, since he had just compared its editorial page to a communist manifesto. Well, I call 'em as I see 'em, Rip thought.

As the rain continued, Rip's thoughts turned from the *Suncoast Gazette* to Carrie Stevens, one of their top political reporters and columnists stationed in Tallahassee. They were opposites in so many ways. He was 40; she was 25. He hated Democrats; she hated Republicans. He was far right; she was way the hell left. They couldn't have a political discussion without hating each other, but the sex was incredible.

Rip and Carrie were trying to be secretive about it, but it was becoming more and more difficult. Tallahassee didn't qualify as a small town in the Iowa sense, but the political community was certainly small enough that secrets and rumors traveled at the speed of light. Rip often wondered if they would be discovered soon, or if people already knew and were snickering about it.

Jesus, would the rain ever let up? Thinking about Carrie made him even more anxious to get going to The Tapper, his personal Cheers. Everyone knew his name there, and the cute bartender, Nickie, would have his beer ready by the time he glad-handed his way to the bar. Besides, Carrie would be there, ready to ream him in public for the communist manifesto comment and do wonderful things to him in private. Yes, Rip was anxious.

And, just like that, the rain quit. Rip turned quickly away from his third-story office window overlooking the Chain of Parks with its magnificent live oak trees and Spanish moss. Off with the lights, lock the door, down the stairs two at a time. He walked quickly to his pick-up truck in the open parking lot. His truck was easy for anyone to spot. The tag proudly announced "RIPPER." If you cared to know his mindset, you could read the big, bright bumper sticker: "One nation under GOD. Don't like it? Bite my ass and leave."

Rip hopped in and started the always-frustrating 30-minute drive to the far north side of Tallahassee where The Tapper was located. There was always too much traffic because Tallahassee preferred trees to roads, and there were too many idiots because the city was thick with Democrats. He knew the traffic would be worse than usual, too. It was 5:30 p.m. on the first Friday in September and the Florida State Seminoles would open the football season at Doak Campbell Stadium tomorrow. The top religion was back in business.

So Rip fought the traffic, cussed the idiots, tossed a line of expletives at a group of black teenagers shuffling across Gadsden Street with their pants dropped down below their butts, and eventually pulled his truck into The Tapper's crowded parking lot just after six. Damn, he thought. He was too late to get a seat and would have to drink standing up.

Carrie Stevens was anxious, too. She knew Rip would be at The Tapper and she wanted to kick his ass. God, he could get under her skin. If they weren't so good in bed together she might just hit him over the head with a lead pipe.

"If you ever stop making the earth move for me," she could see herself whispering to him, "I'll hit you over the head with a lead pipe."

The thought made her chuckle. Some of her tension slipped away, and she printed out the latest version of *The Ripper* and filed it away, as was her habit. She had to give Rip credit. He could be a first-class jerk, but he also knew the political landscape as well as anyone. His newsletters were often the genesis of news stories or columns. Carrie had been filing them away long before she and Rip fell into bed together.

As she was tidying her small desk and preparing to leave the *Suncoast Gazette* office for The Tapper, the only other reporter in the bureau looked out the window and announced the news that the rain had stopped.

"I'm going to the Downtown Getdown," he said. "Wanna come along?"

"No thanks, Carl. I think I'll skip the madness this week."

"Got a date?" He sneered it. Carl was constantly inquiring about her dating habits and she didn't care for it much.

"Not with you."

"Not yet."

"Not ever."

"One of these days, Carrie. One of these days we'll be drinking with other reporters at The Pour House and you'll start lusting after ol' Carl."

With that, Carl was out the door. "Come by Klinger's later, if your date can't rise to the occasion," he called and let the door slam behind him.

What a prick, Carrie thought. Ugh. Carl Splighter was a slimy man. He always looked like an unmade bed, and she was convinced Carl could make a bottle of shampoo last a decade. She was forced to share an office with him in the press building, but nothing could make her socialize with him. Besides, she had Rip to deal with.

Carrie locked up the office and started her own tortuous trip from downtown Tallahassee to The Tapper. Most of the other members of the capital press corps would do their drinking at the Downtown Getdown, a local tradition. Every Friday night before a home Seminole football game, several of the downtown streets were blocked off under the theory that beer served in the street tasted better. Before long, the streets would be packed with rowdies in their garnet shirts predicting mayhem at Doak Campbell tomorrow and spilling beer. All of Rip's political friends would be there, too.

And that's why they each left offices located within a block of each other and two blocks from the Downtown Getdown to meet at The Tapper. None of the patrons at The Tapper were political insiders. Reporters didn't go there, either. The Tapper catered to the meatloaf and mashed potatoes crowd and frankly had too many regulars to make room for new customers. It was a good rendezvous.

Carrie and Rip always arrived in separate cars and always left separately. No signs of affection were exchanged; occasional eye contact was all that was necessary. There were no strangers at The Tapper. Every bar conversation was considered an open meeting and other customers would frequently chime in. Carrie would openly chide Rip over something in *The Ripper* and Rip would offer sympathy to Carrie's parents for being burdened with such a crazed liberal. Laughter was abundant, beer was plentiful, their secret secure. Or so they thought.

As Carrie started to leave the parking lot, she noticed her gas tank was almost empty. Crap! She had no interest in stopping at a gas station to fill up now; she was too anxious to get together with Rip. Carrie was actually going to whisper the lead pipe comment to him after they made love tonight. He might not laugh, but she would.

Carrie thought she probably had enough gas to make it to The Tapper. She could fill up after she left. She fought her way into the traffic and pointed her rusty Saab northward.

On her way, Carrie, too, noticed the group of black teens on Gadsden with their droopy pants showing off their underwear. What possessed them to do this? She didn't understand it, but she mostly shrugged it off. To each his own, she thought.

Carrie wondered if Rip had seen them. He had no tolerance for such things, she knew, and was very vocal about it.

"That's why some people call them niggers," Rip had said to her once. She was shocked to hear the n-word come out of his mouth so openly, and said so.

"I'm just saying," he reasoned. "If they didn't act that way, people wouldn't call them that."

One day, after watching several students amble out of Leon High School with their britches drooping low, Rip had exclaimed to Carrie, "Christ! Do these kids have any parents? Who would let their kids go to school like that? If somebody ran them over, would anybody care? Or would the world be a better place?"

"You should take an anger management class," Carrie had interjected, knowing it would set him off.

"Anger management, my ass! We'd be a lot better off if the people in Tallahassee could get angry at jackasses like those kids instead of whining about somebody trying to name a street after Ronald Reagan. What a screwed-up town."

Yes, Carrie agreed, it was a screwed-up town. But if your game was Florida politics or reporting on Florida politics, it was where you had to live.

Her gas tank was now below empty and Carrie was waiting to turn left into The Tapper's parking lot. She could see Rip's truck was already there. She was going to make it. There were plenty of gas stations nearby, so filling up later shouldn't be a problem. Rip was in there waiting for her, and she was anxious to kick his ass.

2

She could already hear Rip holding court as soon as she opened the door. Rip was standing with his back to her and had the attention of about half the bar. Nickie, the bartender, saw her first.

"Carrie! It's about time, girl. We were about to send out a search party."

Scratchy, from his assigned seat at the end of the bar, offered his usual smile and a wave.

"Now there's a sight for sore eyes," he offered. "You look great, Carrie."

As was her tradition, Carrie ignored Rip and went straight for Scratchy, giving the bear of a man a big hug, though her arms barely reached around him. Scratchy was part of the scenery at The Tapper. He was even on the menu: 'Best Rueben in Tallahassee. Don't believe us? Ask Scratchy.'

"Good to see you, Scratchy."

"What'll it be, girl?" Nickie was asking. "Beer tonight, or fruit drinks?"

It was an inside joke. For them, a fruit drink was a gin and tonic with a twist of lime.

"Yeah, Carrie, what'll it be? You gonna swill beer like the rest of us men or drink like a sissy?"

It was Rip, of course. She ignored him.

"I'll have a fruit drink." Carrie paused a beat. "And put it on asshole's tab."

She brought down the house. Even Rip was laughing as his fellow barflies slapped him on the back and congratulated him for being the first of the night to be called an asshole.

When the uproar died down, it was Carrie who seized the floor.

"I've got a bone to pick with you," looking directly at Rip for the first time. "I'd ask you to bend over so I could kick your ass, but I'm afraid I might lose my shoe in there."

More uproar from the assembled drinkers. They were enjoying this. Always quick with a retort, Rip started to say, "Why don't you bend over instead?" It would have been the perfect comeback, but there were lines they didn't cross in public. He caught himself just in time.

"Oh, yeah? What's got your panties in a bundle?" Rip knew, of course.

"Where do you get off calling the *Suncoast Gazette* a communist manifesto?"

"Well, gee, Carrie. Where do I begin? For starters, they endorsed gay marriage the other day, and gay adoption before that. They hate rich people, which is especially silly since most of their readers are filthy rich. They advocate a Robin Hood tax philosophy – take from the rich and give to the poor. Business owners are scum; the losers at the bottom who probably slept through school or didn't go at all are victims because we Republicans keep kicking them when they're down.

"I think their worst day was when the Soviet Union collapsed instead of annexing the entire Suncoast. How's that for starters?"

Before Carrie could respond, Roger, the professor at Florida State University who frequently spoke with passion about the finer details of the history of bourbon, interjected.

"Actually, Rip, there's nothing communist about gay marriage."

Jesus, Roger, have another bourbon, Rip thought. "What I mean is, the *Suncoast Gazette* is a liberal wasteland. Toilet paper for dogs and parakeets."

"Then that's what you should have called it," Roger announced. "And I'll have another bourbon, Nickie."

And so it went for another hour or so. They bantered and drank and philosophized. They predicted victory for the Seminoles tomorrow. Nickie was a good bartender, and she kept the drinks flowing without much prompting.

At about 7:30, Carrie's cell phone erupted.

"Better answer it, Carrie," Rip intoned. "It might be the Chinese government looking for a manifesto writer."

Most everyone was laughing except Carrie. She was looking at the caller ID. It was that sonofabitch Carl. What the hell did he want?

"Carrie Stevens here."

"Hi, Carrie. It's Carl."

I know, she thought to herself. She could hear the Downtown Getdown in the background.

"Where are you, Carrie?"

"Dammit, Carl, I'm not coming to Klinger's. I…"

"No, Carrie. It's not about that. Can you get to the airport in 30 minutes?"

"Jeez, Carl. I don't know. I'm way up in Killearn. What's up?" She walked outside into the parking lot once she realized the call was important and the slime ball wasn't hitting on her.

"I have a source who tells me Speaker Gonzalez will be arriving on a private jet from Miami a little after eight o'clock. And get this. He's supposed to be carrying a duffle bag full of cash."

"What do you mean, cash?"

"I mean cash, Carrie. Stacks of bills. Greenbacks. Serious juice."

"Why can't you go? You're a helluva lot closer to the airport."

"This is your story, kiddo. The cash is from the Indians. And I'm kinda drunk."

Christ. The gambling casinos. She was a little drunk, too, but this was hot.

"I'm on it, Carl. General aviation?"

"Right. And Carrie? We need a picture with him carrying the duffle bag."

She always carried a little digital camera in her purse.

"No problem, I'm gone." Carrie snapped her phone shut and quickly walked back inside to throw some cash at Nickie and leave. Then it hit her.

Her damn car was on empty! There was no way she could make it to the airport and she didn't have time to stop for gas. Hell, getting to the airport by 8:00 would require some serious speeding. Think!

Rip was watching her stand by the door and she caught his eye. He went over to her.

"What's up, Carrie?"

"I don't have time to explain, but I need your truck. My car is on empty and I need to get to the airport pronto. Can we switch? I'll meet up with you later."

Rip could see the urgency in her eyes. They switched keys. He thought he was helping a friend, a lover. But he might as well have thrown his keys down the toilet. He didn't know it, but that's where his life was heading.

Carrie left and Rip turned back to the bar.

"C'mon, boys. It's time for some serious drinking."

3

Carrie hustled into Rip's truck and cranked it to life. She roared out of the parking lot and jumped in front of the traffic at the stoplight on Thomasville Road. A few horns blared in protest, but she didn't hear them. Carrie Stevens had a chance to catch Speaker Gonzalez in the act of accepting a bribe – to hell with the traffic laws.

She quickly pushed Rip's truck to 60 MPH and was swerving around cars sporting their Seminole tailgate flags, grimacing with the realization that the truck didn't handle as well as her old Saab. Carrie roared southward past the entrance to I-10. It might have been faster to take the freeway to the west end of Tallahassee and curl around to the airport located south of town, but Carrie was already deep in thought about Gonzalez.

Speaker Gonzalez was from Orlando, part of a steadily increasing Latino presence in the Florida Legislature. The Republicans had courted him very heavily four years earlier as part of their highly successful effort to make inroads into the non-Cuban Hispanic population. Gonzalez convinced his GOP colleagues that the quickest way to get the attention of the Latino community was to put him on the leadership team. They elected him assistant majority floor leader during his freshman term. Two years later he was floor leader. When Speaker Robert Klegal resigned to run for attorney general, Alberto Gonzalez became the first Puerto Rican Speaker of the House in Florida history.

Carrie and the *Suncoast Gazette* had paid scant attention to Gonzalez at first, other than noting he was an example of the shrinking influence of the Democrats among Latinos. When he climbed the ladder and became floor leader, it was his assistant who was usually mentioned in political columns. Roxy Jones was far too attractive for her own good. She looked, acted and talked the way dumb blondes with big tits are supposed to look, act and talk. She went straight from being an average student at Florida State University to serving as Chief of Staff to Gonzalez.

The implication, of course, was that Roxy was "serving" her boss in more ways than one. The fact that she was pulling down $90,000 a year infuriated most of the political reporters. They often pointed out that Roxy Jones had posed semi-nude in a "Girls of the Atlantic Coast Conference" calendar. They sometimes used her picture to grab the attention of readers, the one with a lock of hair falling over one eye and her tongue licking her upper lip. They might as well put "ROXY BLOWS SPEAKER" in the headline.

Carrie refused to participate in such nonsense. For her own very personal reasons, she could not in good conscience fault Roxy Jones for either her past behavior or what she was doing with Gonzalez. Besides, it was Gonzalez Carrie was after, not Roxy.

Carrie flew through the intersection known as Five Points, where five streets converged in a crazy madness only Tallahassee natives could understand. The road narrowed and the traffic intensified. It dawned on her that she should have taken the freeway, but it was too late now. Maybe the speaker's plane would be a little late.

Carrie tried to mentally put herself on that plane, to figure out what Gonzalez was up to. Was he really flying to Tallahassee with a bag full of cash from an Indian tribe?

In some of her recent columns, Carrie had been kicking around the idea that Republicans in Florida were softening their opposition to expanding gambling in the state. Legislators were getting tired of saying no all the time but they didn't want to increase taxes. One answer, of course, was to expand gambling and rake in the revenues from the one-armed bandits.

Speaker Gonzalez had publicly repudiated such an idea, noting that Florida voters had twice rejected gambling referendums. He would kill any legislation to expand gambling, Gonzalez promised, and his colleagues took him at his word. Carrie had a few sources, however, who told her that Gonzalez was simply jockeying for the right position. That position, they confided, was to benefit personally by rigging the expansion to favor only one Indian tribe.

Nothing had yet appeared in print about this alleged arrangement, but if Carrie could get a picture of Speaker Gonzalez next to a private jet owned by the tribe in question, she knew her editors would go with it. If he was clutching a bag that certain "anonymous sources" claimed was full of cash, so much the better.

She ran a red light at the intersection of Monroe and College, just a block from where Carl Splighter was nervously checking his watch at the Downtown Getdown. She was thankful for the relatively light traffic on Gaines. It was almost 8:00, as Carrie turned left from Orange Avenue onto the unofficial shortcut to the airport, Lake Bradford Road. She had to hustle.

The "official" road to the Tallahassee Regional Airport bypassed Lake Bradford Road and took a longer route because some of the local residents had convinced Leon County to install speed bumps to keep the traffic away. Rip had often cussed a blue streak over the speed bumps. It always amazed him when some woman in the crowd would speak up in defense of the speed bumps. He would forever brand her as "another worthless lefty."

The speed bumps were designed to keep traffic slower than 20 MPH, but Carrie couldn't spare the time. Besides, she knew the bumps were a little less severe on the shoulders. She hit the first bump at fifty and swore. It was bad, but she could handle it.

It was a typical September evening in Tallahassee. After the downpour earlier in the day, the sun had returned and made everything steamy. It was still too hot and sticky to stay inside a trailer without air conditioning, but Jamal had come to visit. Belinda didn't want her three little angels listening in on their lovemaking, so she sent them outside to play.

"You girls go on outside and get some air while I have a talk with Jamal. Maybe later we can have some ice cream."

"Okay, Momma," Lakesha answered. At nine, she was the oldest and was accustomed to such arrangements. "Can we play on the swings?"

The swings were located down Lake Bradford Road at the church. It was where Lakesha and her two sisters, Shelanda and Lekweeza, liked to go when Momma entertained her visitors.

"Sure you can, sweetie. But be careful on the road."

Her three little angels bounced out of the trailer. She turned her attention to Jamal. It was the last time she saw her children alive.

"Hey, let's pretend we're following the yellow brick road!" Lakesha announced to her sisters. "The church can be Oz!"

"I get to be Dorothy!" claimed Shelanda, who was seven.

"What do I be?" wondered Lekweeza, who at four years old always looked to her sisters for her role in life.

"You be the lion, Weezie," Lakesha decided. "Can you roar like a lion?"

Lekweeza gave it her best shot, and they all laughed. With that, they hooked up arm-in-arm and started down the shoulder of Lake Bradford Road to the church, skipping along and trying to remember the words to "Follow the Yellow Brick Road."

Carrie's cell phone erupted again. She fumbled in her purse to get it, but it was caught on something. She pulled her purse open wider and looked in.

The speed bump caught her completely off guard. The force of the bump knocked the steering wheel out of her hand and jerked the truck to the right. Carrie looked up just in time to see her headlights capture the image of three black girls skipping arm-in-arm on the shoulder of the road. A scream caught in her throat. Panicked, her arms went rigid and she was unable to turn the wheel. Her right foot stayed on the gas. The only limb that seemed to move was her left foot, which reached for the clutch of her rusty old Saab and pressed uselessly against the floor of Rip's truck.

How can things that happen so fast take forever? The scream Carrie wanted to produce came out of her gaping mouth as a low groan. Her eyes met those of Lakesha as the truck slammed square into the three little angels at almost fifty miles an hour. She saw the violence, felt the rage inside her as Lekweeza's arms raised up in a hopeless act of defense against the speeding vehicle of death.

The horrified panic wouldn't go away; Carrie's senses refused to surface. The truck sped quickly off the Yellow Brick Road and into a small lagoon. Still stuck to the front of the truck due to the sheer speed and directness of the impact, the three little angels were pressed into the muck of the tiny lagoon, submerged beneath the squalid water.

The impact of the lagoon bank was finally enough to activate the airbags. At barely over five feet tall, Carrie's head was less than a foot away from the steering column. The exploding air bag snapped her head and neck violently backward. Her stupid cell phone finally quit ringing. The truck stopped moving. The three little angels were nowhere to be seen, and Carrie's world fell into blackness.

4

C arl Splighter closed his cell phone and looked nervously at Roy Fercal, the executive director of the Florida Democratic Party.

"She's not answering."

"It's a little after eight," Fercal noted, checking his watch. "She should be there by now. The speaker's plane should be landing anytime."

"I'm sure she's there," Carl lied. He'd never known Carrie to ignore her cell phone, even if she knew it was him. She would at least pick it up, say she's too busy to talk and tell him to bug off.

"She better not fuck this up, Carl. This is the story of a lifetime and I could have leaked it to anybody. I chose you guys over the *Herald* and the *Times* because you always shoot straight with me. But, honest to God, DON'T – FUCK – THIS – UP!" He punctuated each of the last four words with his most annoying habit – tapping Carl on the chest.

You weasel, Carl thought. He figured Roy chose the *Gazette* because he was trying to do what every man in town wanted to do – get inside Carrie's pants.

"Don't worry, Roy. We're gonna nail the speaker's ass to the wall."

Roy smiled at this and signaled for two more beers.

Speaker Gonzalez was a little nervous as the private jet landed at Tallahassee Regional and taxied to the general aviation hangar. He was an old hand at flying, and the jet was a lot smoother than the props he often got stuck with. Still, he had drained almost half a bottle of Johnny Walker Blue during the flight.

It wasn't the flying that made him nervous. It was his cargo.

Several times Gonzalez had unzipped the oversized duffel bag and fingered the cash. Two million dollars in neat little stacks of hundred dollar bills. Twenty thousand bills. Four hundred stacks of fifty bills each. He had done the math in his head over and over. It was more money than his ancestors had earned in a hundred generations, and it was all his.

But instead of gloating over it, he worried about it. What if it was a setup and the police were waiting to arrest him at the airport? What if someone stole it from him? Where would he keep it? He couldn't just waltz into SunTrust Bank and make a deposit of $2 million. How do the drug dealers handle large amounts of cash? He didn't know any, or he would ask them.

The plane rolled to a stop and Gonzalez, the only passenger, gathered his things.

"What's in the duffel? Is it heavy?"

It was the co-pilot, trying to be helpful, but Gonzalez jumped anyway. "No, it's fine. Just some dirty laundry. I got it."

"Okay, Mr. Speaker. Have a good evening. Watch your step."

"Thank you, sir. I enjoyed the flight."

Gonzalez was already sweating and the Tallahassee humidity didn't help much as he waddled toward his waiting car in the parking lot. Jesus, do they ever get a breeze around here? As he reached the car and stored the duffel in the trunk, the co-pilot hit a speed dial button on his cell phone.

He could hear the sounds of drinking and laughing on the other end, but there was no greeting.

"It's done."

"Did you parade him past the security cameras?"

"Of course."

"Excellent. Do you see a young woman lurking around?"

"No."

Damn! It's a good thing he had a backup plan. Lousy reporters.

"Good work. Watch your mail for a birthday card."

"Thank you." The co-pilot clicked off and watched as Speaker Gonzalez drove away.

"Dirty laundry, my ass."

R ip Snyder was just about getting his fill of beer. He drank it like water, so a good two hours of "pounding the bar with 12-ounce hammers" was pretty much his limit.

"Ring me up, Nickie."

"Okay, Rip. Do you want to pay Carrie's tab, too? She left without paying."

In that instant he knew his secret affair with Carrie was not a secret at all with Nickie. Hell, bartenders know everything.

"Uh, sure, Nickie. Why not? The poor little Commie probably can't manage her money. How much?"

"All together, it's fifty-four dollars."

"Jesus Christ! That's a lot of beer!"

"And fruit drinks, too. Don't forget; Carrie was on the hard stuff tonight."

Rip almost retorted with, "And she'll be on something harder later on." But, he caught himself again. He pulled out three twenties and a five and told Nickie to "keep the change, but don't change much."

Rip was initially startled when he walked into the parking lot and couldn't find his truck. Then, he remembered switching keys with Carrie. He wondered why she needed to get to the airport in such a hurry. It worried him a little; probably some politician about to get caught accepting a free flight to a football game or something. Rip was always amazed that reporters thought votes could be bought for something as cheap as a football ticket or a plane ride. It made him wonder how cheap it would be to buy a reporter's loyalty.

Thankfully, there was a gas station right across the street. Rip, after paying for Carrie's bar tab, was feeling cheap so he only put five bucks worth of gas in the old Saab and headed for home.

R oy Fercal stuffed his cell phone back in his blazer pocket and returned to the raucous crowd of drinkers outside of Klinger's. Carrie's failure to catch Speaker Gonzalez red-handed, if that's what happened, was going to complicate things. He was confident there would be some juicy security camera footage of Gonzalez clutching the loaded duffel bag, and that would be enough to reel in the ditzy television news crews. But it would be tough to make the story stick without getting the major newspapers involved first. He needed time to plan.

"Gotta go, Carl. I'll be in touch." Fercal fixed Carl Splighter with the dead, cold stare of a shark.

"See ya, Roy. Go 'Noles!"

"Yeah, go 'Noles."

Roy didn't care about the Seminoles, but it was dangerous to admit that publicly in Tallahassee. He was already walking swiftly toward his car, his mind working. What was the deal with Carrie? He couldn't, at this time, let Carrie know he was the source of the Gonzalez bribery story. It would spook her, and she'd be suspicious of his motives and start asking the wrong people the wrong questions.

The story needed to break first in a newspaper that was considered respectable by the other members of the press corps, but the paper's reporters and editors couldn't be too thorough. The *Miami Herald, Orlando Sentinel, St. Petersburg Times, Tampa Tribune,* and some of the others would pull too many loose strings and unravel the damn thing in the wrong direction. But if it appeared first and convincingly in the *Suncoast Gazette* and was followed up immediately by the major television stations and the security footage, the story would be off and running with "great legs." The radio talk shows would pick it up, especially the Cuban stations in Miami where the Cubans would be in full throat over a Puerto Rican politician caught taking a bribe.

The major newspapers wouldn't have time to do an exhaustive investigation of the story. In fact, the story wouldn't be, "Did he really take a bribe?" The story would be, "What are the Republicans going to do about it?" Gonzalez would have no choice but to resign in disgrace, becoming the new poster child for Republican corruption in Tallahassee. With any luck, Gonzalez would take a bunch of Republicans down with him.

The game was afoot; Fercal had every intention of winning it.

Confusion.

Carrie came to with no idea what had happened or where she was or why the front of her blouse was covered with blood. She was aware of a pounding pain in her face and head.

It slowly dawned on her that she must have been in some kind of a car accident, since she was in some kind of vehicle and her lap was covered by a deflated air bag. What the hell?

Carrie painfully unbuckled herself and swung the door open, scrambling to get outside. She promptly fell over, her feet splashing into the lagoon and her hands sinking into mud. Crawling on all fours out of the muck, she looked back at the vehicle with its nose wedged into the water. She didn't recognize it.

Carrie stumbled back along the path the truck had taken from the road to the lagoon. She saw a church nearby and there was a light on in the small frame house next to it. Head throbbing, mind numb, she ambled for it.

The Reverend Josiah Franklin had already been interrupted while working on his Sunday sermon by a strange noise. But when he looked out, all he could see was an empty road. He shrugged it off and returned to his desk.

So when a strange woman covered with blood and mud came banging on his office window, sobbing for help, he was doubly alarmed. Good Lord! It looks like the poor woman has been shot!

Josiah quickly went to the window and threw it open.

"My poor woman! Have you been shot? I'm getting help. I'm calling for help right now. I'll be right out. Help is on the way."

Josiah raced back to his desk, to the phone, and dialed 911.

"This is the Reverend Josiah Franklin at the Bradford Road Baptist Church. There's a woman at my door and I think she's been shot! Send an ambulance immediately!"

He didn't wait for a response or questions. Josiah hung up and turned to the window. The woman was staring at him in shock. "Hold on! I'm coming out to get you! Help is on the way!"

Oh my God, Carrie thought. Have I been shot? Am I dying? Who shot me?

Speaker Gonzalez had his air conditioning cranked up as high as it would go but the sweating wouldn't stop. He kept checking his rear view mirror, half expecting to see a patrol car signaling him to pull over. None came.

He decided to pass the usual shortcut with all its speed bumps and take the long way around. It was silly, probably, but the speed limit on Lake Bradford Road was only 20 miles per hour and he sure didn't want to get caught speeding with $2 million in cash bouncing around in his trunk.

Taking the bribe was the first really bad thing he had ever done, and he was starting to realize that being corrupt required a demeanor he didn't have. Maybe he should have turned it down, but Jesus! Two million bucks, just for the taking!

Slowly, his heart stopped racing and the sweating actually did stop. No one was after him; he was alone in his car with a fortune in tax-free cash. Alberto picked up his cell phone and hit speed dial number one. He and Roxy would hit the town tonight; watch the Seminoles beat the crap out of some slow team from up north tomorrow, and then party for the rest of the weekend. And, for once, he wouldn't worry about how to pay for it.

As he waited for Roxy to answer, the speaker's heart jumped into his throat. It was the cops! They were coming for him, lights flashing and sirens blaring, as two Tallahassee police cars raced southward directly at him. Please, God, no!

Gonzalez hung up the phone and jerkily pulled his car to the shoulder. He wanted to cry. His life was over. How could he be so stupid?

The cop cars raced past him, one after the other, and he waited for them to turn around and pull in behind him, guns drawn. They never did. Instead, they turned west on Orange Avenue. They were after someone else! Thank God!

Gonzalez took a deep breath and the stench of urine filled his nostrils. Christ, he had wet his pants. Speaker Gonzalez slowly gathered himself and, shaking badly, pulled back onto the road and headed for his apartment across from the Republican Party headquarters. He needed more Scotch -- and a shower.

The Reverend Josiah Franklin was praying, silently or out loud, he wasn't sure. He didn't know this woman. She wasn't a member of his flock or from the neighborhood, he was certain. She was white. But, Lord, she needed help.

Her face was a bloody mess, her nose all crooked. There was something that looked like a burn on her left cheek. Blood had run from her nose or mouth and soaked her blouse. She was muddy and smelled faintly of sewage.

He gathered her up, brought her into his house and got her to lie down on his sofa. It would be ruined, he knew, but somehow the Lord had directed this woman to him for help. He would do the best he could.

"I called for an ambulance. Help should be here soon. Just try to relax."

Carrie was still in shock, trying to comprehend what had happened to her and wondering if someone had shot her.

Josiah heard the sirens.

"Thank the Lord! Help is on the way, young lady. I'm going out front to meet them."

As he left, Carrie wondered if she was going to die. It made her cry.

Rip Snyder half expected to see his truck in his driveway when he turned off Killearney Way to his home on Langford Drive. Killearn Estates was an aging neighborhood, but Rip loved it. Ancient live oaks with Spanish moss were everywhere. Flowers were plentiful; the yards tended. And best of all, the Killearn Country Club was his backyard.

He knew it was wishful thinking to expect Carrie to be waiting for him, but he wished it nonetheless. Rip was disappointed as he parked the rusty old Saab in his driveway, picked up the mail and headed inside. The lovemaking would have to wait.

He found a leftover sandwich in the fridge, popped open a cold beer, and tried to find a baseball game or some other sporting event on TV. He settled for a tape-delayed broadcast of the European Tour on the Golf Channel. Hey, old golf is better than no golf.

5

The Tallahassee police cruisers pulled into the gravel parking lot of the Bradford Road Baptist Church to find a sweaty and worried Josiah Franklin.

"Where's the ambulance?" he asked, clearly confused. "I called for an ambulance."

"And you are...?" questioned the first officer.

"I'm the Reverend Josiah Franklin. I live here. This is my church."

"You said something about a shooting, Reverend?"

"Yes, officer. That's why I called for the ambulance. There's a woman on my sofa and I think she's been shot!"

"I'm sure the ambulance is on the way. Did you witness the shooting?"

"No. The woman showed up at my house all bloody and everything. I called for help and brought her inside."

"Well, let's get a look at her. Benson, call dispatch and check on the ambulance."

Officer Benson looked confused. "Uh, I think we're actually out of our jurisdiction here, Johnny."

Now it was Johnny Rickdale's turn to be confused. "What the hell are you talking about, Benson?"

"This part of Lake Bradford Road is outside the city limits. We're out in the county."

The Reverend Josiah Franklin was beside himself. "Good Lord! There's a woman bleeding to death on my sofa and you guys are worried about jurisdiction?" His voice was rising out of control, but he couldn't help it. What a night this was becoming.

"Reverend, I'm just sayin', we're out of our jurisdiction," Benson offered. "It doesn't mean we can't help, we just can't arrest anybody."

"GOOD GOD! I DON'T WANT YOU TO ARREST ANYBODY! I JUST WANT AN AMBULANCE FOR THAT POOR GIRL IN THERE!"

Rickdale could see Benson stiffen into a defensive posture. The kid had a lot to learn.

"Sir, we're here to help," Rickdale said in his best reassuring voice. "Benson, call dispatch. Check on the ambulance and tell them to notify the Leon County Sheriff."

Then Johnny turned to look directly at, and only at, Officer Benson. "And be sure to describe the situation fully and completely."

Benson understood the unstated meaning. They couldn't be sure of anything right now. Hell, the angry preacher might even be the shooter.

Rickdale turned to Josiah Franklin and said, "Let's go help the victim."

Officer Benson contacted the dispatcher immediately. "Where's the ambulance?"

"It should be there anytime."

As if on cue, Benson heard the first wails of a siren.

"Okay, I hear it now. But we've got a problem."

"What's that?"

"The crime scene is in Leon County, not Tallahassee. We don't have jurisdiction."

Damn. "That's my fault, officer. I thought it was in the city."

"Well, contact the Leon County Sheriff immediately. Tell them we have one shooting victim and they need to seal off the area. And the guy who called 911 might be involved, we don't know. Out."

Benson met the ambulance and pointed the emergency medical technicians to the house. "The victim is in there."

The medical crew hurried inside the house. Benson saw another vehicle pull up and he couldn't suppress a small grin.

"Hey, Jimmy. You damn near beat the ambulance again."

"I would have, but I pulled over to let 'em pass." Jimmy replied.

It was Jimmy Flain from the local paper. He'd been slaving away at the paper for almost thirty years, covering everything from crime to politics. And Jimmy could tell plenty of stories about "the twofers," when crime and politics intertwined. He was always friendly to law enforcement officers, in person and in his stories and columns. Don't bite the hand that feeds you, was Jimmy's way of thinking.

"What's up here, Benson? Did I hear something about a shooting at the church?"

"Yeah, looks that way. The victim is inside the house."

"Inside Reverend Franklin's house?" Jimmy's ears were really perked up now. He knew Josiah Franklin pretty well. The man was a quote machine when the blacks were marching or otherwise making headlines. "Is it the reverend?"

"No. Some woman."

"A woman was shot inside the reverend's house?" This was getting juicier by the minute.

"Slow down, Jimmy. The reverend says he found her outside, carried her in and called for help."

The medical team was wheeling Carrie out of the house toward the ambulance. Officer Rickdale wasn't at all surprised to see Jimmy Flain chatting with Benson.

"Hey, Jimmy. You didn't beat the ambulance, did you?"

"No, Johnny. Not this time." Jimmy was smiling. He enjoyed his reputation for racing to the scene. His smile disappeared, though, when he got a look at the woman on the stretcher.

"Oh, my God," he managed. "Is that Carrie?" All the reporters in Tallahassee knew each other, of course, and often gathered at Po' Boys for lunch. But the woman's nose was kind of crooked. He looked closer. Yep, it was Carrie.

"You know this woman?" Rickdale asked.

"Yeah, Johnny. It's Carrie Stevens – a reporter with the *Gazette*. Somebody shot Carrie? Out here?"

"No, it turns out she wasn't shot. Her nose is bent and there are burns on her face. I'd say she was in a car accident. But she doesn't remember anything."

"But she's going to be okay?"

"Yeah, she'll live."

The ambulance departed, siren wailing, but it was almost comical to watch as it moved ever so slowly over the speed bumps on Lake Bradford Road. At less than 20 miles per hour, what's the point of a siren?

Now it was Sheriff's Deputy Bill Bowser's turn to arrive at the Bradford Road Baptist Church. He was a big man, getting bigger every year, and everybody called him Bulldog. He was tough, didn't rattle easily, and didn't much care for all the damn Yankees who were finding out about the good life in North Florida.

As was his habit, Bulldog was cleaning his teeth with a toothpick and making little sucking sounds as he ambled over to the gathering of Jimmy Flain, Officer Benson, Johnny Rickdale and that pain-in-the-ass Reverend Josiah Franklin.

"I assume that was the shootin' victim the ambulance just hauled away," Bulldog said, aiming his words mostly at Rickdale because he knew Johnny grew up in nearby Woodville, which made him a local. Benson was some greenhorn from Rhode Island or Maine or one of them damn Yankee states.

"Yeah, that's the victim all right," Rickdale agreed. "But it turns out she wasn't shot, Bulldog. She was either beaten with an airbag, or we got a car accident to look for."

Bulldog pulled the toothpick out of his mouth and spit. "Then why in the hell was it called in as a shooting?"

Josiah Franklin hated this. He had panicked and overreacted, and now he was going to have to admit his mistake to this fat redneck.

"That was my fault. I saw all the blood and thought she'd been shot."

Bulldog stared at Franklin and enjoyed the moment. He let loose with a few more sucks on his teeth and announced, "Well, then I guess we don't need to seal off both ends of Lake Bradford Road and look for a goddamn shooter on the loose, now do we?"

Now eager to be helpful, Josiah remembered hearing the odd noise before the bloody woman showed up at his window.

"Hey, I just remembered something that might be important." Josiah had their attention, but Bulldog was wary.

"I heard a noise earlier and looked outside, but couldn't see anything. It came from down there." Josiah was pointing down Lake Bradford Road, to the south.

"Well, hell, let's check it out," Bulldog said. "There might be other victims." Then he turned to Rickdale and said, "You and the Yankee better let me take the lead. Y'all are out of your jurisdiction."

And off they went, with Bulldog, Benson and Rickdale fanning out with flashlights, Reverend Franklin praying their wouldn't be any other victims, and Jimmy Flain toting his camera to capture the carnage, though a shooting at the home of Josiah Franklin would have been a better story.

Bulldog hated looking into the dark recesses of roadways with a flashlight. It reminded him of the time several years ago when a carload of teenagers went careening off a dirt road south of the

Munson Slough. None of them were wearing seatbelts; three of them were found wrapped around tree limbs. Bulldog was a tough guy, but shining your flashlight on dead teenagers hanging from trees will rattle anybody.

"There it is!"

It was Benson. Bulldog was surprised the kid was the first to spot it.

Bulldog sucked harder on his teeth. "Must've lost control on the road and skipped right into the trees," he observed, though it was obvious to everyone.

The truck was sitting nose down in a small sewage lagoon, the kind meant to supplement a septic tank. The driver's door was open, the bloody, deflated airbag visible. The back of the truck was perched in the air. One of the flashlights caught the tag, and Jimmy Flain recognized it instantly.

"Ripper!" he exclaimed. "That's Rip Snyder's truck!"

"The guy they call Mr. Republican?" Josiah Franklin inquired. "That right-winger who writes that awful newsletter?"

"That's him," Flain confirmed.

Bulldog made his way to the truck and pointed his flashlight inside. "It doesn't look like there were any passengers," he announced. "At least there's no blood on the other airbag. Nothing but a set of golf clubs behind the seats."

Thank you, Jesus, Josiah thought to himself. No other victims. But why was the young lady driving Snyder's truck?

Bulldog reached in and retrieved what looked like an insurance card clipped to the visor of the truck. "Says here Rip Snyder lives on Langford Drive in Tallahassee."

"That's way up in Killearn Estates," Benson noted. "What's his truck doing way down here?"

"Well, I suspect the little lady was drivin' it," Bulldog responded, thinking what a dumbass this Yankee was. He handed Benson the insurance card. "Maybe you can take a little drive and ask him yourself."

Benson wasn't keen on taking orders from a sheriff's deputy, but Rickdale nodded his agreement. "Good idea. I'll help Bulldog secure the scene and such. Maybe this Snyder fella would like to be here when we tow his truck out of the muck."

A bright camera flash momentarily startled everyone, except Jimmy Flain. "Page one," Flain was grinning. "Above the fold."

The Reverend Josiah Franklin decided he wasn't needed anymore and started to make his way back to the house, where a mess was waiting to be cleaned up. Something occurred to him, and he turned back to the officers.

"Is it okay for me to clean up the blood and stuff in my house, or do you guys need to examine it?"

Bulldog pointed at the reverend with his toothpick. "You mean the scene of the shooting? Nah, I think we got that covered, hoss." Bulldog enjoyed a big laugh at the reverend's expense that eventually turned into a coughing fit and a big mouthful of hack that he spit on the ground. It was about half snot and the other half looked like some kind of glaze, perhaps from a long-lost Krispy Kreme.

While Bulldog admired it, Rickdale felt embarrassed for Josiah Franklin. "Reverend, shooting or not, you did real good by calling for help. Thanks."

Josiah nodded at Rickdale and turned for home. Lord, what a night.

Officer Benson pulled his cruiser in behind the Saab in front of Rip Snyder's stucco home. The lights were on.

Inside, Rip had dozed off in front of the golf tournament, something he often did. He heard a car door slam and figured Carrie had arrived.

"Finally," Rip said out loud, looking at the clock and noting it was after 10:30. In his slightly inebriated state, which was normal, he thought it would be funny to greet her at the door with his dick in one hand and a beer in the other. "Which do you want first?" he would ask.

But before he could grab a beer and undo his zipper, the doorbell rang. What the hell? She had a key. He looked outside and saw the police cruiser in his driveway. "This can't be good."

Rip opened the door and stood face to face with Officer Benson.

"Sir, are you Rip Snyder?"

"Yes. What's going on?"

"Do you own a 1999 Ford Ranger with a Florida vanity plate that says Ripper?"

"Yes." Now he was getting sick. "What's the matter?"

"It was involved in an accident."

Rip felt the world start spinning. What happened to Carrie?

"What kind of accident, officer? Where?"

"Were you driving that vehicle earlier this evening?"

"Yes, but I let a friend borrow it. Is she okay? Was anybody hurt?"

"Mr. Snyder, the woman driving your truck has been taken to a hospital. Her injuries are not life threatening. If you'll come with me, we'll see to it that your truck is retrieved from the scene."

Dear God. So Carrie is in a hospital and my truck is wrecked, Rip thought. Fucking great. It dawned on him that Carrie was probably a little drunk when she left the bar. Wow, this could be bad.

6

It was after 11:00 when Officer Benson and Rip arrived at the accident scene. Rip was dumbstruck when he saw his truck stuck head first in the lagoon. Then he saw the blood on the airbag and nearly lost it.

"Mr. Snyder, I assume your insurance is current," Bulldog stated, figuring anyone living in Killearn Estates wouldn't be a deadbeat.

"Yes. Of course."

"Good, 'cuz you're gonna have to pay for all this – the towing, the damages to the trees, the driver's medical expenses."

"Right. I'm covered," Snyder said, though he wasn't looking forward to explaining this to his insurance agent.

"Before we pull your truck out of that shit hole over there, I need to ask you some questions. Did you loan your truck to Carrie Stevens?"

"Yes, sir. She needed to get to the airport and her car was low on gas, so we swapped keys."

"Was she catching a flight? I didn't see any luggage."

"No, sir. I think she was working on a story. You know, for the *Suncoast Gazette*. I don't know any more than that."

Bulldog sucked on his teeth a bit and asked, "Where were you when you swapped keys?"

He's not as dumb as he looks, Rip thought. Rip knew the danger here, but he was a stickler for not lying to the cops.

"We were at The Tapper."

Bulldog considered this. "The bar part or the restaurant part?"

Rip felt his stomach sink. "The bar part."

"So you were drinkin', then."

"Yes, I was drinking." Please stop, Rip thought. No luck.

"And this Stevens girl, she was drinkin', too?"

Rip wanted to dive head first into the lagoon, shit and all. "Yes. She was drinking, too."

A big loud suck on the teeth: "My, my, my. Well, let's tow the fucker out. I'm gonna call in to get a blood sample from the little lady."

Rip closed his eyes and offered up a silent prayer that Carrie's blood wouldn't test beyond the legal limit. Jesus, he thought, I've driven drunk a zillion times. Carrie doesn't deserve this.

Rip, Officer Benson, and Johnny Rickdale watched as the tow truck operator hooked the chain to the pickup and went back to the tow truck to start the winch. Bulldog had moved his cruiser from the church parking lot the short distance to the scene and was on the radio, ordering the blood work on Carrie Stevens. Jimmy Flain was long gone, anxious to put Rip's truck on page one.

Rip grimaced as the winch went to work. It sounded like his truck was going to snap in half. But no horror movie or nightmare could prepare them for what happened next. With the pickup truck groaning, the front rose out of the mucky water, hauling three little black girls up with it. The girls were hooked in the grill and on the bumper. Their heads lolled and their eyes looked frightened even in death.

"Dear God in heaven!" Rip blurted, then turned away.

Bulldog heard him and turned to look. The dead eyes of Lekweeza, though he didn't know her name, stared straight at him.

"Christ almighty!" he said, and promptly vomited his supper onto one of Lake Bradford Road's infamous speed bumps, toothpick and all.

7

Rip couldn't bring himself to look. He was turned away, leaning into a palmetto tree, trying to erase the scene from his head. It wouldn't go away. Jesus Christ. What the hell had happened?

Rickdale was doing his best to assess the scene in a professional manner, but he, too, was badly shaken. The tow truck operator was staring, wide-eyed, at the grisly sight. He had kept it together long enough to stop the winch.

Bulldog was turned away, more out of embarrassment for puking than anything else. This was bad.

"Boys," Bulldog began, surprised at the shake in his voice, "looks like we got us a vehicular homicide – times three." He was regaining control. "Mr. Snyder, I'm afraid we're gonna have to impound your truck. Johnny, would you please escort Mr. Snyder away from the wreckage. I need to call the coroner."

The Reverend Josiah Franklin decided to leave the bloody mess around the sofa for Saturday morning. He was beat and just wanted a hot shower.

He was completely lathered up when he heard his phone ringing. What now? Who would be calling him at 11:30 at night? He could just let it go, but preachers don't have that luxury. Somebody from his flock might need help. Soapy and dripping wet, he scurried to the phone in his bedroom.

"Hello?"

"Reverend? I'm sorry to call so late. It's Belinda."

Belinda, from down the road. Beautiful Belinda. He was suddenly, and rather oddly, aware of his nakedness.

"Belinda? No, it's okay. I was up." And you wouldn't believe what I've been doing, he thought. "How are you, Belinda?"

"Well, Reverend, uh…are my girls still playing on the swings?"

Josiah had gotten used to seeing Belinda's girls on the swings, and other kids from the neighborhood, too. He liked it. The sound of children laughing was as good as music to Josiah.

"Why, no, Belinda. I haven't seen them all night."

The words ripped into Belinda like a saw blade. She had felt guilty enough when Jamal had finally gone; she had to shoo him off. It was the first time she had looked at the clock.

"Oh, my God. Reverend…"

"What's wrong? Belinda? Is something the matter?"

"My angels. I can't find my angels…" her voice drifted away, and Josiah could hear her crying.

What is it about this night, Josiah wondered. "Belinda? When did you last see them?"

"I don't know, exactly," she sobbed. "They went out to play. And Lakesha said they was gonna play on the swings."

Josiah was thunderstruck. It couldn't be, he thought. Please, God, not this. But he already knew something had gone awry between Belinda's trailer and the Bradford Road Baptist Church. Holy Jesus.

"Belinda, I need you to calm down." Was he talking to her, or to himself? "I'll be there in a little bit and we'll get this figured out. Just sit tight."

"Thank you, Reverend."

Josiah quickly toweled off and threw on a pair of jeans and a tee shirt. As he stepped out of the house, he could see there was still activity down at the crash scene. Good God, I hope I'm wrong.

As he hurried down the road to the scene, Josiah was confused by what he saw. The truck was perched oddly, half in and half out of the lagoon. The headlights of the redneck deputy's cruiser illuminated the scene, and the shapes didn't make sense. Then he got close enough, and nothing made sense, nothing at all.

He fell to his knees and couldn't stop the tears. "Oh, dear God, why? Why? Why did you take these three little angels away? Why?" He squeezed his head with his arms, trying to gain control of himself. Belinda needed him now, more than she knew. He would be the one to tell her. God, at least give me the strength to do this, he prayed.

"Reverend?" Bulldog was standing over him. "Do you know these kids?"

"Yes, I know them," he said, haltingly, looking forlornly in the direction of Belinda's trailer. "I know their mother. She's in my flock."

Josiah looked directly at Bulldog. "She just called me. She can't find her kids."

"Aw, Jesus. We'll need her to, you know, identify the bodies."

"No. It's them."

"Well, where does she live? I'll need to go tell her."

"No. I'll tell her. It's gonna be bad, but maybe it'll be easier coming from me."

The Reverend Josiah Franklin started the lonely walk to Belinda's trailer. He prayed for God to give him the right words.

Traffic was light on Lake Bradford Road; it was getting on towards midnight. A car pulled up behind Bulldog's cruiser and he figured it was the coroner, but it was Jimmy Flain.

"Did I beat the coroner?" Jimmy asked as he popped out of his car.

"Jesus Christ, Jimmy. Is this some kind of game with you?" Bulldog growled. "Yes, you beat the coroner. The sonofabitch must've been sleepin'."

Jimmy couldn't see around Bulldog's big body. "So, did you find another victim? A dead one?"

Bulldog wondered if Jimmy Flain would throw up when he saw it; he hoped so. He sucked his teeth a little bit and stepped aside.

Jimmy's hand flew to his mouth as he turned away. His half-digested Whataburger went spraying over the hood of his car.

Attaboy, Bulldog thought; join the club.

"Leave your camera in the car this time, Jimmy," Bulldog advised. "We don't need this picture floatin' around the Internet."

Jimmy could only nod.

The Reverend Josiah Franklin approached Belinda's run-down trailer with a growing dread. He had plenty of experience comforting members of his congregation who had lost family members, but he had never told anyone their three children were dead. He could feel his own sorrow deep in his bones; he wondered if Belinda could even survive it.

"Dear, beloved Jesus," Josiah whispered as he knocked on the door, "Please help us all."

It was obvious Belinda had been crying when she opened the door. Her eyes were wide with fear. She took one look into the eyes of Josiah Franklin and let loose with a shriek, stumbling backwards into her living room sofa.

"My babies! My babies! Oh my God!" Belinda was sobbing so hard she was having trouble breathing. Finally, all that came out was a horrifying wail.

She must have read it on my face, Josiah thought. He rushed to her side and held her. Belinda's tears flowed like the Tallahassee rain, mixing with his own. They rocked back and forth and he tried his best to console her. But the tragedy was too real; the grief was too thick. At some point, Josiah knew, Belinda would calm down enough to ask what happened. He would tell her, and the wailing would write another chorus.

This was by far the worst night of Josiah Franklin's life, and he wasn't the one who lost three beautiful little girls.

8

Saturday, September 6

The phone was ringing and Rip Snyder didn't like it one damn bit. What the hell time is it – 6:30 in the morning? Who was calling at this ungodly hour?

Rip fumbled for the phone and brought it to his ear. He was in the mood to fill somebody's head with a long string of four-letter words.

"What?" was all that came out of his mouth.

"Good morning, Poster Boy!"

Aw, shit. It was Bannerman Lux, his lawyer. Everybody called him Lucky.

"There's nothing good about this morning, Lucky. And what are you doing calling me at 6:30 in the morning?"

"One of these days, Ripper, when you actually take my advice and find out how good it is, you'll thank me. Until then, you keep providing me with clippings for my scrap book."

"What in the living hell are you talking about?"

"Remember, about a year ago, I told you to get rid of that damn vanity plate of yours and get something nobody can remember, like T35VRG or some other nonsense? In case you go speeding through a school zone or something, people won't remember your license plate. You remember that, Ripper ol' boy?"

"Vaguely. I like my vanity plate. And why are you annoying me with this so early in the morning?"

"I take it you haven't read the morning paper, Ripper Boy."

Damn. The awful night came flooding back in a rush. The accident. The newspaper. Shit.

"I take your silence as a no," Lucky observed. "Go get the paper out of your driveway and call me back. I have a feeling we need to talk."

Rip hung up and wanted to puke. Officer Benson had given him a ride back to the house after the three dead girls were discovered hanging from the front of his truck. Rip wanted to go to the hospital and check on Carrie, but Bulldog had expressly forbid it.

"We got us a criminal investigation here, Mr. Snyder," Bulldog had spewed at him. "Until I get a chance to question this Stevens girl myself, you stay the hell away from her." For good measure, Bulldog called his dispatcher and told her to call the hospital and tell them that under no circumstances was Rip Snyder to be allowed to visit Carrie Stevens.

Rip had been back inside his house for no more than thirty seconds before he was pouring a tall glass of straight vodka over ice. Two more glasses had finally done it, and Rip stumbled to his bed and more or less passed out about 2:30.

His stomach was roiling, his head was throbbing and his heart was in his throat as he walked out to the driveway to retrieve the local paper. The stupid paperboy, who was actually a greasy looking man who flung the papers out the side of a dilapidated Grand Tourino, had managed to put the paper underneath Carrie's rusty old Saab.

The throbbing in his head quadrupled as Rip bent down to get the paper. He removed it from the yellow plastic cover and unfolded it.

"Stupid son of a shit-ass bitch!" It was his profanity of choice when something really pissed him off. He must have said it pretty loud because some do-gooder down the street who was putting his recycling bin at the curb looked up at him and scowled.

Rip didn't care. He was staring at a full-color photograph of his truck sitting head first in the lagoon. It was front page, above the fold. Centered across the top of the picture was a headline in bold print: Late Night Drink. The clarity of the picture was impressive, and Rip's beloved vanity plate was plain as day: RIPPER.

Rip's bloodshot eyes moved to the cut line: *Leon County authorities are investigating this accident on Lake Bradford Road. The truck "drinking" from a sewage lagoon is registered to Rip Snyder, 40, of Tallahassee, a top GOP strategist and consultant. A woman who was injured was taken to Tallahassee General Hospital.*

Is that it? Rip quickly looked through the rest of the paper; he saw no mention of it. Of course, he thought. The gory stuff wasn't discovered until it was too late to get it in the paper. The photo was credited to Jimmy Flain.

Well, Jimmy's having fun sticking it up my ass, Rip realized. And Rip knew how the whole thing looked to those who didn't know the rest of the story: Rip gets drunk, wrecks truck, and a woman with him goes to the hospital. "Stupid son of a shit-ass bitch," he said, quieter this time, and went inside to call Lucky.

"Good morning! This is Bannerman Lux."

"You can knock off the good morning shit, Lucky. I'm having a bad day."

"Well, Rip, that's perfectly understandable. Are we facing a drunk driving charge this morning?"

"No, 'we' are not. I wasn't driving the truck, Lucky. Hell, I wasn't even in it. I loaned it to a friend and she wrecked it."

"Some friend. Anyone we know? Was she hurt bad?"

"They took her to the hospital, but they told me it's not life threatening. They won't let me visit her."

"Does the mysterious lady have a name?"

"It's Carrie Stevens, Lucky, a reporter for the *Gazette*. We're friends."

"Ah, I see. So she borrows your truck, wrecks it, and ends up at the hospital. Not too bad. I was afraid we were facing something serious."

"Uh, that's actually not the whole story, Lucky," Rip offered, searching for the right words. "When Carrie wrecked the truck, she apparently ran over three little girls. Killed all three of 'em."

"Jesus, Rip! A woman kills three girls while driving your truck. Now it *is* serious." Lux pondered this for a moment. "Let's see. It was Friday night, so we know you were at The Tapper. We can assume this reporter friend of yours was there with you. So can we also assume she had been drinking before you loaned her your truck?"

"Yes, Lucky. We were drinking."

"Dammit, Rip! This could get ugly. Listen, under no circumstances are you to admit to anyone that you knew this woman had been drinking. No one! Understood?"

Rip was rubbing his eyes instead of answering, feeling stupid.

"Aw, dammit, Rip. Who'd you tell?"

"A deputy sheriff."

"What!?! Are you completely stupid? How many times have I lectured you on never talking to the cops without me there ..."

"I didn't think it was any big deal! Look, Lucky, I didn't do anything wrong! I loaned my truck to a friend and she wrecked it. End of story."

"No. You loaned your truck to a drunk and she used it to kill three innocent victims. That puts you in the crosshairs. Listen carefully, Rip. No more talking to the cops without me. Got it?"

Rip issued a heavy sigh. "Got it, Lucky."

"If anyone calls, refer them to me," Lux advised. "And that includes the press."

9

Carrie Stevens woke up in a cold sweat. Her memory of what happened on Lake Bradford Road was as clear as a bell. It had started coming back to her in the ambulance. Aside from the sickening realization that she had run over three kids was the fear of the many legal repercussions, so she was faking amnesia. She didn't know if it was a good legal strategy, but she needed to buy some time.

The scene kept replaying itself in her mind; she couldn't forget now if she wanted to. Three girls were dead and it was entirely her fault. She had been speeding, drinking, and distracted by her cell phone. Her ass was grass.

In the ambulance, the medical technicians had assured her she had nothing life threatening. The doctors admitted her for observation because of a possible concussion and the apparent short-term memory loss. Then they came and drew blood before giving her a sedative. What time was it now, she wondered? Daylight.

Maybe she should call Rip. God, did he even know? She looked around for a phone; there was none.

The door to her room opened and a big, burly sheriff's deputy wearing an enormous green uniform waddled in. He was cleaning his teeth with a toothpick.

"Good morning, Miss Stevens. I'm Deputy Bill Bowser with the Leon County Sheriff's Department, but everybody calls me Bulldog. How are you feeling this morning?"

"My face hurts."

Bulldog sucked on his teeth and barked a staccato burst of laughter. "I'm not surprised. Hell, it hurts to look at it. How did that happen, by the way?"

"I don't know. I don't remember."

Bulldog grunted and pulled a good, long, sucking whistle through his teeth. Carrie thought he sounded like a hamster an old roommate used to keep.

"I need you to try real hard to remember, Miss Stevens. You see, I got some mighty important questions to ask you, and I don't want to feel like I'm talkin' to a potted plant."

"I've been trying to remember what happened, but I can't. The guys in the ambulance told me I was in some kind of car accident or something, but that's all I know."

Bulldog stared at her hard. "I see. Well, what's the last thing you do remember?"

Danger, she knew. Be careful.

"Uh, I remember being at work, and locking up the office. Then, I guess, I was driving home."

"Do you remember what time that was?" He was using his tongue to rotate the toothpick around in his mouth.

"Well, it was raining, and when it quit raining, I left. About 5:30, I think."

"Where do you live, Miss Stevens?"

"I have an apartment in Killearn Plantation, up on the north side."

"I hear you work for the *Suncoast Gazette*. That true?"

"Yes, sir. In the press center, downtown."

"So when you leave work and drive home, you head north. Some pretty heavy traffic, I'll bet."

"Yes, sir. You get used to it."

Bulldog sucked his teeth some more and continued to stare at her. "I know some folks who like to let the traffic thin out a bit before they tackle it, so they stop off at a bar or something before heading home. Did you do that last night?"

So, Carrie thought, he suspects I was drinking last night. More danger. "No, sir."

He shifted gears. "Does anybody work with you at the *Gazette*, down there at the press center? You know, someone who could help jog your memory?"

"Uh, yeah. A guy named Carl Splighter. He's another reporter."

"You got a number for Mr. Splighter?"

Carrie rattled it off without thinking.

"You got a good head for numbers, Miss Stevens," Bulldog noted as he pulled the toothpick out of his mouth and pointed it at her. "I hope your memory for other things comes back soon."

"Me, too. It's scary not remembering things."

Bulldog grunted again. "Yeah, I'll bet." He turned to leave but spun back around holding his toothpick high in the air. "Do you know a fella named Rip Snyder?"

The mention of Rip's name hit Carrie hard. She couldn't help but widen her eyes and swallow hard.

"Uh, sure. Everybody in my business knows Mr. Snyder. Why – why do you ask?"

"You two pretty friendly, are ya?"

Carrie was avoiding his stare. "Well, I guess so. We get along all right. What does Mr. Snyder have to do with anything?"

"Oh, I've got some questions for him, too, and I thought maybe you had his phone number up in that pretty little head of yours."

"Sorry."

Bulldog pulled the toothpick out of his mouth again and examined something on the point, something he had picked out of his teeth. He flung the toothpick into a nearby trash can. "Keep trying to remember what happened, Miss Stevens. We'll talk later."

Carrie sunk deeper into the pillows and closed her eyes as Bulldog left. She saw the horrible moment she impacted the girls, and opened her eyes back up again. She preferred the image of a fat redneck displaying a tiny piece of breakfast on the end of a toothpick.

Roy Fercal had a worried look on his face as he walked to the end of his driveway to retrieve the morning paper. His mission to bring down Speaker Gonzalez had been made more complicated by the failure of Carrie Stevens to catch the bastard in the act of hauling home his ill-gotten loot. It could still work, but he didn't like complications.

His mood brightened, though, when he extracted the local paper from the protective plastic covering and unfolded it. He actually burst out laughing upon seeing the picture of Rip Snyder's truck sitting nose first in the lagoon. Roy punched the air with a fist.

"Yes! Now you'll get yours, you fucking sonofabitch!"

Such language, thought Hilda Scranton, who at the age of 75 liked to spend Saturday mornings quietly tending to her flowers across Magnolia Drive from Fercal's house. She remembered when people with manners occupied this part of Tallahassee. "Now the whole damn neighborhood is going to hell," she muttered to herself.

Roy was oblivious to the Widow Scranton and anybody else. He was walking on air back to his house. His mind was plotting the end of Rip Snyder.

Rip was a major thorn in the side of most Democrats, but especially Roy Fercal. Every time Snyder mentioned Roy in *The Ripper*, Roy's name was intentionally misspelled as Roy "Fecal." Worse yet, the headline always alerted readers to "Fecal Matter."

Well, who's in the "Fecal Matter" now, you worthless jackass? The news that Snyder had apparently gotten drunk and wrecked his stupid truck hit Roy like Christmas in September. He wondered who the girl was and how badly she was hurt. He hoped it was scandalous, like maybe she was giving him a blowjob when they wrecked. Oh, baby, this was going to be fun!

C arl Splighter's head hurt, even more than usual. He always had some kind of a hangover on Saturday morning, but this was a doozy. The first Downtown Getdown of the year; he always overdid it.

He was trying to brush the crappy taste out of his mouth when the phone rang.

"Hello?"

"Is this Mr. Splighter? Mr. Carl Splighter?"

"Yes, who's this?"

"Sir, this is Deputy Bill Bowser with the Leon County Sheriff's Department. I'm calling about a co-worker of yours, a Miss Carrie Stevens."

Jesus Christ. What now? "Uh, yes sir. Is she, uh, is she okay?"

"When did you last see her or talk to her?"

What was that noise? It sounded like the deputy was sucking on something.

"Late yesterday afternoon, at the office. What's the matter? Is she missing or something?"

"And that's the last time you talked to her, Mr. Splighter?"

Carl wasn't about to get into any details about his phone call to Carrie last night or her failure to answer his second call, not without knowing more.

"That's right, Deputy. Are you gonna tell me what's going on?"

"Mr. Splighter, Miss Stevens was in a car accident last night and she says she doesn't remember anything. I'm trying to piece together what happened."

"Is she all right?"

"She's at Tallahassee General Hospital with a busted nose."

"That's awful!"

"Yeah, and her memory ain't worth a damn either," Bulldog groused. "Do you know a fella named Rip Snyder?"

What the hell? "Yes, I do. The Republican guy. Why do you ask?"

"Did you happen to see them together last night?"

The thought of Carrie dating Rip Snyder kind of pissed Carl off. That must be where she went after work.

"I don't know anything about Carrie being with Snyder."

"Okay, Mr. Splighter. Thank you for your help." The sucking noises stopped when Bulldog hung up.

So, Carl thought. Carrie was with Snyder last night when he called her about Speaker Gonzalez. Then she wrecked her car on the way to the airport and that's why she didn't make it in time.

There was a slow burn in Carl's gut – jealousy or anger or both – as he pictured Carrie with that right-winger. Well, he'd better go visit Carrie. It was his duty as a co-worker, if nothing else.

Carl thought about washing his hair first and decided against it.

S peaker Gonzalez hadn't slept much. It took a lot of Scotch to settle his nerves after thinking the cops were after him. Then, as he lay in bed, he jumped at every sound. The duffle full of cash was stuffed under his bed.

Now, sipping coffee with a couple fingers of Kahlua in it, he was pondering once again what he was going to do with all that cash. Jesus, who could imagine that having two million bucks in cash would be a *problem*?

He thought about opening different accounts at several banks, spreading it around. He knew the IRS was notified of all cash transactions amounting to $10,000 or more. What if he made several transactions at, say, $5,000 each? Would the IRS find out? He didn't know.

What if he made a $5,000 cash deposit at the SunTrust branch on Monroe Street, than another $5,000 cash deposit at the branch out on Appalachee Parkway? Would SunTrust total them as $10,000 and notify the feds? He didn't know that, either. He needed answers to so many questions, but without arousing suspicions.

Jesus, life was easier when all he had to worry about was getting it up for Roxy.

Alberto had punted his plan to get together with Roxy last night after wetting his pants and damn near crapping in them, too. He needed to call her later and take her to the football game. He wondered if he should take her into his confidence on the cash. He was currently leaning against it.

He went for more coffee and Kahlua and decided to go online and read the clips. The Republicans paid for a subscription to a service that clipped every political story from all the Florida papers and put them in a package. All the big hitters, like Speaker Gonzalez, had access to it. The online clips were certainly more convenient than sifting through a stack of actual newspapers, and sometimes the online stories contained information that was too late for the printed version.

There was the usual stuff. A Democrat from Miami was threatening a lawsuit over disparities in education funding. In Orlando, the mayor was forming a committee to explore running for Congress. Kind of early, seeing as how the ballot for this November was already set and the next election after that was 27 months away.

Then he almost choked on a swallow of coffee. The linked headline read: "GOP Heavyweight Involved in Deaths of Three Girls?" Alberto read the teaser with wide eyes: *"Leon County authorities are investigating the tragic deaths of three young girls. All three were run over and killed along Lake Bradford Road by a truck registered to well-known Republican kingpin Rip Snyder, 40, of Tallahassee. The identities of the victims have not been released. Authorities are at a loss to explain why…"*

To read more, Speaker Gonzalez had to click the link. On his browser was a full-color picture of Rip Snyder's truck nose-first in a lagoon. He picked up the rest of the story.

"Authorities are at a loss to explain why the crash occurred or how Snyder's truck managed to run over the little girls, ages 9, 7, and 4. They refuse to confirm or deny if alcohol was involved.

"The apparent driver, Carrie Stevens, 25, of Tallahassee, was taken to Tallahassee General Hospital by ambulance. Her injuries are not believed to be life threatening.

"Authorities say Stevens managed to leave the scene of the accident and seek assistance at the home of Reverend Josiah Franklin, 52, of rural Tallahassee, who notified authorities."

Good Lord, what a tragedy.

Alberto's thoughts about the poor little girls quickly shifted to his own problems. Snyder's political consulting company, The Ripper Group, was on his campaign payroll. He would have to be dumped; Gonzalez didn't want the bad publicity.

Now, what in the hell was he going to do with all that cash?

10

C arl Splighter nearly drove off the road when the local NPR station switched from Weekend Edition to the local news.

"Three small girls are dead following a car accident near the Tallahassee airport overnight. The identities of the girls have not been released. Leon County authorities say the driver, 25-year-old Carrie Stevens of Tallahassee, is hospitalized. The investigation continues. Authorities say they are trying to determine why Stevens was driving a vehicle registered to well-known GOP operative Rip Snyder of Tallahassee. And they say alcohol may have been involved.

"In other news, a sellout crowd in excess of eighty thousand is expected at Doak Campbell Stadium today…"

The news continued, but Carl didn't hear it. Jesus! Had Carrie really killed three kids in that accident? And she was driving Snyder's truck to the airport instead of her rusty old Saab? Why? Snyder must be into her pretty deep. A reporter dating such a high-profile Republican would not sit well in the corporate offices of the *Suncoast Gazette.*

The part about the drinking barely registered with Carl. It was the Friday night before the first home football game; who *wasn't* drinking in Tallahassee?

Carl kept trying to come up with logical reasons why Carrie was driving Snyder's truck on her way to the biggest story of her life, and he couldn't find any. She had some explaining to do.

B ulldog was on his way to the office of the state's attorney when the Krispy Kreme a block away turned on the neon sign that said "Hot Doughnuts Right Now." You might as well wave a steak in front of a lion.

He pulled in and bought two-dozen glazed. He'd take one dozen into the state's attorney's office and keep the other dozen in the front of his cruiser to keep him going until lunch.

Three of the little treasures were gone from his personal stash by the time he pulled in front of the state's attorney's office downtown. Bulldog inserted a new toothpick into his mouth and carried the other box of doughnuts in with him.

"Hey, Jess," Bulldog called, "have you had breakfast? I stopped off for a dozen. They're good and hot."

"Thanks, Bulldog; maybe later. But don't let me stop you."

"Don't mind of I do." Bulldog helped himself to another glazed, storing his toothpick in his breast pocket for later. The doughnut was gone in three bites.

Jessie Malloy watched with amusement. Bulldog could really put it away.

Jessie had been the state's attorney in Leon County for five years now. She had a good relationship with all the law enforcement officers. She had great respect for them and, in return, the officers appreciated her tough demeanor toward the people they arrested. In fact, she knew her supposedly "secret" nickname was "Jailhouse Jess," and she liked it. Let the bastards rot was her philosophy.

Malloy had won re-election this year without spending a cent or campaigning at all. When filing for office had closed, the local

Republicans hadn't even fielded a candidate against her. And, of course, there was no way any of her fellow Democrats would challenge her. She liked it that way. Jessie had bigger dreams, though. She had her eye on Congress, if only that lazy SOB Billy Conner would move aside. She was determined to be the first woman and the first African American to represent her home area in Congress. Patience, she reminded herself constantly, patience.

Bulldog stifled a burp and returned the toothpick to his mouth. "The Stevens girl still claims she doesn't remember anything," he offered, "but I think she's faking it."

"It might not matter, Bulldog. We got her blood test back."

The toothpick stopped moving. "Was she drunk?"

"Just barely – point-oh-nine. But drunk is drunk."

Bulldog pulled a long suck through his teeth. "Okay, she was drunk. We can prove she was driving because it's her blood on the airbag. Her purse was inside the truck and this Snyder fella admits he gave her the keys. And she was speeding, too; had to be."

"What we don't know," Jessie replied, "is what caused her to lose control and what the victims were doing on the road in the dark. But I suspect we'll find out. Go ahead and put her under arrest, Bulldog. Three counts of vehicular manslaughter. Maybe that'll jog her memory."

"Yes, ma'am. She's still in the hospital until tomorrow the doctors tell me. We'll take her down to the jail then."

"Put a guard on her," Jessie suggested. "Announce her arrest to the press at the same time you release the names of the victims. I want the African American community to know justice is being done."

"Gotcha." Bulldog pointed to the box of Krispy Kremes. "You want me to leave those? You know, for later?"

"Nah. Go ahead and take 'em, Bulldog. I'm watching my figure."

Shit, we're all watching your figure, Bulldog thought. Jessie Malloy was a fox. They know how to grow 'em down in Sopchoppy. Yessiree. "Okay. Talk to ya later." Bulldog scooped up the doughnuts and waddled away.

Carl Splighter was shocked by what he saw as he entered Carrie's room. The sexy co-worker he had been leering at for more than a year was almost unrecognizable. She had burns on one side of her face, some kind of thing that looked like a cheap hockey mask over her nose, her hair was a fright, and she seemed incredibly frail.

Carl reached up to run a hand through his own hair and regretted not washing it.

"Hey, Carrie. How goes it?"

"Just great, Carl. Just fucking great."

Okay; so small talk is out. "What in the hell happened to you, Carrie?"

Carrie wasn't about to trust this worm. "I don't remember, Carl. Some kind of car accident they tell me. How did you hear about it?"

"It's all over the news. And besides, a sheriff's deputy called me this morning asking questions about you. And about Rip Snyder, too."

Carrie could see the displeasure in Carl's eyes. "Oh, yeah. I gave him your number. He was here. He's not too happy about my memory loss, but I can't help it."

Carl decided to plunge right into it. "Do you remember me calling you last night? Do you remember why?"

Jesus, Carrie thought, this faking amnesia is a lot of work. "No, I don't. The last thing I remember is leaving the office to drive home."

Carl was about to ask her how she ended up in Snyder's truck when the door opened. It was Bulldog.

"And who might you be?" Bulldog was pointing at Carl with a toothpick.

"I'm Carl Splighter. Carrie and I work together."

"Ah, yes. Tell me, Mr. Splighter, any luck helping the young lady with her memory?"

"No, she doesn't remember anything."

"Well, Mr. Splighter, I'm afraid you need to leave. I'm here to place Miss Stevens under arrest."

"Under arrest? For what?"

"For killin' three kids while she was drunk, that's what. Now scram."

Carl slithered off and Carrie's world went into a tailspin. It was over for her. She had visions of herself in prison for life. Oh, God.

"Carrie Stevens, you're under arrest on three counts of vehicular manslaughter. You have the right to remain silent…"

It was a nightmare; it had to be. But she couldn't wake up. The tears flowed. Then, the deputy was shaking her shoulder.

"I said, do you understand these rights?"

Carrie only nodded.

"Good. I'm putting a guard outside your room. No more visitors. When they release you from the hospital, we'll take you to the jail. You can have a lawyer in here if you want, but that's it. Got it?"

Carrie nodded again.

"Good." Bulldog left the room, headed for his cruiser and another Krispy Kreme.

11

C arl Splighter knew he needed to call the *Suncoast Gazette* and tell them about Carrie's accident and her arrest. But the first person he called was Roy Fercal.

Roy had an annoying habit of answering his cell phone without saying anything. After a few beats of silence, he finally spoke up.

"Who is this?"

"Roy, it's Carl. I just talked to Carrie."

"Did you find out why in the hell she failed us last night?"

"She's in the hospital, Roy. She had a car accident."

"Jesus! It must be going around. I saw that sonofabitch Rip Snyder wrecked his truck last night. Is Carrie hurt bad?"

"Listen, Roy. Carrie is the one who wrecked Snyder's truck. She's hurt bad enough but the worst of it is, she ran over and killed three little girls. She's under arrest."

Roy was silent, trying to digest the enormity of it all. He had been gleefully thinking of a plan to destroy Snyder. Now everything was more complicated.

"Oh, my God, Carl. That's awful. I guess the accident happened on her way to the airport?"

"I guess so. Carrie doesn't remember anything about the accident."

"Why was she driving Snyder's truck? Are they an item?"

"It was news to me, but they must be. I mean, she borrowed his truck, for God's sake."

Something was tickling the back of Roy's brain, the tiny inkling of a plan. But he needed time to think. Obviously, Carrie wasn't going to be much use to him now, at least not as part of his plot to destroy Speaker Gonzalez.

"Listen, Carl. Let's keep the reason she was headed for the airport between us for now. I don't want the cat to get out of the bag too early."

"Right. I was actually thinking that..."

But Roy had already hung up. Christ, Carl thought. He never says hello; he never says good-bye. What a freak.

"I'm sorry to bother you at home, Mr. Bundt. But it couldn't wait."

Carl Splighter had spent some time planning this call before actually dialing the home number of the *Suncoast Gazette* political editor, Jeremiah Bundt. The man was, well, snooty.

"I'm sure you have a good reason for interrupting my morning swim, Mr. Splighter," Bundt intoned. "Whether it's real or imagined, I assume it couldn't wait until Monday?"

"Right. It's about Carrie. She had a car accident last night, a bad one. She's in the hospital."

There was silence on the other end. Carl imagined Bundt standing near his pool, dripping wet.

"How bad is she?" Bundt finally asked.

"A busted nose and some burns on her face from the airbag. And she doesn't remember it, so maybe some kind of concussion."

"Well, she's young and strong. I'm sure she'll recover just fine. Give her my best and tell her to take it easy for awhile."

Carl licked his lips. "It's not that simple, Mr. Bundt. Uh, she ran over and killed three kids. She's under arrest."

Bundt sat heavily into a patio chair. "Holy shit, Splighter! You should know better than to bury the lead! This is horrible!" His mind was racing. "Was she on duty at the time?"

It seemed like an odd question to Carl. "No, I don't think so," he lied.

"I'm just asking, you know, because if she was on duty at the time, there are implications for the paper," Bundt explained. "Keep me informed. I'll notify legal, just in case. And if you get any press calls, for any reason, send them to me. We'll talk Monday morning, if not before."

With that, the phone went dead in Carl's hand. Doesn't anybody say good-bye anymore?

Roxy Jones had been waiting for Gonzalez to call her since last night and she was mildly pissed that he hadn't. It wasn't as though she really enjoyed his company. Even the sex was droll, she thought. But she knew Gonzalez had returned from Miami with a bunch of money from a meeting she had helped set up. She didn't know how much, but she sure as hell expected the fat bastard to use the money to dote on her. All those blowjobs had to be worth something.

So when the phone finally rang at about eleven o'clock on Saturday morning, she hurried to pick it up.

"Roxy here."

"Foxy Roxy! How they hangin'?"

It was Roy Fercal. "You know how they hang, Roy. They don't *hang* at all."

"Don't I know it," Roy agreed. He licked his lips and savored the memory. "Have you talked with Gonzalez since he got back from Miami?"

"No, the fucker hasn't called me. And we're supposed to go to the football game this afternoon."

"Well, when you see him, I have something for you to do."

"Jesus Christ, Roy! Haven't I done enough? I set up the damn meeting with your casino buddies because I felt I owed you something after what we went through. And now you're back for more? You prick."

Roy realized he was breathing a little heavy. God, he loved hearing Roxy talk. "No, Roxy. I'm gonna pay you for this job, and pay you well."

Fercal had her attention now. "Now you're talkin', big boy." She heard his breathing and knew the little pervert was getting excited. "What do you need, sweetie? Tell Roxy what you need."

Roy knew she was toying with him, but he liked it. Jesus, he was getting hard. "First of all, don't wait for Gonzalez to call you. Go over to his apartment. Get him feeling really good, and then spring the news on him that you know about the money. He'll freak, but let him know you think he did the right thing and you want to help him hide it. You know, you're a team and so forth. Screw his brains out and when he agrees to let you help him, get in touch with me. Then we're gonna steal it from him."

"How much money are we talkin' about?"

"Gonzalez got two hundred grand, and you can have a fourth of it," Roy promised.

"A fourth of two hundred," Roxy was doing the math in her head. "Is that like eighty?"

"No. Your share comes to fifty. One fourth of two hundred is fifty."

Roxy thought he might be cheating her. "I want eighty."

Roy rolled his eyes. "Fine. You can have eighty. Just get him to let you take care of hiding it. And don't talk about dollar amounts with him. Just keep it simple."

"Keep it simple, stupid," Roxy said. "The KISS rule. It's my motto in life."

Roy didn't doubt that one bit.

12

The football game against the Golden Gophers of Minnesota was scheduled to start at 3:30, which was a testament to the power of network sports. The game was originally scheduled for that night, when it would be cooler, but the network came calling, dangling wads of cash to change the game to the hottest part of the day. "Yes sir, Mr. Network, whatever you say."

The Golden Gophers had made some noise in the Big Ten the year before, and somehow that qualified them to be slaughtered on national television in a place where championship football is a way of life. There were even some Minnesota fans in town. No doubt they were confused, possibly even frightened, by the spectacle of the Downtown Getdown that had taken place in the streets below their hotel rooms the night before.

It was just past noon and the scene around Doak Campbell Stadium was already coming alive. The footballs were flying, the liquor was flowing, and the local radio stations were starting to predict just how much mayhem would take place that afternoon. One caller, who sounded like his blood was already the color of Budweiser, boldly predicted the score of 77-0. "Go 'Noles!"

Loud music thumped from the houses, big and small, that lined Pensacola Street. Students were everywhere, most with a cup in one hand. Some were clutching wads of money, offering a piece of lawn to park on for twenty bucks. Traffic was thick; nothing unusual there.

Several blocks to the east, in the Leon County courthouse made famous as the backdrop of the 2000 presidential recount, preparations were under way for a news conference. It had been decided that state's attorney Jessie Malloy would announce the arrest of Carrie Stevens and explain the charges against her, as well as release the identities of the three little girls to the media. A one o'clock news conference should give the reporters time to soak up the story of the tragic events on Lake Bradford Road and still make it to The Doak to cover the lead story of the day, Malloy's press assistant had assured her. Two o'clock, though, would be pushing it.

Bulldog was on his way to Josiah Franklin's house, hoping the reverend would help tell the mother of the victims that their names would soon be splattered all over the news, and fill her in on the charges against the Stevens girl. There was still one Krispy Kreme left, but he couldn't face it. He needed some red meat to counteract all that sugar, but there wasn't time.

He flowed with the heavy traffic on Gaines and could see Doak Campbell Stadium up ahead. The smoke from the many barbeque grills was already thickening. It made his stomach growl. Bulldog wanted to be walking around the parking lots, making sure people were behaving, accepting the occasional offer of a bratwurst here, a burger there. He liked Game Day.

Once he was past The Doak, traffic thinned and it wasn't long before he was approaching the Bradford Road Baptist Church, driving on the shoulder to lessen the severity of the speed bumps. He parked his cruiser just as he had the night before when he thought there had been a shooting. What a night.

The Reverend Josiah Franklin, wearing a pair of faded jeans and a tee shirt, emerged from his house before Bulldog could knock on the door. It looked like he hadn't slept much, Bulldog thought, and wasn't surprised.

"Hello, Reverend." Bulldog reached up to his mouth to grab his toothpick and realized he didn't have one.

"Deputy Bowser. We meet again. I assume this is about last night?"

"That's right. Jessie Malloy is fixin' to have a press conference in about 45 minutes to announce the arrest of that Stevens girl. Vehicular manslaughter, three counts. Turns out she was drunk."

Josiah felt his blood start to boil. He had been the leader of the effort to install the speed bumps on Lake Bradford Road, hoping to avoid just this kind of disaster. Now, this drunken white woman had slaughtered three of the tiny lambs in his flock.

"Josiah?" It was a weak voice, from inside the house. "Josiah? Who is it?"

Bulldog looked curiously at the reverend.

"That's Belinda," Josiah said. "The mother of those three kids. I've been trying to comfort her."

Bulldog fleetingly wondered what form the comfort had taken, but decided it was none of his business. "Well, we need to talk to her, Reverend. We don't want her to hear it on the news."

Josiah nodded. "Come on in, Deputy Bowser. We'll tell her together."

B ulldog was grateful for the help of Josiah Franklin. God, the poor woman was a wreck, and who could blame her?

He was on his way back to the courthouse when the growling in his stomach got the better of him. There was a McDonald's handy, and maybe a quick double cheeseburger would hold him until he had time to eat a real lunch. Surprisingly, the drive-through service was fairly quick.

Bulldog was waiting to pull back into traffic, chomping with satisfaction on his double cheeseburger, when a bright green Cadillac went zipping by. Bulldog wasn't sure, but it looked like Reverend Franklin.

The turnout for the news conference was amazing. Tallahassee is full of reporters, of course, with more than a dozen major newspapers from all parts of Florida represented, the Associated Press, a radio network, a television network, and the local folks. Not to mention it was Game Day. But it was unusual for "the big boys" to pay attention to a local story.

This was no ordinary story, though. Rip Snyder was involved somehow, a man despised by most of the capital press corps. And what was happening with their friend, Carrie Stevens? The room was buzzing when Bulldog arrived just before one o'clock. To his amazement, the Reverend Josiah Franklin was in attendance, standing in the back of the room looking resplendent in a cream suit with matching loafers. How did he do that so fast?

The room quieted when Jessie Malloy walked in and made her way quickly to the lectern. She knew the news conference started when she entered the door, not when she began talking. If any of the TV stations used footage of her entrance, the viewers would see a no-nonsense prosecutor in full command of the situation.

"Ladies and gentlemen, thank you for coming," she began, and she immediately noticed the presence of Josiah Franklin. Let the circus begin, she thought.

"Last night, three innocent children were run over and killed on Lake Bradford Road, near the airport. This senseless tragedy could have been avoided, and should have been avoided. Nothing we do now will bring those beautiful children back. But we can, and we will, see that justice is done on their behalf.

"We have placed the driver of the vehicle involved, Carrie Stevens, aged 25, of Tallahassee, under arrest."

Gasps went up from the reporters in the room. Malloy had been expecting the reaction and had deliberately paused to let it happen.

"Miss Stevens has been charged with three counts of vehicular manslaughter. She was drunk."

More gasping, louder this time, as the reporters looked at each other in disbelief. This was more than a news story; this was one of their own.

"Her blood alcohol level was point-oh-nine," Malloy continued. "We also believe she was speeding."

Malloy fixed her gaze on the Reverend Franklin. "Make no mistake about it," Malloy stated firmly. "This office will pursue this prosecution with every available resource. These three little girls were denied a future; they will NOT be denied justice, and I will see to it."

The Reverend Franklin issued a soft "amen" and a nod of the head. The nod of the head was for Jessie. The "amen" was for the reporters, reminding them of his presence.

Jimmy Flain, who was in the front row, turned and caught Franklin's eye. Franklin nodded again, and Jimmy nodded back. The Reverend Franklin was ready to be quoted.

Jessie noticed all of this and wasn't the least bit surprised. That's why she was announcing the arrest early, to keep Franklin on a shorter leash.

"We can now release the identities of the three victims…" Malloy went on. The reporters were dutifully taking notes, still stunned.

When it was time for questions, Jimmy Flain was the first to speak. "Do you know why Carrie was driving Rip Snyder's truck, and what his involvement is in all this?"

It was the same question on the minds of all the reporters.

"Mr. Snyder loaned his truck to Miss Stevens. He wasn't involved in the accident at all."

"Exactly how did the accident happen?" It was Carl Splighter.

"We're not sure," Malloy admitted. "Miss Stevens has apparently suffered a memory loss. And apparently the only witnesses are three little girls at the morgue."

There were a few other questions, mostly mundane. Some of the reporters were looking at their watches. It was Game Day.

The news conference broke up. The Reverend Josiah Franklin was a little disappointed that Jessie Malloy left the room before he could make a show of shaking her hand on behalf of his flock – for seeking justice, swift and certain. He left the courthouse and found a shady spot under a sprawling live oak tree in front, standing with the historic old capitol building over his left shoulder, and waited for the reporters to find him. He knew they would.

The first to get to him was Jimmy Flain, of course. Once the other reporters saw Jimmy talking with Franklin and taking notes, they scurried over to see what they were missing. The Reverend Franklin straightened his tie and waited patiently as the TV cameras focused on him.

"I want to thank Jessie Malloy for seeking swift and certain justice in this case," Franklin stated, strong and sure. "Three innocent members of my flock at the Bradford Road Baptist Church have been slaughtered, like sacrificial lambs, on the alter of sin and excess. We grieve for them and their mother, whose broken heart I have been trying to comfort since the terrible spear of death sped through our community last night."

Josiah reached into his breast pocket and extracted a color photograph of the three girls, taken not three months earlier, their heads alive with colorful beads and ribbons. He held it up, with hands steady as a surgeon, as the cameras focused on it.

"Look at these beautiful angels, so cruelly taken from us by the uncaring hand of drunkenness. I urge you to use this picture, to force the public to stare into the eyes of these poor children. We all know that too often when black folks die, justice is neither swift, nor certain. And when black folks kill each other, it barely makes the news.

"This time, there will be no escaping the justice the black community demands. And we will not rest until justice is done."

Jimmy Flain knew the reverend was holding a picture of three girls, but it looked like the race card to him. My goodness. Where was this headed?

13

Roxy decided it was time to take matters into her own hands. She dressed in a tight FSU polo – no bra – and a tiny pair of white shorts and drove straight to Speaker Gonzalez's apartment. She let herself in with a key.

Gonzalez wasn't too surprised to see her barge right in. They were, after all, supposed to go to the football game in an hour or so. But his eyes bulged anyway at the sight of Roxy in a tight shirt with her nipples on high beam.

"Roxy!"

"I got tired of waiting for you to call," she said. She pulled off her shirt and tossed it on the sofa, exposing her perfect breasts. Her long blond hair teased her nipples. "Let's have it, big boy."

"My God, Roxy! The windows!"

"Forget the windows." Roxy was already kneeling in front of him as he sat in his office chair. "You just sit back and let Roxy do her thing."

And so he did, and it was marvelous. All the tension that had built inside of him over the past two days erupted into a shattering climax as he cried out and held Roxy's head firmly in his lap until the waves of pleasure began to subside. Jesus, she was good.

Roxy looked up at Gonzalez and caught his eye. Grinning, she said, "I know about the money."

Gonzalez sucked in a quick breath. "What money? What do you mean?" His heart was hammering away.

"C'mon, Al. I set up the meeting, remember? The casino money, from the Indian tribe."

Gonzalez was aghast. "But ... I thought ... I mean ... you knew?"

"Look, Al. I'm not as dumb as I look. And before you have a heart attack, I think taking the money was a good idea."

"You do?"

"Hell, yes! Those casino people are loaded with it. If they want to hand out some cash to people in a position to help them, who am I to object? Of course, I'm hoping you'll spend some of it on me."

"Oh, don't worry about that," Gonzalez assured her. "We're in this together."

"Exactly."

"I was actually going to tell you about the money today, anyway," he lied. "I need your help with something."

"What's that?"

"I need to figure out a way to hide it. You know – launder it so I can use it without raising suspicion."

"Actually, I have a friend in the banking business on the Cayman Islands." Roxy didn't really, of course, but it was what Roy Fercal told her to say. And she wanted to earn her eighty grand. "We took some classes together at FSU. In fact, I think he's in town this weekend. Want me to call him?"

"Can we trust this friend of yours?"

"Absolutely. He does this sort of thing for people. And he'll do it for me, I'm sure. People say I have a way with men."

"That you do, young lady. That you do."

Roxy could feel him becoming aroused again. She peeled off her shorts and panties.

"Let's play 'hide the sausage,' Mr. Speaker."

D oak Campbell Stadium was in full roar by the time Rip Snyder arrived at Bannerman Lux's tailgate party. The old lawyer knew how to tailgate, and his better clients were always invited to help themselves to a full bar and catered food.

Despite the horror of the past 24 hours, Rip couldn't help but smile and shake his head. Bannerman had booked a local Hooters knock-off, Uncle Nip's, to cater the event, complete with a half-dozen of their best girls.

"I don't know how you do it, Lucky," Rip allowed as he took a long pull on a cold beer, "but you're a master."

"I'm glad you like it," Lux replied. "I'm especially fond of Buffy over there. She knows what to do with a hot dog, let me tell you."

The joke was lost on Rip. He was staring off into the distance.

"Earth to Rip. Earth to Rip. Are you with me?"

"Oh, sorry, Lucky. I was just thinking about Carrie. And I can't seem to shake the image of those poor little girls."

"Look, Rip, a football game is not the place to discuss a legal case. But I won't lie to you. Things could get dicey for you. But let's talk about it next week. As for now, put it aside and let's go watch the 'Noles. Whaddya say?"

Rip sighed heavily. "Okay, Lucky. But let me get another beer first for the walk across the parking lot."

Rip grabbed a cold one from a cooler and caught up with Lux.

"Hey, Lucky, did you see the way that one girl slides a hot dog into the bun? It's amazing – kind of erotic."

"Yeah, the girl has a way with wieners."

They snickered and joked their way to the entrance of the stadium and, just like most folks, tossed empty beer bottles into a large trash container at the gate. Liquor is not allowed inside Doak Campbell Stadium. Of course, it's a rule that's always broken.

On the way to their seats, Rip stopped at a concession stand to pick up some Cokes. A couple of Minnesota fans were ahead of him in line.

"Ah, Jeez," one of them complained, wiping his forehead, "It's so hot! How can it be so hot in September?"

"Yah, it's a cooker in here," the other one agreed. "And they're kind of stingy with the pop. They're only filling the cups about two-thirds of the way up!"

"Well, gosh darn it! They better fill mine all the way up!"

Rip was laughing to himself. He knew Lux would have a flask hidden away somewhere, just like thousands of other fans. And what good is a flask if your cup of Coke doesn't have room for plenty of bourbon?

The game went about as expected. It was 35-0 at halftime. When the rain came, or in some cases when the bourbon ran out, most of the fans drifted away. Only a few thousand were on hand to witness the posting of the final score: 59-3.

"The coach is getting soft," opined the first caller on the post-game show. "He kinda took it easy on 'em in the second half."

And so it went. Tallahassee was in its element. Football was back and the team was pretty damn good. A storm was brewing over Tallahassee, like a distant hurricane, with three dead girls caught in the eye. But, for today, most folks were oblivious to it.

14

Carl Splighter had been listening to the football game on the radio and cruising through porno sites on the Internet. But his heart wasn't in it. He was thinking about Carrie Stevens and Rip Snyder.

Jesus, how could she date that Republican pig? Rip was against everything Carrie stood for – or was she just a phony?

Carl toasted the FSU victory by chugging a beer, which he chased with another, and another. The more he drank, the more pissed he got.

Then he started thinking about the Speaker Gonzalez story. We can't let it drop, Carl thought, it's too damn hot. And that jackass Fercal will just find another newspaper, anyway.

Carrie probably can't do the story anymore, Carl realized. First of all, her memory might be shot. Second of all, she might be headed for prison. The paper will probably let her go, anyway.

Maybe I should pick up the story, Carl thought. It would be a slimy thing to do – to steal such a hot story from a colleague. But, dammit, it had to be done.

Carrie probably had some notes stashed away somewhere. If I can find them, Carl decided, I can get myself up to speed and move on with the story. It was time to go snooping through Carrie's desk.

Carl drove to the press center. There were more cars than usual for a Saturday evening. Probably writing the Carrie story. His editor, Jeremiah Bundt, was adamant that the *Gazette* would report nothing about Carrie in Sunday's paper. It seemed silly to Carl. All the other papers would clearly identify Carrie as a reporter for the *Gazette*. Pretty hard to stick your head in the sand on this one, Jeremiah.

Carl didn't really want to deal with questions about Carrie, so he entered quietly, moved quickly to his office in the near corner of the building and locked the door behind him. He used only the natural light from the window to conduct his search.

Where would she keep her most valuable notes? He opened the lower right-hand drawer of her desk first. It was full of files, and Carl couldn't believe his eyes. The biggest file folder was labeled *The Ripper* and as he thumbed through it, Carl realized she had filed away every issue of that jerk's newsletter. God, she has it bad for that prick.

The last file folder, way in the back, contained nothing but a key. It looked like a standard key used to lock desk drawers. One drawer on the left side of the desk was locked; the key opened it.

There was a stack of reporter's notebooks, labeled by date. They appeared to contain notes on several different topics. He'd have to read through them later. Way in the back, under some copy paper, was a book with a soft leather binding. Jesus! It's a diary!

It wasn't locked, which both surprised and pleased Carl. He opened it greedily.

March 1: Rip used the 'n-word' again today. He knows it bothers me, too, but he just let it fly. I should just walk away, but there's something about him I can't resist. He's good to me, overall, and I like the sex. He has some money, too, which doesn't hurt!

The reference to sex raised Carl's blood pressure a bit, but he was intrigued by this "n-word" business. He flipped to a new page.

April 23: Rip did it again. We were riding together — kinda risky, given our relationship — when some black kids came out of a school. They had their pants hung low, below their butts. Rip was screaming at them! "Look at those dumbass n---ers! We'd be better off without 'em!" I was embarrassed. I mean, sure, it's a stupid look, but they're just kids! But then we went to Rip's place and had great sex. What's wrong with me? Is sex more important to me than social justice?

So, Carl thought, Rip is a racist. Now there's an interesting tidbit to chew on. He flipped ahead.

August 10: Rip is starting to ask the wrong questions. Today he asked about my parents, and what I did in high school, and what classes I took in college — stuff like that. I shut him up with a BJ, but I don't like him asking about my past. What if he finds out who I really am? He might walk away and I'll be left to date ugly people like Carl. God, I'd rather die!

Carl snapped the book shut and tried to regain his composure. But it was a losing battle. He was actually shaking.

"You bitch," he spat into the air. "You'll pay for that, by God!"

Carl locked up the desk and returned the key to the file folder. He took the diary with him.

Roxy and Speaker Gonzalez watched the football game from a luxury suite, courtesy of a large lobbying firm in Tallahassee. The firm was only too happy to entertain one of the most powerful people in all of Florida.

Gonzalez had trouble concentrating on the game, what with $2 million in dirty cash stuffed under his bed and Roxy spending most of her time on her cell phone, just out of earshot. Probably making arrangements with her banker friend, the money-launderer. It wasn't the first time he wondered about Roxy, and whether he could trust her. But she already knew about the money! He had no choice but to bring her into it, and she might prove useful.

Roxy caught his eye after snapping her phone shut and motioned for him to join her in a corner of the suite.

"It's all arranged," she whispered. "My friend has a condo on St. George Island. We can drive over there after the game and spend the weekend. He already has some ideas on what he can do to hide the money."

Things were moving too fast for Gonzalez and he was shaking his head. "Roxy, I can't just hand a duffle bag full of cash over to somebody I don't even know."

Roxy was expecting this. "Of course not! We won't bring the money with us. We'll just get to know him and listen to what he has to say. If we like what we hear, we can arrange to meet him again later and do the deal."

Do the deal. She made it sound so easy, he thought.

"Okay, Roxy. We'll go to St. George and meet this friend of yours. But no money gets handed over unless I'm comfortable with it."

"You got it, Al. In fact, let's leave now. This game is boring. We could be on the beach in two hours."

And off they went, with Speaker Gonzalez dreaming about what he would do with $2 million and Roxy making plans to steal it from him.

Gonzalez dropped her off at her apartment to pack an overnight bag. "I won't need much more than a bikini," she winked.

Al wasted no time driving to his own apartment. He was relieved to see the bag of money was still under his bed. He packed for the weekend, stole another glance at the money, and motored off to retrieve Roxy. He badly wanted the money to be hidden away in an account somewhere. Hiding money under his bed was not his style.

The drive to St. George Island took over an hour, even with Gonzalez paying no attention to the speed limits. The condo Roxy was talking about was on the far eastern edge, the most remote part of the small barrier island in the Gulf of Mexico. It was one of eight units in a grouping, all with a private entrance in the front and a couple of parking spots each.

It was early Saturday evening of Labor Day weekend, but many of the parking spots were empty. The tourists still hadn't discovered St.

George Island like they had Panama City or Destin or other nearby vacation spots. Here, the beach was still natural and not at all crowded.

The man who answered the door was about Roxy's age and looked like a surfer dude, with bright blonde hair and a deep tan. Roxy immediately threw her arms around his neck. The man responded with a playful squeeze of Roxy's butt, which made Gonzalez feel a little stupid as he stood and watched these two friends greet each other.

"Good to see you again, Roxy," the surfer dude said, and then offered a hand to Gonzalez. "And you must be Al. I'm Joe."

Speaker Gonzalez was unaccustomed to being called "Al" by a complete stranger, but perhaps the informality was a good idea, given the illegal nature of what they planned to discuss.

"Nice to meet you, Joe. Thanks for the invitation."

As they entered the condo, it was immediately obvious that Joe the Surfer Dude had some money. The furnishings were fine leather, the carpet thick and luxurious. The living room flowed openly over a granite bar into a well-appointed kitchen. Beyond the kitchen was a wall of windows looking directly over an oversized deck and the Gulf of Mexico.

"My God, Joe! This is tremendous!" Speaker Gonzalez couldn't help himself. He was accustomed to enjoying the luxuries of others, but this was making a huge impression.

"Thanks, Al, but I can't take full credit for it," Joe admitted. "I'm a part-owner with three other bankers who specialize in helping certain clients with hard-to-manage assets. We share it."

Gonzalez found this interesting, and comforting. So it wasn't just Joe the Surfer Dude he was dealing with. Perhaps at least one of the other guys had some gray hair and actually looked like a banker, he thought.

Joe opened a cabinet door in the kitchen and uncorked a bottle of Johnny Walker Blue, pouring Gonzalez a generous portion over ice. He knows what I drink, he thought. Roxy must have filled him in.

They took their drinks onto the deck, and again Gonzalez was impressed. To the left was the solitude of a state park. Immediately ahead was the beach and the shimmering, emerald green waters of the

Gulf. To the right was the deck of another condo, separated by a privacy fence.

Joe saw him looking at the fence and said, "We own the condo next door, too. We let our clients use it, but not when we're here. Privacy, you know."

Gonzalez took a healthy sip of Johnny Walker Blue and let the smoothness of the liquid spread through him. He smelled the salt air, listened to the surf, and looked at the sky beginning to color with the approaching sunset. He thought about the condo next door and imagined having a key to it – as a client.

"You've done awfully well for yourself, Joe," Gonzalez said. "And you're still young."

Joe waved his hand dismissively. "I fell in with the right people. We're all fraternity brothers. And there aren't very many people who do what we do, and do it successfully."

Gonzalez took another sip and realized "do it successfully" meant "without getting caught." It was a good thought. He looked lazily to his left and realized for the first time there was a car parked nearby, well hidden behind some bushes. A wooden walkway led from the solitary parking spot to a set of stairs entering the deck.

"That's my rental car over there," Joe explained. "This is the only condo in this complex with a completely private parking spot. You can't see it from the road, the park or the beach. We like our privacy."

Roxy appeared on the deck in a striking leopard skin bikini. "You boys can talk business all you want. I'm going to the beach."

Roxy didn't need to listen to the conversation. She knew her "friend" Joe – whom she had never met – would convince Al to go back to Tallahassee and retrieve the money at some point during the weekend. Joe wasn't a banker, Roxy knew. He wasn't a graduate of FSU, either. He wasn't a lot of things, but Roxy didn't care. He was a thief and that's all that mattered.

Joe and Al watched as Roxy sauntered her way to the beach in front of them. Well, leered is more like it. The surfer dude looked away first. "Let's have another drink, Al, and talk some business."

Another drink sounded good. "Make it a double."

15

Speaker Gonzalez was amazed. Joe made it sound so easy, so plausible. Could it really be this easy to launder $2 million?

Joe explained that the condo next door actually served two purposes. They let clients use it as a perk, as he had mentioned earlier, but they also used it as a vehicle to launder money. Joe and his partners would agree to loan Gonzalez $2 million from a shell corporation to buy the condo, which is way more than the condo is worth, but who cares?

All the papers would be signed and Gonzalez would actually own the condo for a period of one month. Then, another shell corporation owned by Joe and his buddies would buy the condo from Gonzalez for $1.8 million. The $200,000 difference represents Joe's "fee."

"You end up with a million eight in the bank, free and clear," Joe assured him. "And you can even write the two hundred thou you lost on the property off your taxes."

"But what about the loan?"

"The loan isn't real, Al. It doesn't exist. The only real money is the cash you give me and the money we pay you to buy the condo back."

Maybe it was the three glasses of Johnny Walker Blue, but the plan sounded brilliant to Speaker Gonzalez. And, who knows? Maybe there's more cash to be had out there!

"I like it, Joe. I like it a lot."

"Great. Hey, here comes Roxy. Let's take a walk down the beach to the Leaky Tiki for some seafood. I'm starved."

While Speaker Gonzalez and Joe the Surfer Dude shared blackened grouper and expensive liquor with Roxy Jones, Carl Splighter spent his Saturday night with a twelve-pack of Old Milwaukee's Best, a double Whataburger and Carrie's private diary.

Carl was relieved to discover no further references to him, but it was no picnic reading about Carrie's sexual appetite for Rip Snyder. The diary was sprinkled with references to "my former life" and "my dark little secret," which was intriguing. There were also numerous references to Rip's private comments, many of which would be damaging to Rip personally. Carl started to realize that his initial idea of using the diary to ruin Carrie was shortsighted. After all, Rip was a bigger target.

And Carl thought he knew just the sleaze ball willing to make use of it.

Roy Fercal picked up his cell phone and listened. Joe knew better than to wait for "hello." He was in one of the condo's three bathrooms. Roxy and Al were on the deck.

"The fishing was good today, boss. I hooked a good one."

"Fantastic. Are you going to have it mounted?"

"Should have everything taken care of by Monday morning. Would you like to see it?"

"Bring it by Monday night," Roy said, grinning. "We'll celebrate. And don't forget to clean up. You know how I hate it when fishermen leave evidence of their weekend activities behind."

"Don't worry, boss. Your condo will be clean as a whistle."

As Roy hung up he thought for about the millionth time that "Joe" was a damn good operative.

When Joe returned to the deck, he found it empty. He could see Speaker Gonzalez and Roxy frolicking in the water in the moonlight. They were naked. He turned away and let them have their privacy. Roxy was the wrong sex, and Gonzalez was too fat for his tastes. But it did remind him of the condo his real buddies were gathered in about a mile away. He would join them tomorrow night and start his own celebration of reeling in the big fish.

16

Roy was in Apalachicola, a quaint old fishing village just across Apalachicola Bay from St. George Island. No way was he going to be in Tallahassee – more than an hour away – at a time when he was directing the theft of a $2 million bribe from the Speaker of the Florida House of Representatives. And Apalachicola, with its antique shops, decent restaurants and the best oysters on the planet was as close as he could safely get.

He grabbed a beer from the mini-fridge in his suite and plopped himself into a white wooden rocker on his balcony overlooking the Apalachicola River, which he couldn't see because of the darkness, and enjoyed the cool breeze floating in from the bay. He had stayed in this wonderful old hotel many times before, when he was still married. Roy started remembering the days when he would stroll through the antique shops with his wife, arm in arm, looking for the perfect something and usually not finding it. But it was fun for them anyway, especially when they would enjoy a wonderful seafood meal and return to this very suite.

Stop it! Those days are over, he reminded himself bitterly. Politics can be bad for marriages, Roy knew, and politics had ended his. There were too many young, eager women interested in going to bed with people of power, and too many weak men unable to resist the temptation. Roy Fercal was one such man. And it was times like these, on a beautiful Saturday night, alone in a romantic suite, when the memories grew thick and the loneliness thicker.

His thoughts turned to Roxy Jones. She had been the straw that broke the camel's back. He had enjoyed the company of several interns for years without getting caught, but it was Roxy that his wife knew about and left him over.

A few years ago, Roy had been drinking with some buddies at The Pour House, a fairly large bar near the FSU campus where college kids went to get stupid drunk and people like Roy went to get lucky with stupid, drunk college girls. Roxy had just appeared in the girlie calendar, bare breasts and all, and there she was. Roy and his buddies were snickering about it when one of them bet Roy a hundred bucks he couldn't get Roxy to leave the bar with him.

"You're on," Roy had said, and strolled right up to her. He introduced himself as the chief of staff to Congressman Billy Conner, which wasn't true, and that the congressman wanted to talk to her about an internship in Washington, which was also a lie.

"He's up at Klinger's right now," Roy lied. "I could introduce you to him, if you want."

Roxy took the bait and they left The Pour House for Klinger's a few blocks away. While they were walking, Roy admitted he didn't work for the congressman and that he was really trying to win a bet with his friends.

"I know who you are," Roxy said without breaking stride. "And you're much more important than a congressman's lackey."

"Then why did you come with me if you knew I was lying?"

"Because I'm hoping you can make my eyes roll back in my head a few times tonight."

And the affair was on, as hot as a blast furnace for about a week. Then his wife confronted him about it, and he found himself unable to lie to her. She demanded Roy break it off with Roxy, which he did. Then she divorced him and took him to the cleaners.

Shaking away the memory, Roy fetched another beer and resumed his observation of the darkened river. Rehashing the loss of his wife was agonizing, but conjuring up his affair with Roxy was stirring him in a different direction. He licked his lips. Roxy was over there with that fat bastard Gonzalez tonight, but if everything went according to plan, Roxy would be alone tomorrow night. Perhaps he would pay her a visit.

C arrie Stevens was having the worst Saturday night of anyone, of course, with the possible exception of Belinda, who was feeling guilty about being with Jamal while her babies were getting run over in the road.

Carrie figured her life was over. She wondered if she would spend the rest of her life in prison – dying there – or just the best part of her life, getting out just in time to be a bitter old maid. Maybe she should plead guilty for a lighter sentence. But how light could it be? She had run over and killed three little girls while she was drunk!

She had avoided prison once, when she was just a teenager, by ratting out some people the authorities wanted more seriously than her. Could she do it again? But there wasn't anyone to rat out this time, was there?

Was there?

R ip Snyder had fallen asleep in front of the Golf Channel again, a half empty glass of vodka on the rocks melting into water.

Before sauntering off from Bannerman Lux's post-game tailgate party, Rip made Bannerman promise to help Carrie get the best deal she could.

"I'll pay the bill, Lucky," Rip assured him. "I'll pay."

"Look, Rip. You didn't wreck your truck, Carrie did. You should be looking out for your own interests."

"I am looking out for my interests, Lucky. I'm looking out for Carrie."

Bannerman watched him go, shaking his head. Then he looked around for the Uncle Nip's girl who was so talented in the area of serving up a hot dog. She was gone.

17

Sunday, September 7

Sunday morning in Tallahassee. Most folks went to church. Quite a few played golf. And everybody was talking about the top story of the day – the Seminoles. But because it was such an impressive victory – and expected -- most of the talk involved laughter and didn't carry on very long. If the team had lost, the cussing would have lasted a week.

Besides, there was another big story afoot. The local paper made the story hard to miss. A picture of the Reverend Josiah Franklin holding a picture of three dead little girls took up two-thirds of the above-the-fold space. The headline to the right read LOCAL MINISTER DEMANDS JUSTICE FOR THREE DEAD ANGELS.

The sub-headline below read *Local Woman Arrested for Manslaughter.* The story, of course, carried the byline of Jimmy Flain.

> *(Tallahassee) – The Rev. Josiah Franklin, long-time civil rights activist and pastor of the Bradford Road Baptist Church, is demanding justice in the wake of the tragic deaths of three young sisters in a car accident near his church.*
>
> *"When black folks die, justice is neither swift nor certain," Franklin said at a news conference in front of the Leon County Courthouse on Saturday. "This time, there will be no escaping the justice the black community demands.*
>
> *"We will not rest until justice is done."*
>
> *An arrest has already been made in the case. State's Attorney Jessie Malloy announced Saturday that Carrie Stevens, 25, of Tallahassee, has been charged with three counts of vehicular manslaughter. Her blood alcohol level was .09 – above the legal limit of .08.*
>
> *"Nothing we can do now will bring those beautiful children back," Malloy admitted. "But we can, and we will, see that justice is done."*
>
> *Franklin said he appreciated Malloy's swift filing of charges against Stevens, but it wasn't enough.*
>
> *He said the three little girls were "slaughtered like sacrificial lambs on the alter of sin and excess."*
>
> *Franklin led the fight to put speed bumps on Lake Bradford Road, but he's angry that the "terrible spear of death" is still allowed to speed through the community.*
>
> *"The police wouldn't tolerate this happening in Killearn," Franklin claimed. "Why must we put up with it where the black folks live?"*

The story went on, but by now most folks had drifted away to the sports pages, to read half a dozen stories describing a football game they already knew about.

Traffic was especially thick along Lake Bradford Road on this particular Sunday morning. Most cars were carrying black families headed to hear the Reverend Josiah Franklin preach for the first time. Three of their own had been "slaughtered," as the Reverend said, and it was time to pull together.

Several of the cars carried white folks looking to gawk at the sewer where it all took place. The rest were people just trying to get to the airport, cussing both the traffic AND the speed bumps.

There were more people than the church could hold, and most of the men gave up their seats to the women and stood outside, as close as they could, to listen through the open windows. When Belinda walked in, dressed in black, the wailing was profound. While the women wailed, the men outside quietly promised each other that this time, justice would be done, praise the Lord.

The Reverend Franklin wasn't surprised by the large turnout, but he was certainly pleased. The sermon he had been working on when Carrie Stevens appeared at his window could wait for another day. This one would flow from the heart.

And flow it did. He went on for almost three hours, evoking cries of "Amen!" and moving most of the assembled to tears more than once. He wrapped it up with a flourish, renewing his call for justice.

"Let the angels in heaven, including the three little ones slaughtered from this flock, hear us loud and clear! Let justice be done! Let justice be done! Let justice be done!"

And the crowd picked it up, the women standing as one, tears turning to anger and determination. Even the men outside, who had taken to sitting in the shade, answered the call and joined the chorus.

Bulldog, who was out patrolling Lake Bradford Road at the time, looked over at the spectacle with awe, and fear. He forgot about the speed bump up ahead and hit it too fast. His toothpick twisted and stabbed the inside of his cheek.

"Shit!"

Damn these speed bumps, he thought. And it occurred to him that maybe the speed bumps had actually caused the accident instead of preventing it. Of course, that doesn't excuse the drinking, but there you have it.

Bannerman Lux spent his Sunday morning at the hospital. He presented himself as Carrie's lawyer and was ushered into her room.

"I didn't call for a lawyer," Carrie said after Lux introduced himself. "I can't afford a lawyer."

"You can afford me. Your friend Rip Snyder is paying the bill."

This touched her, deeply. "How is he?"

"He's worried about you, about how you're doing and what's going to happen. He tried to visit but they wouldn't let him."

Carrie swallowed hard. "I'm in a world of hurt here, Mr. Lux."

"Call me Lucky."

"Lucky, huh? Well, that makes one of us."

"Actually," Bannerman allowed, "you might be luckier than you think."

"Me, lucky? I just ran over and killed three little girls while I was drunk. What, am I supposed to feel lucky it wasn't four? Or a whole busload?"

Bannerman pulled up a chair. "I did some checking. There might be a chain of custody problem with your blood test. I don't think they can prove beyond a doubt that the blood they tested was actually yours.

"So we might get the blood test thrown out. If we do, they can't prove you were drunk."

"Great, Lucky. Now I'm legally sober when I run over the girls with a speeding truck. Maybe I'll get the key to the city."

"Tell me what happened, Carrie, and don't leave anything out. I'm your lawyer; you can trust me."

Carrie took a few deep breaths and told the story to another person for the first time. She told Lux about everything except *why* she was racing to the airport.

"Why were you racing to the airport, Carrie?"

"I'm working on a story and I needed to get to the airport in a hurry. That's all you need to know."

Lux didn't like it, but he moved on. "So your cell phone distracted you and you hit a speed bump. You lost control and hit the girls."

"That's about it, yeah."

Lux thought it over. "So I wonder why the girls were walking on the road."

Carrie looked directly at him. "I've wondered that, too. And I've wondered what the *mother* was doing while the girls were walking on the road."

Lux grinned at her. "Do you make a habit of throwing gasoline on a fire?"

"What do you mean, Lucky?"

"Well, you're kind of cut off from what's happening out there, but this whole thing is turning into a race issue. Accusing the mother of not watching her kids would be scalding hot."

"Good, God! I didn't run over them because they're black! I ran over them because I was drunk!"

Lux had to laugh at that one. "I think you'd better leave the defense strategy to me, Carrie."

It was a drop-dead gorgeous day on St. George Island. Speaker Gonzalez was sitting on the deck of the condo, letting the sea breeze knock down some of the cobwebs from a night of too much Johnnie Walker Blue.

As he watched the constant movement of the Gulf of Mexico, Gonzalez recalled how much fun it was to splash around in the water completely naked with Roxy Jones. The moonlight, the water as warm as a bath, and the stars! But the night had ended badly for him, as he was unable to perform sexually. Too much Johnnie Walker Blue.

Roxy didn't seem to mind too much, but now she was on the beach with Joe the Surfer Dude and it bothered him. It shouldn't, he told himself. They're old friends. And what hold did he have on Roxy anyway?

Well, I pay her ninety thousand goddamn dollars a year for doing next to nothing, he thought. And now she's going to have her hooks into some of my millions, too. It occurred to him that Roxy was very expensive. Maybe too expensive.

Joe looked back at the condo and saw Speaker Gonzalez on the deck. He started to get up from his beach chair and said quietly to Roxy, "I need to finish up some details with Gonzalez. If I play my cards right, he'll be heading back to Tally today to retrieve the money. You can stay."

Now things are looking up, Roxy thought. "Well, gee whiz, Joe. You and me all alone in this big condo on the beach, what in the world will we do with ourselves?" She was getting wet just thinking about spending the day in bed with this hunk.

"Don't get the wrong idea, Roxy. You're not my type."

"I can be any type you want, Joe. You name it."

"Can you grow a penis?"

"What, you're gay? Jesus, it figures. All the best looking guys are gay and I end up sleeping with fatsos like Gonzalez. Thanks a lot, Joe."

Joe plodded to the deck and greeted Gonzalez warmly. "Are you ready to make some money?"

18

It was early on Sunday afternoon when Bulldog showed up at Carrie's hospital room, with Bannerman Lux a close second. It was obvious the big deputy wasn't pleased at being shadowed by the lawyer, judging by the increased intensity of the way he sucked around the toothpick in his mouth.

"Miss Stevens, I'm here to take you to jail," Bulldog announced, pointing at her with the toothpick. "This other fella says he's your lawyer."

"Yes, Deputy, he's my lawyer."

"You don't need to say anything, Carrie," Lux advised, "and there's no good reason for you to say anything to Deputy Bowser."

Bulldog looked at Lux like he might stab him in the eye with his toothpick. He turned back to Carrie and inquired as to whether her memory was good enough to remember the rights he had explained to her yesterday.

"Yes, I remember."

"Well, ain't that nice. Did your memory come back about the accident while you were chattin' with your lawyer here?"

"That's none of your business," Lux chimed in. "Your job is to take her to jail, and nothing else. Let's get on with it so I can get her bailed out and back among friends."

Bulldog snorted. "I'll get on with it as soon as a nurse comes in here and unhooks everything and clears her for release."

Lux produced a bag that he said contained some clothes for Carrie to wear while she was leaving the hospital. "Your other stuff was pretty much ruined."

"Thanks, Lucky."

Bulldog had a laugh at that one. "Lucky, huh? You get liquored up with a man named Rip, run over three kids and hire a lawyer named Lucky. Somebody ought to be writing a fuckin' book." More guffaws. "I'm going to the nurses' station to see what the hold up is."

And off he went, with tears welling up in the eyes of Carrie Stevens. Lux thought she looked like the most defeated person he'd ever met.

Gonzalez and Joe the Surfer Dude were going over the details of the money-laundering scheme again when Joe's cell phone erupted. He glanced at the caller ID and looked nervously at his condo guest.

"I need to take this, Al, sorry. It's one of my partners."

Gonzalez expected him to go inside the condo for privacy, but he simply opened the phone and said hello. I guess he trusts me, Gonzalez thought.

Joe kept looking at Gonzalez while he talked. "Well, I was planning on catching the Tuesday morning flight from Tallahassee through Orlando, which would put me back in the Caymans that afternoon."

There was a pause. "Are you sure it can't wait a day? I'm with a client."

Another pause, then a sigh. "Alright. I'll catch the Monday flight. I should be good to go by four tomorrow afternoon."

Joe hung up and looked apologetically at Gonzalez. "There's a big meeting at the bank tomorrow afternoon, and my partners are insisting I be there."

"A meeting at a bank on Labor Day?"

Joe grinned. "It's not Labor Day in the Caymans, Al. Anyway, I'm sorry but we'll have to finish our business another time. I should be able to get back here in a couple of weeks or so."

Gonzalez was dumbstruck. The idea of keeping the money under his bed for a few weeks was unacceptable.

"But why, Joe? I'm sold on this plan. I'm ready now. I don't want to wait a couple of weeks."

"But you didn't bring the money with you, and I need to get out of here first thing in the morning. Relax. A couple of weeks won't change anything."

"No!" Gonzalez was starting to panic. "I'll drive back to Tallahassee this afternoon and get the money. I can be back with the money tonight."

Joe thought it over. "Okay, Al, let's do it this way. I have something I need to do tonight, so there's no point in rushing back here right away. But I need to leave here by nine o'clock in the morning. Why don't you just bring it here before then – say about 8:30 in the morning. That'll give us time to take care of the paperwork. Then you and Roxy can hang out here for a few days and relax."

Gonzalez was nodding with relief. "That's good, Joe. I'll be back here no later than 8:30 in the morning."

Gonzalez waddled out to the beach where a glistening Roxy Jones was laying on her stomach, obviously topless.

"Roxy, I'm going back for the money. I'll bring it down early tomorrow morning and do the deal with Joe. Do you want to come back to Tally for the night or stay here at the beach?"

"What a stupid question, Al. Tallahassee or the beach? Gee, I think I'll stay here."

And keep Joe company, Gonzalez thought. Oh, well. A night away from Roxy didn't sound half bad. "Alright. Joe said we could stay here for a few days after he leaves tomorrow. Do you want me to bring you some more clothes?"

"No. I think I'll just stay naked most of the time, if that's alright with you."

Jesus, Gonzalez thought as he ambled off. For a chief of staff, she's a pretty odd duck.

L ife had turned into a blur for Carrie Stevens. She was grateful for Lucky, who managed to convince Bulldog that no handcuffs were necessary, but the process of being admitted into the Leon County jail was like an out-of-body experience.

Some slimy man who called himself Buddy Frolic fingerprinted her. Under different circumstances, Carrie would have laughed at the name, which reminded her of a male stripper she used to know. But this Buddy Frolic was about 60 with more fingers than teeth.

Eventually, the ordeal ended with Carrie in a jail cell and Bannerman Lux saying something about keeping quiet until he came back. Carrie nodded and tried to blend in with the concrete walls. She fought the memories, refusing to let them in. But they were like demons, darting into her mind seemingly at will.

Jailhouse demons. I guess every jail has them, Carrie thought, and cried.

A s soon as Gonzalez's car disappeared from sight, Joe went to where Roxy was laying on the beach. She had fallen asleep. He put a hand on her bare back and gently shook her awake.

When Roxy realized it was Joe, she sat up, exposing her bare breasts. "Have you changed your mind?"

"About what, Roxy?"

"About being gay."

"Sorry, Roxy. It's who I am. Look, I'm leaving and won't be back until morning. Gonzalez is gone until morning, too. You've got the place to yourself, except Roy Fercal will be stopping by tonight."

"Gee, I wonder what he wants. I swear that little pervert can smell pussy a mile away."

"What happens between you and Roy is none of my business. But keep this in mind – we're only a few hours away from a big score. So maybe a little celebrating is in order."

"Whatever, Joe." She pulled on a tee shirt and gathered her things. "But if you ever stop being gay, I'll be all over you until your ears bleed."

19

John Billings was a creature of habit. He was one of the few people who actually lived on St. George Island full time. He'd been a postal worker in Rochester, Minnesota, for more than thirty years and was smart enough to invest a little money in a company called Minnesota Mining and Manufacturing. His postal retirement and his money from 3M added up to a pretty good nest egg – enough to buy a house on St. George and leave behind the Minnesota snow.

But John was unable to leave behind the daily need to walk a route. He couldn't deliver the mail anymore, but being a creature of habit, John liked to stroll around the beach and the state park with a pair of binoculars and look at birds. His wife, Margaret, had bought him a really nice digital camera last Christmas with a zoom lens, and he was building up quite a collection of bird pictures.

On this Sunday, with a few thunderstorms starting to build out over the Gulf of Mexico, John was expecting a colorful and unusual sunset. He was positioned for it, standing on the beach between the state park and a condo complex. John's heart skipped a beat when he looked at the back of the last condo. There, standing on the deck and looking off at the approaching sunset was a very beautiful *and very naked* blonde.

John checked her out with the binoculars and silently thanked Margaret once again for the digital camera. He zoomed in and snapped a few shots. I'll have to hide these from Margaret, he thought. Then, as he was about to snap a few more, the door to the condo's deck opened and a man appeared, grinning. The woman was not at all startled to see him. As they embraced, John snapped one more picture before turning his attention to the sunset. It was, as he expected, glorious.

He took one more look at the condo, but the man and woman were gone.

S peaker Alberto Gonzalez actually enjoyed the drive back to Tallahassee. He even stopped at a ramshackle seafood restaurant in the fishing village of Panacea for fried oysters and pecan pie. The closer he got to Tallahassee, though, the more nervous he got. He was worried about the money, of course.

He was relieved to find the duffel bag full of money, undisturbed, under his bed. Relax, he told himself. Tomorrow morning it'll all be over.

Gonzalez found a bottle of Scotch in his liquor cabinet and poured some over ice. It wasn't Johnny Walker Blue, but it would do in a pinch. He vowed that once he had access to his millions, he would stock the good stuff by the case.

His answering machine was blinking. There were three messages – two from his colleagues in the Legislature who wanted to discuss legislation (that could wait) and one message from his wife in Orlando. Gonzalez realized he hadn't spoken to his wife in – what – four days? Had it been that long?

Gonzalez forced himself to call his wife and endured another strained conversation with her. They had stopped loving each other long ago, but Gonzalez needed a wife for his political career and Mrs. Gonzalez, he was certain, enjoyed being the wife of the speaker. And she'll enjoy being the wife of a congressman, too, if everything goes well, he thought. Perhaps I should buy her something shiny and expensive with my millions, he mused, to keep her in the fold.

Another glass of Scotch later and Gonzalez started thinking about Roxy. Last night's sexual failure with her was a first for him, and he started imagining Roxy with Joe. It was a very clear picture of two very beautiful people having incredible sex, and it angered him. Then Gonzalez conjured up the notion that Roxy would tell Joe about his failure to get it up, and they would make fun of him. Now he was getting really pissed.

The apartment started closing in on him. Why in the hell should he wait until morning to return with the money? Why not go back right now and reclaim what was rightfully his?

Gonzalez drained his glass of Scotch, poured another in a go cup, grabbed the duffel full of cash, and headed back to St. George Island in the dark.

Gonzalez was plenty drunk by the time he crossed the bridge to St. George Island, and he had to piss something fierce, but he refused to stop until he got to the condo. He was driven by jealousy and anger and the need to reclaim his territory from Joe.

Gonzalez decided to drive around the side of the condo to the private parking spot and was surprised to find it empty. Joe must be gone, but he could see lights on in the condo. Perhaps Roxy was alone and would welcome him with open arms!

The first thing Gonzalez did when he got out of the car was unzip his trousers and water the hedges. Jesus, I'm drunk, he thought. Please, God, not another case of whiskey dick.

His back teeth no longer floating, Gonzalez zipped up and waddled down the boardwalk to the deck. He got one foot on the deck when he looked inside and froze.

Roxy wasn't alone after all, but the man with her wasn't Joe. Gonzalez couldn't believe what he was seeing. Roxy was sprawled naked on the sofa, and the man putting his clothes back on was *Roy Fercal!*

What the hell? What's Roy Fercal doing in Joe's condo, banging my chief of staff? For God's sake, Fercal runs the Democratic Party! He's my enemy! And for that matter, why is my chief of staff having sex with the enemy?

Gonzalez had never felt so betrayed, so angry. He watched from the darkness as Fercal finished dressing and headed for the front door. Then, through an open window, Gonzalez heard Roxy ask Fercal, "When do I get my share of the money?"

"After I get the money from Joe."

"Tomorrow?"

"Yeah, Roxy. Tomorrow. I'll see you tomorrow."

With that, Fercal let himself out.

Gonzalez felt like he'd been hit in the chest with a baseball bat. He had no doubt whose money they were talking about – his. So Joe was going to take the cash and give it to Fercal, that bastard. It was a setup! And Roxy was in on it!

He heard Fercal's car drive off and watched as Roxy, still naked, walked into the kitchen. And he snapped.

Gonzalez threw open the door and stormed into the kitchen. "You bitch! You fucking goddamn traitor! To hell with you!"

Startled, Roxy turned wide-eyed as she saw Gonzalez pick up a cast iron skillet from the kitchen stove and swing it at her. The skillet slammed into the side of her head with a sickening whack. There was the sound of a skull cracking open, and Roxy collapsed to the floor like a rag doll.

Gonzalez stood over her for a full minute, trying to regain control of his breathing, the skillet still in his right hand. The enormity of what he had just done started to sink in and he dropped to his knees.

"Oh, God, Roxy. I'm sorry. Oh my God."

Slowly, Gonzalez checked her for signs of life. There were none. Roxy Jones was dead, and he had killed her.

20

Gonzalez was in shock. He was not a violent man, yet he had just killed his chief of staff in a fit of blind rage. What now? He needed to act. He needed to *do something*, but what? Well, he can't keep kneeling over Roxy's nude body with a skillet in his hand. Surely not.

He rose unsteadily and with great effort, his knees popping and protesting, and put the skillet back on the kitchen stove. He thought there was a noise from one of the bedrooms. Oh my God! Was Joe here? A witness!

"Joe?" Gonzalez offered. "Are you here, Joe?"

Nothing.

Gonzalez walked slowly down the hall and through the bedrooms. The condo was empty, save for him and Roxy.

And Roxy was dead.

Then Gonzalez went out on the deck, looking up and down the beach for any signs of people. There were none. Thunderstorms were rattling just offshore, with brilliant flashes of lightening putting on quite a show. No, this was not a night to be frolicking on the beach.

So, Gonzalez felt it was safe to assume that no one had seen him swing the skillet at Roxy's head and kill her. Now what?

Well, Joe could be coming back at any moment. He had to get rid of Roxy's body, and pronto. He went to his car and moved the duffel bag full of cash from his trunk to the back seat. Then, with great effort, Gonzalez managed to wrap Roxy's body in a blanket and lug it to his trunk.

Remarkably, Roxy had bled only a little, from her left ear. Gonzalez simply wiped it up with a paper towel and flushed the bloody towel down the toilet.

He moved more quickly, worried that Joe would appear any second. Gonzalez gathered up the few things he had brought to the condo for the weekend and went back to the car. It was starting to rain and a loud thunderclap nearly made him cry out.

He backed out of the private parking space and sped off, sobbing at the enormity of what he had just done and how his life had turned to shit since he accepted the bribe from those damn casino thugs.

Thinking of the money brought back the feelings of betrayal. How in the hell had this happened? As he drove away from St. George Island, Gonzalez pondered it.

He had accepted a meeting with some casino executives in Miami without knowing what to expect. He certainly wasn't expecting a bribe. Roxy had set up the meeting, and later said she knew about the bribe. Did she know about the bribe ahead of time? Doubtful, he thought. If you're going to bribe the Speaker of the House of Representatives, you don't go blabbing about it to the chief of staff ahead of time.

That means somebody else knew about the bribe and brought Roxy in on it. Clearly, Roxy's role was to convince him to hand the cash over to Joe in an effort to launder it. And from what he had overheard at the condo, Joe was going to hand the money over to that slimy bastard Fercal. What was Fercal going to do with the money? Probably keep it.

Gonzalez shuddered at how close he had come to being duped into handing over $2 million in cash to a thief. And what will happen when Joe realizes the money isn't going to be handed over? And when will Roxy be missed?

And then it hit him like a thunderclap. *Roy Fercal knows about the bribe!* The head of the Democratic Party knows the Speaker of the House took a bribe! Holy shit. How?

Well, either the casino thugs told him, or the whole thing was a setup from the beginning to bring him down. This was bad. This was very, very bad.

As Gonzalez approached the city limits of Carrabelle, he spied a police car partially concealed behind some brush just off the road. He braked a little, but didn't need to. For a change, Gonzalez wasn't speeding, and the cop ignored him.

Jesus. I'm the Speaker of the House driving around in the rain with the nude body of my chief of staff in the trunk and a $2 million bribe bouncing around in the back seat, he thought crazily. And just how does a person explain *that?*

The thought of Roxy's body in the trunk started closing in on him like a ghost. He needed to dump it, but where?

Up ahead he saw a sign pointing the way to an official hurricane evacuation route. He and Roxy had driven the lonely road once before, just for the heck of it, after spending the day on St. George Island. It went through Tate's Hell Swamp, and Gonzalez remembered how desolate it was. They didn't meet a single car.

It was perfect. Gonzalez turned north and drove in isolation for several minutes. He pulled over where a single-lane road that was nothing more than packed sand intersected with the highway and killed the headlights. The darkness was absolute and the trunk light looked like a beacon when he opened it.

Gonzalez struggled to lift Roxy's body, still tightly wrapped in the blanket, out of the trunk. He dragged it to the edge of the swamp and let it roll in. Then he returned to the car, closed the trunk, and threw up.

21

Monday, September 8

Monday morning stirred slowly in Tallahassee, it being Labor Day and all, even though it's not much of a labor town. About the only thing manufactured on a regular basis in Tallahassee is legislation. Still, a holiday is a holiday.

But the holiday didn't make a bit of difference to Bannerman Lux. He was in his downtown office bright and early, working the phone to get Carrie Stevens out of jail. He tried Jessie Malloy, the state's attorney, at home and didn't get an answer. She wasn't in her office, either, so he wondered if she was spending some time with her parents in Sopchoppy. Lux knew the number because Jessie's father was a frequent golf partner. She was there.

"Look, Jess, it's not Carrie's fault that it's a holiday," Lux reasoned. "She doesn't belong in jail."

"She killed three kids, Lucky."

"Allegedly, Jess, allegedly. And Carrie's not going to run from this. We'll face it head on."

They jostled back and forth for a few minutes and eventually negotiated a compromise to present to a judge for Carrie's release.

After the judge rubber-stamped the agreement, Lux wasted no time driving to the west side of town and retrieving Carrie from the Leon County jail. Buddy Frolic looked like he was sorry to see her go.

"Where can I take you, Carrie?" Lux asked her. "Home?"

"I want to talk to Rip. Take me to Rip's."

So that's where they went.

B uddy Frolic was indeed sorry to see Carrie leave his jail. He could tell she was a good-looking woman, even with her face all bandaged up. And he knew something about her that others didn't, and it only deepened his interest in her. Boy howdy!

When he ran Carrie's fingerprints through the system, he at first thought he'd made some kind of mistake. So he ran them again with the same result. Carrie Stevens wasn't Carrie Stevens at all. Her real name was Shelby Hoagensteiner and there was a file on her. Buddy called an old friend in St. Louis who filled him in on the juicy details.

S helby was born in a hospital in Jefferson City, Missouri, to a single mother who lived in a tiny town nearby called Henley. Her home life must not have been very good, because Shelby ran away at the age of fourteen. She went back home six months later but ran off again on her sixteenth birthday and shacked up with some fellow outcasts in the St. Louis area.

Shelby was a looker, even then, and one night a man she met at a party offered her a job dancing at a strip club he managed in Sauget, Illinois – just across the Mississippi River from St. Louis.

"You're eighteen, aren't you?" he inquired.

"Of course," she lied.

"I thought so," he lied back, and the next night Shelby Hoagensteiner was stripping herself naked at a club called Peckerheads. It was like nothing she'd ever seen or heard about.

Peckerheads was only one part of a complex of businesses called the Pecker Palace in what used to be a neighborhood grocery store. There was also the Knothole Club, an adult bookstore with private booths for viewing movies and "knotholes" between the booths. In the back was an all-nude male club called Boner's. But the business that got the Pecker Palace in the most trouble was the Rub-a-Dub Hot Tub Club, which presented itself as a place where you could buy a hot tub and – as a popular service to its clientele – dancers from Peckerheads or Boner's could help you try it out for size right there at the Pecker Palace!

It was an enormously popular and lucrative business operation. Dancers worked for tips only, and they had to pay the Pecker Palace owners for the privilege. Even so, on a good night, a good-looking dancer who was open to suggestions could walk out with a thousand bucks in cash. There was a $20.00 cover charge and the drinks were outrageous – eight bucks for a Budweiser.

Word got around, with the help of the Internet, about Shelby Hoagensteiner, although she went by the name "Paradise." She was a big hit and a frequent visitor to the Rub-a-Dub, where she charged eager businessmen a minimum of $200 to find out if they liked having sex in a hot tub. They always did.

Eventually, the feds started taking an interest in the Pecker Palace. They didn't really care so much about what people were doing in there, though there was some hand wringing about that. No, the feds were interested in the idea that an awfully lot of money seemed to be pouring into the Pecker Palace with only a fraction of it being reported as income. Prostitution was a nuisance; cheating on your taxes was a federal offense.

The Pecker Palace was owned by the Barboni family of Chicago, which had a long history of sucking money out of the Metro East area of St. Louis with a variety of sleazy businesses. Taking down the Barboni family also piqued the interest of the feds.

So they sent a nice-looking agent in his thirties into the Pecker Palace with a wad of cash. When he walked up to the bar at Peckerheads and ordered a beer, he did so by pulling out the large wad of cash and peeling off a hundred dollar bill. All the dancers who weren't otherwise occupied saw it, of course, and the agent was marked as a cash cow. Shelby was the first to snag him.

She took $100 from him for a couple of lap dances in the back, and he tipped her a couple of twenties while she was on stage dancing. Eventually, he asked about the Rub-a-Dub Hot Tub Club. She escorted him into the Rub-a-Dub.

Two other federal agents had been across the street, in a van, listening to everything the inside agent was doing through his wire. They had snickered all the way through the lap dances, what with the grunting and all, but they were paying close attention now.

They recorded the exchange between the agent and Shelby. It was almost pitiful the way Shelby laid it out so plain and simple.

"For two hundred bucks we can both get naked and play around with each other," she said. "If you want to have actual sex, it's another hundred."

The agent didn't get naked or have sex with her, though he might have if not for the stupid wire. She was hot. He simply looked at her sympathetically and said, "You're busted, Paradise." And in no time at all, the Pecker Palace was full of federal agents.

At the other end of the Rub-a-Dub, there was a fat old man who was actually in the throes of orgasm when the agents burst in. He looked like he wanted to drown himself. The dancer jumped up, slapped him hard across the face and yelled, "Rape!" But nobody bought it.

22

A lot of people got hauled off to jail that night, including Shelby Hoagensteiner, and it scared her. The Pecker Palace was shut down and the feds started the long process of sifting through boxes of paperwork, looking for evidence of tax evasion and money laundering. They were willing to let the local cops worry about the prostitution angle.

But then the news came back that the dancer known as Paradise was only 16, and the feds took a renewed interest. This was the leverage they needed against the Barboni family.

The feds approached Shelby with a deal she couldn't refuse. In exchange for her sworn testimony and full cooperation, she could walk away with nothing to show for it but her memories. It was a chance at a fresh start! And Shelby had squirreled away almost $30,000 in cash, a fact she didn't bother to share with her new friends, the feds.

So Shelby ratted out the Barboni family as best she could, even swearing under oath that the manager of the Pecker Palace knew she was only 16 and didn't care. In fact, she said, he liked it.

It took awhile, but with Shelby's help and a lot of long hours running down leads from the paperwork, the feds got indictments for tax evasion, money laundering and racketeering against several members of the Barboni family. Once the first member of the family pleaded guilty and started to sing, the rest of the family followed suit. There were prison sentences all around.

Shelby Hoagensteiner ceased to exist. Paradise had the business card of a very appreciative customer and magazine publisher who lived in Tampa. He was thrilled beyond belief when Paradise called him and, of course, he would help her relocate to Florida.

So Paradise moved to Tampa and became Carrie Stevens, the youngest writer on the staff at *Living Tampa Bay*, an upscale magazine geared to the local elite. Even without formal training, Carrie was a pretty good writer and she honed her skills on such riveting topics as fine dining and art exhibits. Her work ethic, plus the occasional roll in the hay with the magazine's owner, moved her up the ranks to managing editor.

Eventually, the wife of the magazine owner started getting suspicious and Carrie figured it was time to move on. With the help of a glowing reference from *Living Tampa Bay* and a phony resume, Carrie landed a job as a reporter with the *Suncoast Gazette*. Finally, her past was behind her – or so she thought.

So, Buddy Frolic thought, Carrie Stevens is really Shelby Hoagensteiner, and she used to strip under the alias of Paradise at a place called the Pecker Palace. She was busted for prostitution at the age of 16 and the charges were dropped for cooperating with the feds and putting the owners of the Pecker Palace behind bars.

It was heady information to have, and Buddy had used information a lot less juicy than this to coerce sexual favors from some of his jailhouse guests. It disappointed him greatly that Carrie or Shelby or Paradise – or whatever the hell you wanted to call her – had slipped away before he could use it against her. Still, the information was valuable. If he couldn't get some jollies out of it, then maybe someone else could make use of it. He dialed the phone number from memory.

Buddy knew better than to wait for a greeting. When he heard background noise, he started talking.

"Hey, Roy. It's Buddy."

"Buddy Frolic! What's up, Buddy?"

"I got some juicy stuff for ya. On a local celebrity."

"I'm all ears, Buddy."

And Buddy passed along the lurid details of Carrie's past to one Roy Fercal, who listened with sharp interest and filed the information away for future use. Sooner or later, it seemed, dirt always came in handy in the wild, wild world of politics.

"Listen, Buddy, will this information become public? Or can we stash it away somehow?"

"I can stash it, if you want. As far as the court knows, she ain't nothin' but Carrie Stevens unless I fill 'em in."

"Good, Buddy, let's keep a lid on it. Look for a birthday card in the mail."

Buddy didn't bother saying goodbye; he knew Fercal's phone habits. He set about the business of destroying the paper trail identifying Carrie Stevens as Shelby Hoagensteiner.

23

J oe the Surfer Dude had partied with his buddies until almost dawn. He finally crashed on a sofa to catch a couple of hours of sleep before meeting Gonzalez, but he overslept. It was almost ten o'clock by the time he cracked open an eye and found a clock.

Jesus Christ! He cursed himself for letting things get out of hand last night with so much riding on his meeting with Gonzalez. Damn it!

Joe showered and dressed as quickly as he could and drove the short distance to the other condo. What would he tell Gonzalez? Had he blown the deal?

Joe looked around the parking lot but didn't see Gonzalez's car anywhere. That worried him. He parked in the private spot around back and hurried into the condo.

"Roxy? Al? Hey, sorry I'm late. Something came up. Hello?"

It didn't take Joe long to discover the condo was empty. He checked the beach – nothing. Had Gonzalez gotten spooked when Joe wasn't there this morning and left with the money? It's possible. But what about Roxy? Damn it, she was in on it. Couldn't she figure out a way to keep Gonzalez busy for a couple of hours?

Joe went through the condo more carefully. Hmm … Gonzalez's clothes and toiletries were gone, but Roxy's were still there, including her leopard skin bikini, which she had strung over a shower rod to dry.

So, it looked to Joe like Gonzalez had gotten spooked this morning and left. Roxy was a mystery. Damn, this was bad. It was time to call Fercal.

"Roy? It's Joe. We got a problem."

"What do you mean, problem? He should have given you the money by now. What's going on?"

"He didn't show, Roy. I've been waiting all morning," Joe lied, "and there's been no sign of him."

"Jesus! He's over two hours late! Call him, or something. Find out where the hell he is!"

"I don't have his number, Roy. You got it?"

"Hell no, but I'm sure Roxy does. Get her to call him."

"Well, that's another thing, Roy. She's not here, either."

"What? What the fuck are you saying?"

"I'm telling you Roxy is gone, too. There's nobody here but me."

"That doesn't make any sense," Roy said, pacing his suite in Apalachicola, his head starting to throb. "She was there last night. I was with her. Where the hell would she go?"

"I don't know, Roy, but she's gone. What now?"

"Christ, I don't know. You stay put, Joe, in case Gonzalez finally shows up with the damn money, though I doubt it. I'm gonna call Roxy and find out what the hell is going on."

Roy found Roxy's cell phone number in his phone's address book and hit dial. She better have a damn good reason for being AWOL.

When the phone was answered Roy started right in. "Roxy! Where are you? And where is Gonzalez? Damn it, this wasn't in the script!"

"Hi, Roy. It's me, Joe."

"Joe! What are you doing answering Roxy's phone?"

"I heard it ringing. It was in her purse."

"Her purse is still there? Then she couldn't have gone far. I'm on my way over. We'll find her and get this shit straightened out."

It was almost noon when Gonzalez jerked awake with a start. Where the hell was he? He was confused by the unfamiliar surroundings, and then it all came flooding back to him along with a wave of grief and guilt. Gonzalez had figured Fercal and Joe would be looking for him, so he decided to drive all the way to Orlando instead of returning to Tallahassee after dumping Roxy's body. But he only got as far as Gainesville before fatigue forced him to find a local motel.

He looked around for the duffel full of money, but it wasn't there. Had he carelessly left it in the car? Stupid!

Gonzalez was even more alarmed when he got to the car. It was unlocked! Amazingly, though, the duffel was still there and the money was still in it. Jesus! Anybody could have stolen it!

And for a brief moment, he almost wished they had. The money was nothing but trouble. His life seemed so much better a few days ago when he was nothing but an honest politician. Well, mostly honest anyway.

Gonzalez put the car in gear and resumed his trip to Orlando. He figured hell would freeze over before anyone spotted Roxy's body in that godforsaken swamp.

24

As luck would have it, hell actually did freeze over in that godforsaken swamp just a few hours later.

Billy Ray Schlotzin, one of the few people to actually live within the official confines of Tate's Hell Swamp, was spending his holiday hunting for alligators. He had come to the task fully prepared, with his best rifle, plenty of ammo, a good pair of binoculars, and a twelve-pack of Bud Light on ice. Well, at noon it was a twelve-pack. Now, it was closer to a six-pack and Billy Ray had to piss.

He stopped his truck and started peeing over the side of the road into the swamp, but it didn't sound right. It kinda sounded like he was peeing on a drum, or something. When he finished, Billy Ray took a closer look and realized he had been peeing on a blanket and something was rolled up in it.

With no small amount of trepidation, Billy Ray found a dry spot on the edge of the blanket and gave it a tug. He tugged harder and gravity took over. The nude body of Roxy Jones came tumbling out and Billy Ray forgot all about hunting for alligators.

A cell phone in the middle of Tate's Hell Swamp was about as useful as a canker sore, so Billy Ray hightailed it back to his trailer and called the sheriff. Then he hurried back to the spot of the body, to make sure it was still there and the gators hadn't gotten it. She was still there, and Billy Ray stood guard over her until the sheriff arrived.

Johnny Tobin had been the sheriff of Franklin County for 28 years. He didn't rattle easily, but the idea of a body in the swamp made this day more interesting than most.

"Good afternoon, Billy Ray. I guess you're the one who found the body?"

"That's right, sheriff. I was lookin' for gators."

"You touch anything?"

"Yeah, I touched the blanket. I was trying to see what was in it and she came rolling out. Scared the bejesus out of me."

Sheriff Tobin squatted down to examine the blanket. "Smells like somebody peed on the damn thing."

Billy Ray blushed. "Uh, that was me, sheriff. I peed on it."

"Jesus Christ, Billy Ray! What are you doing peeing on a crime scene?"

"I didn't know it was a crime scene when I peed on it!"

"Alright, Billy Ray. Calm down. Do you know this girl?"

"No, I don't," Billy Ray said, "but she's a looker. Even dead, she's a looker."

Sheriff Tobin had to admit that, yes, even dead, she was a looker. But the way Billy Ray said it made his skin crawl just a bit.

"You sure you didn't touch her, Billy Ray?"

"Yes, I'm sure! What do you think I am? Some kind of pervert?"

"Well, you peed on her, Billy Ray."

Sheriff Tobin enjoyed a good laugh as he walked back to his cruiser to call in the crime scene boys with Billy Ray loudly proclaiming his innocence in the peeing department.

Ordinarily, John Billings made his bird-watching rounds later in the day, to avoid the heat. But the memory of the naked blonde was too much, and he was back in St. George State Park just after lunch hoping for another peek.

He found a secluded spot where he could zoom in on the deck of the condo without being seen. There was movement inside, he could tell, but the deck was empty. Then someone walked out onto the deck and started looking anxiously up and down the beach. John recognized him as the same man who had embraced the woman the evening before. Just for the heck of it, John clicked off a few pictures. It was good practice, if nothing else.

The man, obviously angry, stormed back inside and shut the door. John kept watch for a while, but it was obvious the naked blonde was not going to make an appearance. Disappointed, and sweaty, he went back home.

Rip Snyder and Carrie Stevens were spending a quiet Labor Day together at Rip's house. They had asked Bannerman Lux to stay and sit on the deck and watch the golfers go by, but he begged off, sensing a need for them to be alone.

Rip had almost melted when he first laid eyes on Carrie and her burned face inside a miniature hockey mask. Here was the woman he had treated as little more than a sex partner just a few days ago, but what he felt today was deeper. He wrapped his arms around her and held her. They wept, silently, together.

Eventually, Carrie told Rip about the accident.

"I'm so sorry, Carrie. What a horrible thing. We'll get you though it, though, with Lucky's help. It'll be okay."

"No it won't, Rip. It'll never be okay. I killed those kids. I wish I could take it back."

"Don't talk like that, Carrie. We'll figure out a way. We'll make it happen."

Carrie just shook her head and burrowed deeper into Rip's arms. He didn't understand, she thought. Even if she beat the charges, her mind would be imprisoned forever by the memory of those three little girls hitching a ride from life into death on the hood of a truck.

R oy Fercal was livid. Jesus, he was having a bad stretch of luck. His plan to get a picture of Gonzalez toting his bribe into the *Suncoast Gazette* went belly up because Carrie Stevens had a damn wreck on her way to the airport. Then his brilliant plan to steal the bribe from Gonzalez goes bust because of – because of what? He didn't know, and that angered him, too.

And Roxy Jones was nowhere to be found, like she was abducted by aliens or something. What was going on?

Eventually, Joe decided to click through Roxy's address book on her cell phone. He found an entry called, "Alcell" and figured it was the speaker's cell phone. He hit dial.

Hundreds of miles away, on the outskirts of Orlando, Gonzalez heard his phone chirp and checked the caller ID. He gasped as the name "Roxy" showed up on the screen. Jesus! What the hell? He shut the phone off and threw it into the back seat. Christ almighty! His skin was crawling and it was all he could do to keep the car on the road.

Roxy's dead. So who was calling him on her phone?

He figured it had to be Joe. Gonzalez didn't even bother going to his house. He drove straight to his district office in downtown Orlando. It was closed for Labor Day, of course, but he let himself in and used the phone to call a friend of his who owned a private flying service.

Gonzalez begged his friend to fly him to Puerto Rico, that very evening. It was urgent family business, Gonzalez pleaded, and he would pay cash. The friend agreed and the arrangements were made.

It was a smooth flight, made all the smoother by the presence of Johnny Walker Blue. They landed at a private airport near Ponca, in the south. As Gonzalez deplaned, clutching his oversized duffel, he turned to the pilot.

"One more favor, my trusted friend," Gonzalez implored.

"And what is that?"

"You flew me here yesterday."

"I did? Yesterday?"

"Yes, my friend, and we spent time together in Ponca, drinking rum."

"And did we have fun together? In Ponca?"

"We did indeed, my beloved friend," Gonzalez assured him, handing him a stack of one hundred dollar bills.

"And it is a memory I shall cherish forever, Alberto. To Ponca!"

"To Ponca!" And they parted ways, with Gonzalez looking for a car and his pilot friend wondering what the hell was going on. He shrugged, stuffed the bills in his shirt, and changed the date on his logbook.

Sheriff Johnny Tobin had a mess on his hands. The medical examiner told him the woman found in the swamp hadn't been dead for very long, probably less than a day. It was a miracle she was found so quickly, the medical examiner said.

Sheriff Tobin wasn't sure he'd classify Billy Ray Schlotzin managing to take a leak on a newly discarded body as a miracle, but God does work in mysterious ways.

It was obvious to everyone that the poor woman had been killed someplace else, wrapped in a blanket and dumped there. The cause of death was easy, too – her head was bashed in with something big and heavy.

"And somebody had a good time with her beforehand, Sheriff," the medical examiner noted.

"Really? How's that?"

"We found semen, and plenty of it. Looks like the sex was pretty rough, too. Bruising and stuff."

"You think she was raped?"

The coroner nodded. "More'n likely."

The sheriff pondered this. "Got enough semen to get DNA?"

"More than enough. Find yourself a suspect, sheriff, and if the DNA matches, we'll send the bastard to Stark where he can ride Old Sparky."

"You know nobody rides Old Sparky anymore. They get the needle now."

"Yeah, and it's a damn shame. All because a few weenies couldn't stand the smell of burning flesh."

"Any news on an ID?"

"Well, her prints aren't in the system. I guess we'll need some help from the public on this one."

So Sheriff Tobin called the local media, which doesn't amount to much in Franklin County. He also sent word to the sheriffs in the surrounding counties of Wakulla, Liberty and Gulf, along with a picture of the deceased. He also sent a couple of deputies around Carrabelle, Eastpoint and St. George Island with pictures.

And Billy Ray Schlotzin, who enjoyed his celebrity status as the one who found the body, also spread the word. He told the story with great gusto at Biggy's Bar and Grill in Carrabelle, leaving out the part about peeing on the crime scene, of course.

25

Eventually, Roy Fercal decided Joe was a liability. The gig was up, anyway. Something had spooked Gonzalez and there was no way he was going to hand two million bucks over to Joe anymore, and Roy told him so.

"Do I still get paid?" Joe asked. "I put a lot of work into it."

"Your share of the money was coming out of the cash, Joe. Right now, nobody gets paid."

This pissed Joe off, but there was no point in lashing out at Roy. Besides, Joe blamed himself for oversleeping. Maybe he's the reason Gonzalez got spooked.

"Well, that sucks a big one, Roy. If you ever get your hands on the cash, I still expect my share."

"Whatever. I'm going back to Tally and figure this thing out. You clean up the condo and make sure it's locked up tight before you leave."

"What about Roxy's stuff, Roy? Maybe she'll come back for it."

"Toss it in the dumpster, Joe. That bitch has some explaining to do."

So Roy left, stomping angrily on the gas and spraying sand in the direction of John Billings, who was on his way back to St. George State Park on his bike.

"Stupid bastard," John whispered to himself, then corrected his statement. "Stupid DEMOCRAT bastard," taking note of the old "Reelect Gore" bumper sticker on the car as it sped away.

Joe did as he was told, cleaning up the condo and gathering Roxy's things to throw away. He couldn't bring himself to discard the leopard skin bikini bottoms, though, because he liked the feel of them. He even stripped off his clothes and put them on. They barely covered his crotch, which was clean-shaven, and left most of his behind exposed. He liked it, and figured his buddies at the other condo would, too. So he left them on and finished up the cleaning job.

But Joe's thoughts were turning to more earthly pursuits and he was careless. He completely missed a semen stain on the living room sofa and took no notice at all of some blonde hairs stuck to the bottom of a cast iron skillet.

By the time Joe finished up he was whistling a happy tune and walked out to the dumpster wearing nothing but the bikini bottoms. He so startled John Billings that the old postal worker forgot all about his fancy new camera as he wondered what in the hell was going on in condo number eight.

On the way back to Tallahassee, Roy developed a theory as to what happened to Gonzalez and Roxy. He decided Roxy somehow figured out the amount of cash Gonzalez had was two million instead of two hundred thousand, as Roy had told her, and she got pissed. She probably spilled the beans to Gonzalez – or played the hero and told him she had smelled a rat – and they took off.

So it was Roxy's fault. But why would she leave without her purse and cell phone? She must have left in one heck of a hurry. Trying to beat Joe, most likely. Damn! They had come so close. Time for a new plan.

His reason for arranging the bribe was to bring down Speaker Gonzalez just in time for the elections this fall, casting a stain on the Republican Party and impacting on the election results. Stealing the money was pure greed.

So forget about stealing the money for the time being and go back to the original intent – casting a stain on the Republican Party. How could he do that? What tools did he have at his disposal?

Then it hit him like a brick – Rip Snyder! Rip was loosely tied to the tragic deaths of three black kids because he loaned his truck to a drunk who ran them over. And the drunk who ran the kids over is a former teenaged prostitute with an arrest record. Jesus! This is better than bribing the speaker! And a lot of powerful Republicans had Rip on the payroll as a political consultant. By throwing mud on Rip, Roy could spread the mud to a lot of top Republicans.

It's hard to make mud without dirt, but Roy had the dirt on Carrie Stevens. Roy's mood brightened and the rest of the drive to Tallahassee went quickly. There was work to be done.

Roy's first call was to Carl Splighter.

"Hey, Carl. What's the latest on Carrie?"

"They let her out of the hospital on Sunday and took her straight to jail. Three counts of vehicular manslaughter. She'll get twenty years, at least."

"She's not in jail anymore, Carl. They let her out this morning." Roy knew this from his conversation with Buddy Frolic.

"Jesus! That was fast. And on a holiday, too."

"Yeah. She must have a helluva lawyer. Listen, Carl, I need to meet with her, pronto."

"You want to meet with Carrie? Why?"

"None of your business. Just set it up. Tell her to meet me at eight o'clock tomorrow morning at the entrance to Maclay Gardens. Got it?"

"You gonna look at flowers together?"

"Tell her it's about the biggest story of her life, Carl. Understand?"

Carl understood. He figured it was about Gonzalez. "Listen, Roy, on another topic. I was gonna call you anyway. How would you like some dirt on Rip Snyder?"

Jesus! What was Carl doing, reading Roy's mind?

"Whaddya got?"

Carl filled him in on Rip's liberal use of the n-word.

"And how do you know this, Carl?"

"It was in her diary. Carrie's, I mean."

"You've been reading her diary?"

"It was at the office! I stumbled onto it and read a little bit and it pissed me off. So I took it."

"You stole her diary? Jesus, Carl!" Roy considered this for a moment. "Anything juicy in it?"

"You mean besides the nigger stuff? Sex stuff mostly, with her and Rip."

Roy was almost giddy. "Does she mention anything about a woman named Shelby?"

"Shelby? No. Is it someone I should know?"

"Never mind, Carl. Hey, thanks for the dirt on Rip. I owe you. Make sure you set up that meeting with Carrie. Okay?"

"Okay. Listen, about this Gonzalez thing ..."

But Carl was talking into an empty phone. Roy Fercal was gone.

Roy contacted Jessie Malloy, the Leon County state's attorney, on her cell phone.

"Jailhouse Jess! You ready for a big victory tomorrow?" The first Tuesday in September is the primary election.

"Gee, Roy, I hate to get cocky. But since I'm the only one on the ballot, I feel pretty safe."

"How would you like to go to Congress in two years?"

"What? Is Conner retiring? I haven't heard anything about it."

"Yeah. Consider him gone. You interested?"

"Of course I'm interested; you know that."

"Then I need you to meet with me – tonight."

"Tonight? Does it have to be tonight? I'm in Sopchoppy with the family."

"The sooner the better. Old Man Congress is calling, Jess, and we mustn't keep him waiting."

"Okay, Roy. I'm on my way."

That done, Roy called Billy Conner's chief of staff. The congressman was planning to vote for himself in the morning and catch a mid-morning flight to Washington.

"I need a few minutes of the congressman's time in the morning."

"Can you meet him at the airport?" the chief of staff inquired. "His plane leaves at 10:15."

"I'll be there at 9:30," Roy announced and clicked off.

Roy popped open a beer and waited for Jessie Malloy. He was hoping her political ambition was stronger than her sense of civic duty. That would make her normal in Roy's world, and he liked normal.

The meeting with Jessie Malloy was not going as smoothly as Roy had hoped. He had started by explaining to her that Billy Conner was going to retire after one more term, but that the decision "was only somewhat voluntary." Malloy was instantly on edge, anxious to get elected to Congress, but not really interested in pushing someone aside to get there.

"Listen, Jess. Conner has a serious skeleton in his closet and the door is about to fall open. He has no choice but to retire, whether you decide to replace him or not. I'm giving you first crack at it."

"But once the announcement is made, there'll be lots of people lining up to run. I can think of half a dozen Democrats off the top of my head."

"Ordinarily, that would be true, yes. But we can fix that."

"What do you mean, fix it? Are you saying you'll clear the field for me? You'll stop others from running?"

"That's exactly what I'm saying, Jess. All you have to do is say the word and you're as good as elected."

The room got quiet. Roy stared at her, waiting. Jess returned the stare, then: "Why me?"

"Because I need a favor."

Jessie nodded. It made sense that Roy Fercal wasn't about to hand over a congressional seat without expecting something in return. "And that would be what, exactly?"

This is where Roy was going to discover which was larger – her ambition or her sense of duty.

"Well, what I need, exactly, is for you to drop the charges against Carrie Stevens. Let her go."

"Are you crazy, Roy? The woman killed three kids! Three BLACK kids! I can't do it. You're asking too much."

"Think of the good you can do in Congress, Jess. You'd be great."

"I'd be a laughingstock! How does turning loose of a killer get me elected to Congress?"

"I told you. I can fix it."

"Can you bring those kids back to life, Roy? Huh? Bring the kids back, and I'll let your little girlfriend go."

"She's not my girlfriend."

"Then why are you asking me do this?"

"Because the party needs Carrie back at work. She's on the verge of exposing corruption in some very high places. If she goes to prison, a lot of Republicans will get away with it."

"Get away with what?"

"They're stealing us blind, Jess. And listen – if Carrie nails these bastards in the *Suncoast Gazette,* you'll get to prosecute 'em. Do you think putting a governor behind bars will get you noticed?"

"The governor?"

"Yes, I said the governor. And others."

"I don't know, Roy. How would it work? I can't just waltz into court and let the girl go."

"You'll have help."

"What kind of help?"

"From Busby."

"Judge Busby Brown? He's in on this, too?"

Roy nodded. "He'll issue a ruling that cripples your case. You'll have no choice but to drop the charges. You can even criticize Busby if you want. He won't care."

"And what does old Busby get for his trouble?"

"Well, if everything shakes out right, a seat on the state supreme court."

Jessie was stunned. "Are you saying you expect all of this to lead to a Democrat being elected governor in two years?"

Roy couldn't contain his smile. "That's right, Jess. I'm talking about a sea change here. The Republicans will be too crippled by corruption to stop us." Roy waited a beat. "And it all starts with you."

The room got quiet again. So this is what politics is like among the big boys, Jessie thought grimly. Am I ready for this? "Okay, Roy. It's a deal. And this meeting never happened."

26

John and Margaret Billings were just leaving the Leaky Tiki after consuming their usual Monday night fare of blackened grouper, waffle fries and cole slaw, along with a pint of Budweiser for John and a glass of chardonnay for Margaret. They were walking hand-in-hand in the gathering darkness, as they often did, toward home along the island's main drag.

A deputy sheriff's car approached them and stopped. The deputy got out.

"Evening, folks. Nice night for a walk."

"It sure is, officer," John said, taking the lead as usual. "Everything quiet?"

"Well, I need to ask you folks about something, and it's a little disturbing."

"Oh? Did something happen here on the island?" Bad things almost never happened on St. George Island.

"Well, I need to show you a picture of a woman to see if you recognize her. But I should warn you folks – the woman in the picture is dead."

"A dead woman?" Margaret asked, unbelieving. "Here on the island?"

"Well, we don't know about that, ma'am." He handed the photograph of Roxy Jones, taken at the crime scene, to Margaret. "Have you ever seen her before?"

Margaret winced. "No, I don't know her. Dear God, such a beautiful woman. What a shame!"

Margaret handed the photo to John and he almost fell to the ground.

"Oh my God! I know this woman!"

The deputy looked at him sharply. "You know her?"

Margaret was aghast. "You know her? How?"

John took a step back. He couldn't take his eyes off the photograph. "I mean I don't exactly know her. I don't know her name or anything, but I've seen her. Here on the island."

The deputy asked John where he had seen her, and under what circumstances. John was instantly unnerved. He didn't relish the idea of describing his telephoto intrusion into the woman's nudity the night before in front of Margaret. But the woman he saw last night was dead, and didn't he have an obligation to tell what he knew?

While John debated what to do, he pretended to study the photograph some more.

"Sir? I need to know where you saw her. It's important."

John handed the photograph back to the deputy. Resigning himself to an ass chewing from Margaret, he started in.

"You know that condo complex at the end of the road here, next to the state park? I saw her there. She was, uh, sunbathing on the deck. Last night. About sunset."

"John!" Margaret started in on the scolding. "You were supposed to be taking pictures of the sunset, not spying on people!"

"I did take pictures of the sunset! I showed them to you!"

The deputy jumped in. "Hold on, folks. Sir, which condo?"

"The last one, next to the park."

"And you don't know her name? Had you ever seen her before?"

Margaret was glaring hard at him now, waiting for the answer. John answered the deputy but looked directly at his wife. "No, I don't know her name and I never saw her before."

The deputy asked more questions and John described his habit of walking in the park, looking at birds and snapping pictures of the sunset. The deputy took their names and phone number and said he'd be in touch.

"If you think of anything helpful, Mr. Billings, give us a call."

Still hiding the fact that the woman he saw was naked, and that he had pictures of her, John felt an immediate rush of guilt. But he swallowed it and only nodded.

"Will do, deputy."

Billings watched as the deputy pulled away, the Budweiser tasting stale in his mouth.

The deputy radioed Sheriff Johnny Tobin who was just across the bridge in Eastpoint.

"I'll be there in five minutes. Sit tight."

Now Sheriff Tobin was there, along with the deputy who had talked to John Billings and another officer who had been working the west side of the island. They knocked on the door of condo number eight. There was no answer.

Tobin sent the deputies to knock on the other condo doors, but they were also deserted. Flashlights in hand, they walked around back and stood on the deck.

"Nice and private back here," one of the deputies observed. "No one can see you."

"Well, that Billings fellow managed to see our victim sunbathing," Tobin countered, shining his flashlight into the kitchen, but seeing nothing out of place. "This could be where she was killed. Maybe we should have another talk with Mr. Billings. He might know more than he's telling."

Sheriff Tobin directed one of his deputies to find out who owned condo number eight and to make arrangements to search it. He and the other deputy paid a home visit to Mr. and Mrs. Billings.

It was Margaret who answered the door. "John! The deputy is here, and the sheriff, too!"

John felt sick to his stomach. He wasn't cut out for this lying crap.

Sheriff Tobin said he had some questions, but John didn't wait to hear them. Instead, he dropped a bombshell. "I think I have a picture of the man who probably killed her, if you're interested."

It was past ten o'clock by the time Sheriff Tobin and the deputy left with a handful of pictures of their victim standing naked on the back deck of the condo, including two shots showing the face of a possible suspect, a man in his thirties who nobody recognized. John Billings just gave in and printed his entire file of pictures he had taken of her, which he had stored on his computer under "Tax Stuff," so Margaret wouldn't look through it.

The other deputy had tracked down the owner of the condo – a tribal casino down by Miami called the Golden Arrow. They were reluctant to authorize a search.

"Fine," a tired Sheriff Tobin offered. "We'll get a warrant. I'm going home. I reckon our victim will still be dead in the morning."

To the dismay of the other deputies, though, he ordered them to keep an eye on the condo all night. "We don't want anybody carting off evidence now do we?"

The phone call from the Franklin County Sheriff's Office to the tribal casino management was not a welcome one. A condo they owned on St. George Island was a possible crime scene? This was not good.

The word spread up the chain of command in a hurry and reached two executives, both awakened by nervous underlings, who had given the $2 million in cash to House Speaker Alberto Gonzalez. They conferred and decided that even though there was no evidence of a connection, it was still uncomfortably possible, especially since they knew the condo had been loaned to Roy Fercal for the Labor Day weekend as a gesture of goodwill for his part in arranging the bribe.

A member of the legal staff was immediately dispatched to Tallahassee via private jet to monitor the situation and make sure no evidence of the bribe surfaced. On the flight to Tallahassee Regional Airport, the lawyer asked the pilot if he happened to be the same one who flew Speaker Gonzalez last Friday. He was.

When they taxied to the general aviation terminal in Tallahassee, the lawyer asked if this was where Gonzalez had deplaned.

"Exactly the same place," the pilot said. "He waddled past the building to the parking lot over there."

The lawyer spotted the security camera and silently thanked his boss for teaching him the most important legal lesson of his career: A casino lawyer should never leave the office without a briefcase full of cash.

27

Tuesday, September 9

Roy Fercal inhaled deeply, closed his eyes and enjoyed the fresh air of morning at Maclay Gardens. He loved it here. It was, arguably, the prettiest spot in Tallahassee. But he chose it for his meeting with Carrie Stevens for a different reason. He liked the privacy.

Then he saw Carrie's burned face in a miniature hockey-looking mask.

"Jesus Christ! You look like Freddie Kruger!"

"Fuck you, too, Fercal."

"I'm sorry. You just kind of startled me is all. How do you feel?"

"Nowhere near as good as I look. What's up, Fercal? I didn't come to the gardens to make small talk about my lovely face. Carl said something about a big story."

"Yeah, right." But Roy couldn't keep from staring. "The biggest story of your life is what I think I said."

"Something like that. So let's have it."

"Let's take a walk down this path."

Roy had walked this path many times. It was pretty now, but it was absolutely breathtaking in March, when the azaleas bloomed.

"You've gotten yourself in quite a pickle, Carrie. Three counts of vehicular manslaughter. You'll spend the best years of your life in prison."

"I already know that, Fercal. What does that have to do with anything?"

"But then again, a girl like you knows how to wiggle out of a pickle like this, don't you Carrie? Or should I say Shelby?"

Carrie stumbled and fell clumsily into a nearby park bench. She had trouble breathing.

"Oh, I'm sorry." Roy offered his hand with exaggerated concern as he sat beside her. "Perhaps you'd prefer your stage name – Paradise."

Carrie looked at him, wide-eyed, her mouth agape. Her eyes were tearing up.

"Tell me a story, Paradise. Tell me about the Rub-a-Dub Club."

"You – what – I, uh, no, I don't know what you're talking about."

"Yes you do, Paradise. I know all about it. But it was a long time ago and your secret is safe with me – for now."

"Stop calling me that. My name is Carrie Stevens. And I don't know anyone named Paradise."

"Whatever you say, Carrie. If that's how you want it." Roy got up as if to leave, then turned back to Carrie. "I wonder what the

Suncoast Gazette will do when they find out their rising young reporter who killed three kids used to be a hot tub whore?"

"Shut up!"

"Oh, that's right. It doesn't matter, because you're going to prison anyway. Do they have hot tubs in prison, Paradise?"

"Stop it, you sonofabitch! Stop it!"

"You know what you need? You need someone with enough juice to help you get out of this jam. You need someone with the ability to get you started on a clean slate. You need someone willing and able to make it happen."

"What the hell are you saying, Fercal?"

"Well, for starters, I can make the whole thing about your time at the Pecker Palace go away. Nobody ever has to know about that. Second, I can arrange things so your manslaughter charges go away."

"What do you mean, go away?"

"I mean like it never happened. You'll walk out of the courthouse a free woman, or at the very worst with a traffic citation for careless driving."

"Bullshit." Carrie was shaking her head. "Nobody can do that, not without bribing the judge."

"I can do it, Carrie."

The reality of what Fercal was saying started to sink in. She eyed him suspiciously. "But why? Why are you offering to help me? I don't even like you."

"Because if I help you, you'll help me."

I guess I should have expected that answer, Carrie thought to herself. "Assuming you were able to help me, and assuming I let you, what would you want me to do, Roy?"

"I need you to tell me everything you know about Rip Snyder. The juicy stuff – his kinky sexual habits, how often he uses words like nigger and spic, ugly things he has said about people in private. Stuff like that."

"You want me to rat out on Rip? Why?"

"I have my reasons."

"I don't know, Roy. I don't think so. Rip and I..." Carrie struggled with the words. "I mean, he's been good to me. I don't have any reason to rat him out."

"I can give you two good reasons – the Pecker Palace and Lake Bradford Road. Not exactly your two best moments in life."

"I just don't think I can do it, Roy."

"Listen. Rip is going down with or without your help. So why not help yourself in the process? If you don't do something, your life is going straight into the shitter."

Carrie was silent, staring at the ground.

"Okay, Carrie, here's my best offer. By the end of the week, you will be a free woman. I guarantee it. When that happens – when the charges against you are dropped – I expect you to meet with me and spill the beans on Rip. If you don't, the Pecker Palace will be front page news."

This time, when Roy turned to leave, he kept going.

The activity on St. George Island on Tuesday morning was sparse. The two deputies had kept watch over condo number eight by sleeping in shifts. They were both awake now, drinking coffee and eating some very mediocre doughnuts from the grocery store down the street.

A car pulled up alongside and a fairly young man in a suit emerged and introduced himself as Case Dickman, a lawyer representing the casino that owned the condo.

"Is that your real name? Case?" one of the deputies inquired.

"Yeah. Why?"

"I don't know. Guess you were born to be a lawyer."

"Both my parents were lawyers. They thought it was cute."

Sheriff Johnny Tobin arrived with the search warrant. Case Dickman made a point of locking his car. There was a briefcase on the front seat with piles of cash and a very valuable security tape showing Speaker Gonzalez toting his duffel bag from a private jet to his car.

Sheriff Tobin and the deputies searched the condo after Case let them in, being careful where they stepped and what they touched. The first thing they found was an apparent semen stain on the living room sofa. A few minutes later, Sheriff Tobin discovered the blonde hairs sticking to the bottom of a cast iron skillet, and what he thought might be the remnants of a small blood stain on the kitchen floor.

"We got us a crime scene, boys," Tobin announced. "And I think I'm looking at the murder weapon."

"Murder?" Case Dickman was incredulous. "Nobody said anything about murder!"

Sheriff Tobin showed Dickman a photo of the dead woman. "This woman was raped and killed and dumped in a nearby swamp. We think she was killed right here. Do you know her?"

"No, I don't." He was lying, but being a casino lawyer, he was good at it. Anybody who paid close attention to politics, as he did, knew about Roxy Jones. Jesus! Roxy was dead?

"Who was staying at this condo over the weekend?"

"I don't know." More lying. "The owners use it as a perk for top employees, our best customers, stuff like that."

"Can you find out?"

"Let me make some calls." No lying this time, just stalling.

"Please do. In the meantime, I'm calling in the crime scene boys to pick this place clean like it's a Thanksgiving turkey."

Roy Fercal was on a roll. In less than 24 hours he had bribed a judge and a prosecutor and successfully blackmailed – he hoped anyway – a newspaper reporter. He was jazzed. He had the congressman figured for easy pickings.

They met in the corner of a comfortable seating area provided free to the public by Florida A & M University. It was a great place to sit and wait, though it was sparsely used, mostly because there wasn't much reason to sit and wait at the Tallahassee airport.

"How you doing, Congressman? I see you're up by 10 points in the tracking polls, so I feel safe in congratulating you on your election to a tenth term."

"From your lips to God's ear, Roy. I hope you're right. I want to thank you for all your help."

Roy waved his hand dismissively. "Happy to do it. You've served us well, Billy. What do you plan on doing after you retire?"

Congressman Conner laughed. "That's a long way off, Roy. I haven't even thought about it. I'm only 57 years old!"

"You should think about it, and soon."

The jovial tone in the congressman's voice disappeared. "What are you saying, Roy? With one breath, you're congratulating me. With another, you're telling me to retire. What the hell are you trying to say?"

"I'm saying you should retire after this next term. Twenty years are enough, Billy. You're done."

"The hell I am! You've seen my polling numbers. I can serve this district as long as I damn well please!"

"No, Billy, you can't."

"Do you know something I don't?"

"Yes, Billy, I do." Roy leaned in close and spoke in a coarse whisper. "Three years ago I loaned you the use of a condo on St. George Island. No wife, no kids. Just three days of rest and relaxation for an overworked congressman. You met a young man on the beach, a real golden boy. I think his name was Joe. And I believe the two of you had a gay old time together."

Congressman Billy Conner's mouth had gone dry. Roy's breath on him felt sickly and hot. His scalp started to sweat.

"I know all this, Billy, because there are pictures. Lots and lots of pictures." Roy leaned back and smiled. "Joe tells me you were quite a tiger – a hungry tiger. He still talks about it."

"You bastard!"

"Call me any name you want, Billy. But tomorrow you're going to announce your decision to retire at the end of your next term.

And it won't be so bad. Hell, I'll bet FSU offers you a teaching job in political science."

Conner knew he was trapped. It was true about his three days on St. George Island. My god, the things he and Joe had done together in that condo! Things he had never done before or since – but Joe was so damn gorgeous! He made it all seem so *right*. And it must have been a setup all along.

How many other politicians had Roy set up like this, just to be able to manipulate them? Jesus. The man is evil.

"Fuck you, Roy. I'll do it, but fuck you anyway."

"Better hurry, Congressman. You don't want to miss your plane."

With that, Roy Fercal strolled away, his exhilaration complete. He was right about the congressman – an easy mark. Good thing, too, because there weren't any pictures. There never had been.

28

Alberto Gonzalez did indeed have family in Puerto Rico. They were thrilled to see him, even unexpectedly. They were initially confused when he said he had been in Ponca since Sunday morning, attending to business without calling them, but they understood. Gonzalez was a hero in his native land precisely because he knew how to take care of business.

The cash, except for some walking around money, was safely stowed in a large safe deposit box in a Ponca bank – a real one, not some product of Joe the Surfer Dude's imagination. Gonzalez was still kicking himself for almost falling for that one.

He used the family phone to call his office in Tallahassee and inform them of his whereabouts.

"I came down Sunday morning to attend to some family business," Gonzalez told them. "I might stay here all week if nothing important comes up. I'm sure Roxy can handle things."

C arrie Stevens was badly shaken by her run-in with Roy Fercal. The life she thought she buried somewhere between St. Louis and Tampa had crawled back out of the grave, like some kind of B movie monster. She needed to kill it again.

She had no choice, really. If Fercal delivered on his promise to get the manslaughter charges dropped, how could she do anything but cooperate in his scheme to ruin Rip Snyder? She could refuse, but then her dirty little secrets would come out and she'd forever be known as the hot tub whore from the Pecker Palace.

Carrie hated the idea of doing this to Rip, but damn it, she'd built a pretty decent life here. She would do what was necessary to protect it. Plus, she was worried about the Barboni family. She helped put several of them behind bars. Would they come after her if her true identity was revealed?

Why take the chance?

I t was the middle of the afternoon and pretty hot on St. George Island. Sheriff Johnny Tobin was enjoying a cigarette in the parking lot of the condo complex. The search of condo number eight hadn't turned up very much additional evidence, but he did know a few things. The semen on the sofa matched the blood type of the semen they found in the victim's body. And the blonde hairs on the skillet were from the victim. So this is where he raped her and killed her.

That little dweeb of a casino lawyer was spending most of the day in his car on the phone, but wasn't being much help in finding out who had used the condo for the weekend. They were stalling, Tobin knew, but you can't push a rope uphill.

Tobin stubbed out his cigarette and watched as a garbage truck backed into the parking lot and prepared to collect the trash from a dumpster. Jesus, he thought, am I stupid or what? And how did the lab boys miss it?

He ran to the dumpster, waving his hands and shouting for the garbage men to stop. They did. Sheriff Tobin opened the top of the dumpster and peered in. It stunk a little, but not too bad. There was one trash bag that was tied up neater than the others and sitting on top. He removed it and dumped the contents on the parking lot.

There were some skimpy-looking clothes, including a kick-ass leopard skin bikini top. But it was the purse that caught Tobin's attention. He opened it and found a driver's license bearing the picture of the victim.

"Roxanne Jones," he announced to the bewildered garbage men. "From Tallahassee. We're gonna find out who did this to you, Roxanne. And when we do, the bastard is gonna fry."

R oy Fercal was feeling good. All the pieces were in place. Tomorrow, Congressman Billy Conner would announce his intention to retire in two years, signaling to Jessie Malloy that the plan was afoot. Jessie would drop the manslaughter charges, showing Carrie it was time to spill the beans on Rip. Then it would be Roy's turn again, and he would derive great pleasure from turning Rip Snyder into a bitter, hate-filled racist in the eyes of the public.

There was nothing to do but wait, so Roy decided to drive over to Roxy's apartment on the off chance that she was there. He still wanted to steal the $2 million in bribe money from Speaker Gonzalez, of course, but he was also remembering the carnal pleasures he and Roxy had enjoyed two nights earlier. Maybe she was ready for another round.

Roy parked in front of Roxy's building and trudged up the outer stairs. A skanky-looking woman from one of the other apartments walked by with a load of laundry and Roy gave her a wide berth. He stood in front of Roxy's apartment and listened. There was no sound. He rang the doorbell – nothing. He knocked – still nothing. Damn it; where was she? Roy stepped away from the door and peered in the lone window. Empty. He flipped open his cell phone and called Roxy's home number. When her antiquated answering machine picked up, he spoke in a terse whisper.

"Damn it, Roxy! Where are you? I swear to God, you'd better not fuck me over on this. I play for keeps, and you know it. Call me."

Roy clicked off and watched through the window to see if Roxy emerged from the bedroom or something. Nothing happened.

The absence of Roxy Jones was becoming uncomfortably obvious at the Office of the Speaker of the Florida House of Representatives. The governor's chief of staff wanted to set up a meeting for Friday morning. She had called three times.

So the receptionist dialed Roxy's home number. When the machine picked up, the receptionist sounded desperate.

"Roxy? We need you, girl. The speaker is in Puerto Rico all week and said you could run things and we've got the governor's office calling for you. Are you sick or something? Better give us a call."

Then she called Roxy's cell phone and it startled Joe the Surfer Dude, who had absentmindedly kept it after using it to try and reach Speaker Gonzalez. He briefly thought about answering it, but decided he wasn't even supposed to have it, so he turned it off and threw it in the trash.

Carrie Stevens sat in front of her telephone for a long time, shaking. Could she really go through with it?

Yes, she decided. She had no choice.

She picked up the phone and dialed. The receptionist put her through.

"This is Bannerman Lux."

"Hi, Lucky. It's Carrie Stevens."

"Carrie! How are you? Everything okay?"

She sighed heavily. No sense beating around the bush. "I've been thinking, Lucky, and I've decided you're right."

"Of course I'm right. I'm always right," Lux bragged with a grin. "What exactly do you think I'm right about?"

"I think you're right about the blood test. You know, that they screwed it up. And I think you should file a motion to have it dismissed."

"I plan to – at your arraignment."

"Don't wait for the arraignment. Do it now."

"You mean like right now? This minute?"

"Yeah."

"Look, Carrie, you don't need to be in a hurry on this. You're out of jail, and . . ."

"No, Lucky. Do it now."

There was a pause. "Okay, Carrie. I'll do it now and let you know."

"Thanks."

"Jessie? It's Bannerman Lux. Do you have a minute to talk about Carrie Stevens?"

Jessie's heart skipped a beat. "Uh, sure, I guess. What's up, Lucky?"

"I'm preparing a motion – right now – to have her blood alcohol test thrown out. They messed up the chain of custody."

Jessie didn't know what to say. Was this it?

"Jessie? Are you there?"

"Yeah, Lucky. I'm here. Did you say you're preparing the motion right now?"

"As we speak, Jess."

"So you're in a hurry?"

"My client is pushing me on this, yeah."

"Okay, Lucky. I'll call Judge Brown and see if he'll hear us on the motion tomorrow. Will that work?"

"Thanks, Jess. See you then." Lux hung up and thought Jailhouse Jess was being incredibly accommodating.

29

It was almost six o'clock when Sheriff Johnny Tobin and his two best deputies arrived at the apartment complex of Roxanne Jones, accompanied by a cranky Deputy Bill "Bulldog" Bowser. It turned out the apartment complex was just outside the Tallahassee city limits on Miccosukee Road. Bulldog was along as a courtesy of the Leon County Sheriff's Department.

"I hope this ain't gonna take too long," Bulldog groused. "I usually have supper waitin' by 6:30."

Sheriff Tobin looked at the big man in his green uniform and thought missing a meal might not be a bad idea. "A woman who lived in this complex is dead, Deputy Bowser, and I aim to find out who did it and why."

Bulldog wiggled his toothpick and grunted. "Well, let's get to it then. And you might as well call me Bulldog. Everybody does."

The building manager let them in. Bulldog was wheezing from the flight of stairs.

The apartment was fairly neat, though it was obvious the occupant wasn't expecting company. There was a laptop computer, turned off, on the kitchen counter.

"We'll need to secure this and go through it," Tobin said, and one of his deputies scooped it up.

In the only bedroom was a security badge on a lanyard hanging from a hat tree. "Roxanne Jones, Office of the Speaker," Tobin read aloud. "It's a badge issued by the Capitol Police. So I guess she worked for Speaker Whatsisname. Who is it again?"

"Gonzalez," piped up one of his deputies. "Speaker Gonzalez."

"Isn't he Puerto Rican or something?" Bulldog was still wheezing, just a bit.

Sheriff Tobin waited for Bulldog to explain the significance of this, but all he got were some sucking noises.

"We'll need to have Capitol Police get with the speaker's office right away, see if they know about next of kin," Tobin observed, and dispatched a deputy to make the call.

"There's an answering machine over here, Sheriff," the deputy announced. "It's an old one, by the looks of it. No time stamps or anything."

Sheriff Tobin hit the rewind button, then play.

"Damn it, Roxy! Where are you? I swear to God, you'd better not fuck me over on this. I play for keeps, and you know it. Call me."

Tobin hit stop, rewind, and play again. After the second time, he hit stop again and the room was quiet. Bulldog even stopped sucking on his toothpick.

"Does anyone recognize that voice?" Tobin asked, looking at each of them. No one did.

"I don't recognize it," Bulldog offered, "but it sounds like the voice of a killer to me." His stomach let loose with a loud growl that seemed to last forever. Bulldog withdrew his toothpick, pointed to his watch and said, "Six-thirty. Right on the fucking dot."

Clay Chester was numb. As the deputy chief of staff, he was the only one still working in the office of Speaker Gonzalez when Franklin County Sheriff Johnny Tobin showed up just after seven o'clock with the news that Roxy was dead.

Murdered, he said. Roxy had been murdered!

Clay actually liked Roxy, even though it was Clay who did the real heavy lifting around the office while Roxy kept her job with "other" talents. She was fun to have around – lots of laughs – and dazzling to look at.

But not anymore. Roxy was dead. Murdered.

"Please don't release this to the press, Mr. Chester," Tobin directed. "Her family doesn't know yet, and we need to make contact with them. Do you know where we can reach them?"

"Her parents live over in Ponte Vedra Beach. I'm sure the contact information is in Roxy's file."

Chester retrieved the information for Sheriff Tobin and his two deputies.

"Mr. Chester, when did you last see Miss Jones?"

"Last Friday, I believe. When she left the office."

"Do you know why she was on St. George Island last weekend?"

"St. George?" Chester was mildly surprised. "She didn't mention it. Usually, when she's going to the island for the weekend she talks about it all week. She loves the island. Her parents live right on the ocean over in Ponte Vedra. The beach is in her blood."

"When she goes to the island, who usually goes with her?"

Chester was instantly uncomfortable with the question. He didn't want to go there, but lying was out of the question.

"Well, sheriff, she usually goes to the island with the speaker."

"With Speaker Gonzalez? Just the two of them?"

"Sometimes they take other friends with them. Other times, it's just the two of them, yeah."

Sheriff Tobin took a moment to digest this. "So where was Speaker Gonzalez last weekend?"

"He went to the football game on Saturday. Then he apparently flew to Puerto Rico on Sunday morning for some family business."

"Where is he now?"

"He's still there."

"You said he 'apparently' flew to Puerto Rico on Sunday," Sheriff Tobin observed. "Why do you say *apparently*?"

Jesus, Chester thought. Is Gonzalez a suspect? Then – did he do it?

"Well, sheriff, we didn't hear from him until today. He called in to let us know he might be there all week. I say 'apparently' because I don't know for certain what flight he was on."

"Are you sure he was calling from Puerto Rico?" the sheriff inquired.

Chester was shaken by the direct, accusatory nature of the question. "Oh, yes. We have caller ID. You know, to track down crank calls. The speaker's call definitely originated in Puerto Rico."

"I'll need to speak with him."

"Of course, Sheriff Tobin. I'll have him call you."

"One more thing," Tobin said as he was preparing to leave. "I'll need a DNA sample from every man in this office, including you and Speaker Gonzalez. Can I assume you'll cooperate so we can get to the bottom of this?"

Chester had planned on standing, but his ass suddenly weighed about eight tons. "Of course, Sheriff. This is a terrible tragedy. This office will fully cooperate."

Clay Chester sat in his office and waited for his ass to shed the extra weight. He buried his face in his hands and grieved for his co-worker.

Eventually, the grieving turned into questions. Who killed Roxy? Was it Gonzalez?

What was she doing on the island? Is that where she was killed? Would Roxy accept a spur-of-the-moment invitation to go to St. George Island for the weekend? Absolutely. Would such a last-minute invitation come from Gonzalez? Never. Weekend trips for the speaker to the island or anywhere else were always paid for by lobbyists and arranged in advance.

So maybe Chester's boss didn't kill his co-worker. But who did, and why?

Chester had no problem providing a DNA sample. They wouldn't find any of his DNA at the crime scene or inside the body of Roxy Jones. Not for the lack of wishing it so, you understand. But all of that DNA had long ago washed itself down the shower drain.

He had assured Sheriff Tobin of the speaker's cooperation in providing a DNA sample. Was he too hasty? After all, Chester knew Roxy and Gonzalez had been sharing DNA since the job interview. Would Gonzalez have to admit to the sexual nature of his relationship with Roxy and would it become public? It would ruin him.

So many questions. Chester looked at his watch and realized it was almost nine. Time to call Gonzalez.

The scene at 26 Ocean Drive in Ponte Vedra Beach was totally out of sync. There was a police car in the circle drive, something that never happened before. Inside, an attractive woman just three days shy of her fiftieth birthday had collapsed into the arms of a confused rookie police officer. The other officer, who had years of experience imparting bad news to the stunned parents of black kids in neighboring Jacksonville, was letting the man of the house vent his anger.

"Whoever did this to my little girl better hope the cops find him before I do!" the man bellowed, waving his hands and spilling Scotch on the marble floor. "Because if I get him, I'll make him bite his own goddamn nuts off!

"I want the fucker dead! You hear me? Dead! And I ain't talking about some weenie-ass execution with a lethal injection machine. Fuck that! Put the sonofabitch in the hot seat and let his hair fry!

"Send this bastard straight to hell!"

The yelling continued for a time and made less and less sense, but the veteran officer knew what was going on. The father had two options – yell or cry – and he didn't want to cry.

Later, when the comforting arms of the rookie cop and the willing ears of the old veteran were gone, Mr. and Mrs. Jones went looking for solace in the bottom of a Scotch bottle.

30

Clay Chester tried the speaker's cell phone first, but it rang harmlessly in the back seat of the speaker's car in the parking lot of an Orlando flying service. Then he tried the Gonzalez residence in Orlando, hoping that Mrs. Gonzalez would have a number where the speaker could be reached in Puerto Rico.

What Clay discovered was that Mrs. Gonzalez was very drunk and very surprised that her husband was in Puerto Rico.

"We talked a few days ago," she slurred. "He didn't mention it."

She didn't think she had a phone number for him there, and Clay was certain she couldn't find it if she did.

Finally, he went to the receptionist's desk and scrolled through the caller ID log until he found the number that registered when Gonzalez had called in earlier that day.

Clay's Spanish was bad, but he managed to convey his need to speak to Alberto Gonzalez. He was there.

"Good evening, Mr. Speaker. It's Clay."

Gonzalez launched into a routine he had been rehearsing in his mind, hoping it would solidify his alibi. He hadn't expected a phone call quite so soon, but he didn't hesitate.

"Clay! I'm glad you called. I know it's late, but we need to have Roxy set up a meeting with McKenzie over in the Senate for Monday morning, first thing. You could do it, of course, but you know how Roxy is. She seems to get her way with that old fart. Is she there? We ought to get started on this right away."

There was a long pause as Clay struggled to find the words. "Uh, I have some bad news, Mr. Speaker." His voice was shaking badly. "I'm afraid Roxy is dead. She was murdered."

"What? That can't be right. I just saw her at the football game on Saturday! My God in heaven! When did this happen?"

"Sometime Sunday night, Mr. Speaker."

"Do they know who did it?"

"Apparently not. There was a sheriff in here and he wants all of us to provide DNA samples. I told him we would."

There was a pause. "Why would they need DNA samples from us?" Gonzalez inquired. "Surely they don't suspect it was someone from the office!"

"I don't know, Mr. Speaker. But the sheriff wants to get to the bottom of it, and I told him this office would cooperate fully."

"Of course, Clay. Of course we will. You were absolutely right." Inside, though, Gonzalez was seething – and worried. How long does DNA hang around inside a woman's body? Would his sample tie him to the murder? Thank God he couldn't get it up Saturday night!

"Uh, Mr. Speaker, the sheriff wants you to call him. He said he needed to speak with you."

"Does he know I'm in Puerto Rico? And that I've been here since Sunday morning?"

"That's what I told him, sir."

"Well, I'm not going to call him tonight. This is too much of a shock. I'll catch a flight of some kind in the morning and make my way back."

"Do you want me to go ahead and set up that meeting?"

"With the sheriff?"

"No, with McKenzie. On Monday."

"Oh! No, forget it. McKenzie can wait." And the phone went dead.

Clay looked at it for a long time. The speaker asked if they knew *who* did it, but not *where* or *how*. Perhaps he already knows, Clay thought, and the Office of the Speaker suddenly felt like a very cold place.

The Reverend Josiah Franklin stood in the pulpit of his darkened church. Tomorrow morning, his little church would be packed with mourners. At least twice that many more would be forced to take part from the lawn. The media would be well taken care of; he saw to that. In fact, making arrangements to handle the media had required Belinda to push the funeral back to Wednesday morning.

Reverend Franklin convinced her it would be better for the girls if the media were present and accounted for. So they brought in a riser for the television cameras. The footage would be powerful – a packed church, three little caskets draped with flowers, and the booming voice of a commanding preacher.

Franklin closed his eyes and pictured the scene, hearing his words. He had an idea of what he would say tomorrow, but his heart would do most of the talking. Such a lack of preparation would frighten some preachers, but not Josiah. He had a gift, and the gift served him best when it was a bit unpolished.

He was ready. This was a moment in time that was waiting to be seized. He might as well seize it and make it his own.

Tomorrow.

31

Wednesday, September 10

J immy Flain had a love-hate relationship with elections. He was a
political junky – he had once watched the North Dakota State of the
State Address on CSPAN – and elections were a necessary fix for all
political junkies. But he hated the long hours of Election Day,
followed by yet another work day. He liked the notion of moving
Election Day to Saturday, so all the political junkies like him could
sleep in the next day.

There were no surprises the night before and the results had
been tabulated fairly early. It was a presidential election year, so there
wasn't much up for grabs in Florida except part of the state senate and
the entire house. None of the incumbents lost, and none had been
expected to lose. Ho-hum.

Flain checked his calendar. The funeral of the three black girls was at 10:00, which Flain expected to be a media circus. Would the Reverend Franklin continue to play the race card? Probably so. Well, it made for an interesting story.

Flain yawned, stretched, and checked his watch. He needed to leave for the Bradford Road Baptist Church in about an hour. He filled his coffee cup, returned to his desk and checked his e-mail. There was one from the office of Congressman Billy Conner.

"Ah, yes," Flain said to himself. "Always the first to brag about an election victory."

But when he opened the message Flain was shocked. It was a news release announcing Conner's decision to retire at the end of the next term. There was the usual stated desire to "spend more time with family" and so on, but they always said that.

"What has gotten into you, Billy?" Flain wondered aloud, reaching for the phone. He was just starting to dial when his editor came over all excited, waving a piece of paper.

"Got a hot one, Jimmy. It just cleared the wire."

"I already know about it," Jimmy said.

"You do? Then what the heck are you doing sitting behind your desk?"

"I'm calling him."

"Calling who?"

"Billy Conner. I want to know why he's retiring."

"Billy Conner is retiring?"

"It says so in his news release," Flain said, listening to the phone ring in his ear. "What does the wire copy say?"

"This is bigger than Billy Conner, Jimmy," the editor replied as he tossed the wire story on Flain's desk. "The speaker's chief of staff is dead. Roxy Jones. She was murdered."

Flain let the phone drop and it rattled across his desk. He clumsily hung it up.

"Somebody murdered Roxy Jones? Jesus Christ!" Flain snatched up the wire copy and read it. "Mother of God. Raped and bludgeoned and dumped in a swamp. Holy Christ."

"See what I mean, Jimmy? It's bigger than Billy Conner."

"Damn right it is. I'll get on the horn to the speaker's office, see if they have a statement." Flain reached for the phone again. "Can you put somebody else on the Conner thing? One of the rookies?"

"Sure, Jimmy. Conner picked a helluva day to drop this little sugar cookie. Hope he doesn't mind being next to the obits."

Judge Busby Brown had a trial starting at nine o'clock, but he had agreed to hear Bannerman Lux's motion in chambers at 8:30. Lux and Brown were making small talk when Jessie Malloy entered, looking nervous and harried.

"Sorry I'm late, Your Honor." Malloy didn't bother to mention the reason she was late. She was sitting in her car, listening to a news report concerning Congressman Conner's decision to retire.

"Not at all, Jess," Judge Brown said dismissively and waved them into chairs. "This shouldn't take too long. You first, Mr. Lux."

"I assume you've read the motion, Your Honor. The hospital messed up the chain of custody on my client's blood test. The people can't prove the alcohol test was performed on her blood."

Judge Brown turned his gaze to Jessie Malloy. "And what do the people have to say about this?"

"Your Honor, some of what the motion claims is true. The blood test was not exactly by the book, but it's ridiculous to jump to the conclusion that the blood that was tested belonged to anyone else."

"So the chain of custody was broken?"

Jess looked at the floor. "Yes, Your Honor, the chain of custody was broken."

"Then I have no choice but to grant Mr. Lux's motion. The blood test is out."

This is too easy, Lux thought. Maybe it's time to buy a lottery ticket. "Your Honor, without the blood test, my client wasn't drunk. The people have no hard evidence to suggest that my client was speeding. And for that matter, the kids could have jumped in front of the truck, causing the accident. There are no eyewitnesses. I move you dismiss the case for lack of evidence."

The room was quiet. Judge Brown was waiting for Jessie Malloy to play her part, but she seemed dumbstruck. He decided to shoulder the burden himself.

"I'm sorry, Miss Malloy, but Mr. Lux has a point. Without the blood test, the people really don't have much of a case. I'm dismissing the charges."

Malloy finally found her voice. "But, Your Honor, the uproar. The black community will never stand for this. Where do they go for justice?"

"I understand the need for justice, Miss Malloy, but the law is the law." They looked at each other and the irony of the words seemed to strike them both. "I'm sorry, Jess. This isn't your fault. Tell the hospital to be more careful next time."

Carrie Stevens hung up the phone in disbelief. Fercal had actually done it! Bannerman Lux had called her with the news – the blood test was thrown out, the charges dropped, and the state's attorney was not going to appeal the ruling. She was free!

Ordinarily, she would have immediately called Rip and made arrangements to celebrate. But not today. She couldn't face him. She remembered the time when she was twelve years old, back in Henley, Missouri. Her dog, a collie named Buster, had gotten sick and needed to be put down. But her mother was too cheap to pay the veterinarian and insisted it was Shelby's duty to shoot the dog.

So her mother loaded the shotgun and handed it to her daughter. Shelby thought ever so briefly about shooting her mother, and maybe she should have. Buster didn't understand and was actually trying to play with the gun barrel.

"Shoot, God damn it!" her mother yelled. "Shoot!"

And so she pulled the trigger. The memory was still harsh, but this time her mind's eye saw the face of Rip Snyder being blown away instead of Buster.

32

Roy Fercal heard the same news report Jessie Malloy heard. Billy Conner had announced his retirement. The plan was afoot. This was going to be a very good day.

But a few minutes later the same news announcer came on the air with a breathless bulletin:

> *"First News has just learned that the chief of staff to House Speaker Alberto Gonzalez has been found raped and murdered in Franklin County. Authorities say Roxanne Jones of Tallahassee was apparently assaulted and bludgeoned to death on St. George Island Sunday night and dumped in Tate's Hell Swamp. Franklin County Sheriff Johnny Tobin is urging anyone with information related to the case to contact his office immediately. There are no suspects in custody at this time."*

The radio station went back to playing music but all Roy could hear was the buzzing in his ears. Somebody murdered Roxy and dumped her in a swamp? Sunday night? Impossible!

Think, Roy, think! Who would do such a thing? He tried to get his mind around it.

Roy had been with Roxy Sunday evening, of course, and when he left her she was very much alive. The news report said she was killed on the island, but he didn't know if that meant inside the condo, on the beach, or somewhere else on the island.

He remembered it was getting stormy when he left Roxy in the condo that evening, so he was reasonably sure she wouldn't have gone to the beach. That probably meant she was killed inside the condo. That narrows it down to about three scenarios.

First, Joe killed her. This was highly unlikely. Roy knew Joe was gay, and when they were together on Monday there was no indication that Joe knew Roxy was dead. Forget scenario one.

Second, a stranger entered the condo and killed her. Possible, but not likely. Crime like that doesn't happen on St. George Island.

Third, Speaker Gonzalez killed her. That would explain why Gonzalez failed to show for his appointment with Joe. But why would he kill Roxy? Perhaps he had somehow discovered what Roxy was really up to. It was the only option that made sense.

Could it be true? If so, it was manna from heaven! The third most powerful man in the Florida Republican Party was on the take AND a murderer!

Roy had been driving to his office but changed his mind at the last minute. He headed for the airport instead.

Jimmy Flain was furiously typing up a version of the Roxy Jones murder story for the newspaper's website, including a statement from Speaker Gonzalez expressing his "shock and outrage" at the brutal murder of his most trusted employee. His office would "cooperate fully" with investigators to find the "monster that ended such a beautiful life" and hoped prosecutors would go for the death penalty.

Another reporter was busy with the Billy Conner retirement, dutifully working up a feature story highlighting the congressman's many accomplishments – which were actually few – and speculating about future plans – which seemed awfully vague.

Flain finished up and dashed out the door to the Bradford Road Baptist Church. He needed to spend more time on the murder story, but he couldn't miss the funeral. After the funeral, he planned to drive down to St. George Island and do some digging.

Jimmy Flain was in his element. News was happening and happening fast.

"It's a great day to be a news reporter," Flain said to no one in particular, and no one in particular paid him any attention.

The Reverend Josiah Franklin was ready. He peered outside and watched as the huge crowd gathered to pay their respects to three little angels who had been run down by a senseless drunk. They were seeking solace from the Lord and wanted justice from the state.

His phone rang and Reverend Franklin frowned at it. He didn't like interruptions when he was mentally preparing to preach, but he picked it up anyway.

"Reverend, it's Jessie Malloy, from the state's attorney's office."

"Good morning, Miss Malloy. Are you coming to the funeral? I might still be able to save you a seat, but not for much longer."

"I'm sorry, Reverend, but I can't get away. Duty calls, you know."

Franklin nodded. "I'm sure you're a busy woman, Miss Malloy. We'll say a prayer for you. We're counting on you to bring us justice."

Jessie felt a stab in her heart. "Uh, Reverend, that's why I called. There's been a development in the case. I wanted to tell the mother but I can't reach her. I thought you could help me."

"Certainly, Miss Malloy. What kind of development?"

"Well, Judge Busby Brown this morning dismissed the charges. The case against Carrie Stevens is gone."

"What? How could he do such a thing? She was drunk and speeding and careless! What kind of fool could dismiss such a case?"

"I'm sorry, Reverend. I truly am." And these words were true. The next words, however, were not. "I fought as hard as I could and pleaded with Judge Brown not to do this. But the hospital goofed up the blood test, and the judge threw the whole thing out. There was nothing I could do."

Franklin could feel his blood starting to boil. "This Judge Brown who did this. He's white, isn't he?"

"Yes, Reverend, but I don't think..."

"I'm sorry, Miss Malloy, but I really have to go. I have a flock to tend to. They have come to me seeking comfort and justice. The comfort will have to come from the Lord. But as for justice, well, we'll just see about that."

The line went dead and Jessie found herself wondering if the phone call was a big mistake.

Roy Fercal had gone from jubilation to disbelief to anger in a matter of minutes. When he got to the airport, Fercal went straight to his inside source within the Transportation Security Administration to retrieve a copy of the general aviation security tape from last Friday. The TSA worker came back to him looking sheepish.

"It's not there."

"What the hell do you mean it's not there? Where is it?"

"We don't know," the worker whimpered. "There's some talk about a malfunction. I don't know."

"Jesus Christ," Roy fumed. He dug into his pocket for three hundred dollars and waved it in front of the worker's face. "You see this, dickhead? This is the money you're not getting because of this."

Fercal stormed off, and the worker watched him go. He would have sold the tape for three hundred dollars, no question. And he was damn glad somebody else had come along with five thousand dollars earlier in the week.

"Forget you and your three hundred dollars," the worker mumbled and returned to his job of watching for terrorists.

33

Jimmy Flain had to park on the shoulder of Lake Bradford Road and walk almost a quarter of a mile to reach the church. He got a few angry looks from the mourners who were forced to gather outside in the mounting heat as he walked inside to his seat in the press area.

The Reverend Josiah Franklin emerged from behind a curtain in the front of the church and the congregation settled down. Flain thought the reverend looked angry. The reporter clicked on his miniature tape recorder and snapped a photograph of Reverend Franklin standing behind the three small caskets.

The choir launched into a heart-wrenching rendition of The Old Rugged Cross and the crying started.

As the choir finished, Reverend Franklin strode purposefully to the pulpit. The church was dead quiet, except for the sobbing.

"Praise be to God and only to God."

The congregation responded with a chorus of amens, and Flain could hear the mourners outside who responded more loudly. If they can't be seen, Flain figured, they were damn sure going to be heard.

"I come to you today with a heavy heart, and a troubled heart, and an angry heart. My heart is heavy, as is every heart on this day, for the senseless tragedy that took these three little angels from our midst. They were so perfectly innocent, unstained by sin, borne of love, and gifts from God Almighty to brighten our world with their blessed presence in our lives."

Franklin paused and looked at the caskets for a long moment. The crying escalated.

"And brighten our lives they surely did, but for far too short a time. And that's why my heart is troubled, because the brutal act of violence that swept these angels away from us could have been avoided and should have been avoided."

The women, who were doing most of the crying, could only nod. The men, however, found their voices to fill in the amen.

"So we come to the Lord seeking comfort for our heavy and troubled hearts. And we pray, too, that the Lord will find special solace for Belinda, in her hour of terrible grief."

Franklin looked straight at Belinda and softened his voice.

"Hold tight to your faith, my child. Cling to the Lord's hands and let Him heal your heart. And lean on us, Belinda, for we are here to serve you in your time of need."

More amens. Franklin turned his attention back to the congregation at large and Flain could see his face harden.

"But I must tell you why I come to this pulpit today with a heart that is also angry. The anger I feel boiling in my heart today is from the knowledge that once again, the black community will be denied justice in this case."

No amens this time. Just a lot of confused looks.

"My friends, I have learned this morning that these three little angels will be denied justice for no other reason than they are *black* angels."

More confusion and a growing murmur from the assembled masses.

"Last Friday night, a white woman, drunk and uncaring, came careening through our community and wiped these three beautiful angels from the face of the earth. This morning, a white judge dismissed the case and set this careless drunkard loose on the community without so much as a fine or a slap on the wrist."

The congregation gasped as one and turned to each other in angry disbelief.

Franklin let the anger grow before continuing. "I'm as shocked and angry as you are. We were hoping and praying for justice in this case because one of our own – Jessie Malloy – would see to it. But what can one black woman do in the face of white injustice? It's out of her hands."

The anger was growing. Jimmy Flain was becoming alarmed. He wanted to take out his cell phone and call his editor with the news about Carrie Stevens, but feared he might be stoned for the sacrilege.

"But the Lord works in mysterious ways, my friends. Those of you who worship here often have heard me countless times refer to this church as the working hands of God."

There was a chorus of amens from some. They must be the regulars, Flain thought.

"So what do we do as the working hands of God now? Do we sit back, bury these little angels, and whisper among ourselves about the lack of justice from the white establishment? Do we do nothing?"

"No!" the congregation responded.

"Or do we take to the streets and demand that justice be done?" the reverend boomed, his fist stabbing the air.

The crowd stood as one and yelled, stabbing the air with fists of their own, except for Belinda, who was too racked with grief, and the reporters, who watched in disbelief.

"We came today to return these angels to the Lord, and we will do that. Their final resting places have been prepared in the cemetery outside. But the Lord isn't finished with these lovely children. My friends, the Lord wants them to lead us in our quest for justice!

"My heart is seeking justice and my feet are in the mood to march! Will you join me?"

"Yes!"

"Then follow me as we march to the courthouse, holding our fallen angels high over our heads, and see if we can open some eyes!"

With that, the Reverend Josiah Franklin left the pulpit and walked down the aisle to the front door. The congregation started to follow, with the men taking up the caskets.

Jimmy Flain and the other reporters were scrambling to get ahead of the mob. He ran across the church yard to the road and got to his car. Flain turned back, snapped a photograph of the Reverend Franklin leading three hundred marchers out of the church lot and turning northward on Lake Bradford Road, with three little caskets held high.

He called his editor. "Get some reporters over to the courthouse," Flain said. "We got trouble."

The church was empty, save for a lone young woman who was sobbing in the front row. All she wanted to do was bury her children, Belinda thought. What in the hell was happening?

34

The news about the marching congregation spread fast. A businessman on his way to the airport, already cussing the damn speed bumps on Lake Bradford Road, went apoplectic when he found his way completely blocked by three hundred black people carrying coffins. He turned his car around and called 911 on his cell phone.

The 911 operator notified the sheriff's office, and the sheriff's office dispatched Deputy Bill Bowser to investigate. By the time Bulldog arrived, the marchers had turned east on Orange Avenue, snarling mid-day traffic on the busy thoroughfare. It was all he could do to fight his way through it. He pulled to a stop in front of the mob and struggled his way out of his car.

"God damn it, Reverend, what the hell is this about?"

"It's about justice, Deputy. It's about demanding justice for these three little girls." Reverend Franklin pointed to the caskets being held high in the air behind him.

"You mean those bodies are actually in those caskets? Good God, I thought it was just for show. Have you lost your mind?"

Car horns were starting to blare from both directions. It was a mess.

"Deputy, are you aware that a judge has dismissed the charges against Carrie Stevens? She gets nothing, not even a scolding."

"A judge dismissed the charges?" Bulldog was confused. "Impossible! That's just a stupid rumor."

"Jessie Malloy told me herself, just this morning."

This caused Bulldog to suck on his toothpick harder than usual. He was there when the little girls were pulled out of the sewage lagoon. The idea that a judge would let the Stevens girl go seemed ludicrous to him.

"I can understand your anger, Reverend, but we can't have you marching in the streets and messing up traffic. It ain't safe."

"Deputy, we have every intention of marching to the courthouse and demanding justice. A little snarled traffic means nothing to us."

"All the way to the courthouse?" Bulldog couldn't believe it. He hadn't walked that far in his entire life put together. "But you're breaking the law, Reverend. You ain't got a permit."

"Then arrest us, Deputy," Franklin said, and swept his hands to indicate the marchers behind him. "All of us."

"Hell, Reverend, I didn't come here to make a scene." Bulldog couldn't believe what he was about to do, but he was pissed about the Stevens girl getting off, so he did it. "Give me a minute, Reverend, to call this in. Then I'll escort you and your marchers to the courthouse. But you gotta stay on the right side of the road so we can move traffic on the other side. Is that a deal?"

"It's a deal, Deputy." Franklin turned to those behind him and the word spread backwards.

Within a few minutes, Bulldog found himself in the position of leading a parade of three hundred angry black folks toting three small coffins. A foursome of golfers on the Seminole Golf Club stood on the twelfth tee and gawked at the crazy scene.

"Well, if that ain't the damnedest thing I ever saw," one of them said, and proceeded to pull his tee shot into a huge live oak tree between the fairway and Orange Avenue. "Damn! I should have waited. How's a guy supposed to play golf with all that nonsense going on?"

The marching continued, with many of the ladies pulling off and finding places to rest. They hadn't been prepared to do any marching and the high heels just weren't working. As the crowd moved its way down Orange Avenue and up Springhill Road, they picked up marchers who didn't know what was going on but joined in anyway.

By the time they turned east again on Gaines Street, their numbers had swelled to 400. Jimmy Flain had requested a photographer position himself at the top of Doak Campbell Stadium, which was smart. The picture of 400 black people, three coffins and the deputy's cruiser would eventually run in every major newspaper in America.

It was past noon and hot as blazes by the time the marchers, now 450 strong, turned north on Monroe Street and arrived at the Leon County Courthouse. They had been marching mostly in silence, but now they found their voices and started chanting, "No justice – no peace!"

Tallahassee police officers had shut down Monroe between Apalachee Parkway and Tennessee Avenue, just to be safe. A small crowd of gawkers had gathered on the piazza in front of a downtown bank that afforded a clear view of the goings-on. The noise attracted the attention of several dozen people who were having lunch outdoors on Adams Street a block way and they ate more quickly – some anxious to go watch the show and others anxious to get out of the area.

Judge Busby Brown heard the commotion, too, and looked out his window in great fear. "Bring a car around back," he barked at his clerk, "and haul my ass out of here!"

Jimmy Flain was perfectly positioned to dutifully take note and report the activities in the morning paper, standing just in front of the courthouse door. There were only a few officers standing sentry, but several more in full riot gear were waiting inside the courthouse in case they were needed.

The marchers formed a loose mob in front of the courthouse and continued their chanting, punching the air with their fists. TV cameras showed up, and the chanting got louder.

One of the onlookers on the piazza was Rip, and he was torn. He had been thrilled to hear the news about the charges against Carrie being dropped. But she wasn't answering her phone or returning his messages. Didn't she want to celebrate?

And how was he going to deal with all this in *The Ripper* this week? Ordinarily, he would have a great time poking fun at the black marchers carrying the coffins of little girls around town. But how does he handle Carrie's involvement – and his own?

It was sticky, that's for sure.

Bulldog entered the courthouse and made his way to Jessie Malloy's office.

"The Reverend says a judge dropped the charges in the Stevens case. That true, Jess?"

"Yeah, Bulldog, it's true. It was Judge Brown, this morning."

"Busby did this?" Bulldog couldn't believe it. "What the hell did he do, take a stupidity pill this morning? What are we gonna do with this mob out there, Jess? For chrissake, there must be five hundred of 'em, and they're pissed as hell."

"They have a right to be pissed, Bulldog. They want justice and they're not going to get it."

One of the marchers outside – a black teenager who had joined in along the way because it looked like fun – found a rock and hurled it toward a second story window. The rock found its mark and shattered the glass in Jessie Malloy's office. Bulldog was so startled he actually coughed his toothpick across the room and it clattered to the floor.

"Holy shit, Jess, we might have a riot on our hands!"

More rocks were thrown and the police in riot gear wasted no time in pouring out of the courthouse and forming a ring in front of it. Jimmy Flain started to wonder if he was in such a good spot.

Jessie Malloy wasted no time. She rocketed out of her office and headed for the stairs. "Somebody find me a bullhorn!"

The appearance of the riot squad stopped the rock throwing, at least momentarily. But the chanting continued, louder than ever.

One of Jessie's aides handed her a bullhorn as she emerged from the courthouse doors, but she didn't use it. Instead, she motioned for Reverend Franklin to meet her in front of the doors. Jimmy Flain slid over and listened in.

"This is getting out of control, Reverend. Someone's going to get hurt."

"Three little girls are dead, Miss Malloy, and we want justice. We demand it!"

"Well, you're not going to get justice by standing in front of the courthouse and waving coffins in the air. It's ridiculous, Reverend! Don't you see? You're hurting your cause, not helping it. And those little girls deserve to be put to rest, not used to start a riot."

"But what about justice? Where do we go for justice?"

"I'm with you on that, Reverend. Believe me, I want justice, too. And somehow we'll find it. But, please, stop waving the bodies of those little girls in the faces of the riot police. For God's sake."

The absurdity of having brought the coffins along seemed to strike Franklin for the first time.

Malloy handed him the bullhorn. "Stop the protest, Reverend. Lay the little girls to rest."

"We'll need buses," Franklin said. "We've walked a long way."

"You'll have your buses, Reverend. And I won't stop searching for justice, either."

Franklin nodded and raised the bullhorn. The crowd quieted almost immediately.

"My friends, we have made our voices heard. I have been assured there will be justice, praise the Lord."

There was cheering.

"But right now, we need to get back to the job of returning these three little angels to the Lord. There will be buses brought in to bring us back to the church, where we will lay these girls to rest. Thank you for marching with me, but our marching must come to an end now. I'll see you back at the church."

35

R oy Fercal was so pissed he could hardly see straight. The stupid, cud-chewing, mouth-breathing, good-for-nothing asshole bastards at the airport had failed to get Speaker Gonzalez on tape with his duffel full of cash. He couldn't even think of enough swear words or scream them loud enough to himself inside his car to feel better.

Then he was driving down Lake Bradford Road and came up behind the hoard of marching black people streaming out of the church. Idiots! He turned his car around and hurled more profanity into the air. Jesus, he felt like he might pop a blood vessel.

Without the security tape and without the still picture that bitch Carrie Stevens was supposed to get last Friday, the Gonzalez bribery story was pretty much ka-put. And his efforts to steal the money for his own personal greed had gone up in smoke, too. Jesus! He just arranged for Speaker Gonzalez to get two million bucks in cash and the SONOFABITCH IS GETTING AWAY WITH IT!

Roy slammed his fist into his horn and blew it a few times as he drove aimlessly along Capital Circle Drive.

"You're getting away with taking a bribe," Fercal spat into the air of his car, "but you're not getting away with murder, you bastard!"

He reached for his cell phone and started to dial information to be connected to the Franklin County Sheriff's Department and tip them off about Gonzalez but stopped cold. There was a danger sign flashing in his mind; what was it?

The news report said Roxy had been raped and murdered. How did they know she was raped? They must have found evidence of it. And what might that evidence include? *The presence of semen.*

And whose semen would they find inside Roxy Jones last Sunday night? *His.* And how much of his semen would they find? *Enough to fill a bucket, most likely.* And where would they find it? *Everywhere there was an opening, including her nose if they looked hard enough.* Hell, they might even find it on the damn walls.

This could get very sticky, pardon the pun, if they find out I was there, Roy thought. Am I the reason they think she was raped? Could they be looking for me *right now?*

Wait one damn minute, he thought. I'm innocent! I didn't kill anybody. All I did was have sex her. *Yes, his mind responded, but you also used her to set up a bribe for Gonzalez and conspired to steal it. That brings Joe into the picture and he's a wildcard. Joe knows a lot of things. We wouldn't want him talking, now would we?*

But what if Joe could be the one to tip off the authorities about Gonzalez? It was risky, but Roy thought it through. Let's say Joe was supposed to meet Gonzalez and Roxy at the condo Monday morning, early. True enough. And to make it easier for the speaker, he and Roxy were going to spend Sunday night at the condo, courtesy of a friend or something. But when Joe got to the condo Monday morning there was no one there.

And why was Joe meeting Roxy and Gonzalez on St. George Island on Labor Day morning? To discuss the possibility of Joe working on a campaign. That could work, Roy decided. And Joe would be under strict orders to keep Roy out of it.

He dialed Joe's cell phone number.

"Joe, I need a favor."

"Sure, boss," Joe responded casually. He was wearing Roxy's bikini bottoms again, sitting with a couple of his buddies on the back deck of their condo. "Whaddya need?"

"Any word from Roxy?" Roy knew Joe paid little attention to the news. He was hoping today was no different.

"Nothing."

Roy was relieved. This could work. "I need you to call the Franklin County Sheriff's Office and tell them you're worried about Speaker Gonzalez. You were supposed to meet him Monday morning to talk about working on a campaign but he was a no-show. And you haven't been able to raise him. You're afraid something might have happened to him. Make sure they know the meeting place was the condo and that Gonzalez had planned to stay there Sunday night with Roxy. Understand?"

"What's the deal, boss? Why the cloak and dagger routine?"

"I'm trying to flush them out, Joe. And listen, if this works, I'll double your share of the money."

"Now you're talking!"

"One other thing, Joe. Keep my name out of it completely. It's politics. You understand."

"Sure. I'll let you know …" But the phone had gone dead.

Joe was going through the conversation with the sheriff's office in his head, like he was rehearsing, when another one of his buddies who had made a beer run returned all excited.

"You'll never guess what! Some young blonde woman was raped and murdered on the island last weekend! They dumped her body in the swamp. A guy at the store said she was some big hee-haw with the Speaker of the House!"

Joe wanted to vomit. All he could do was stare at the messenger who had delivered the awful news.

"That's terrible!" another buddy declared. "Do they know who did it?"

"Well, a deputy was showing a picture around of some guy they want to talk to. I gotta tell ya, Joe, he looked a lot like that one friend of yours. What's his name? Fecal or something?"

This time the wave of nausea was overwhelming. Joe bolted out of his chair, made it to a bathroom and puked. As he knelt in front of the toilet, catching his breath, it all became clear to Joe. Roxy was dead and Roy wanted to use Joe to cover his ass, or maybe even take the fall. What a bastard.

Joe looked down at the leopard skin bikini bottoms. They didn't feel good against his skin anymore; they felt spooky. He stripped them off and started to throw them in the trash, but stopped himself.

Would the authorities come looking for him, too? Would he be a suspect? He was innocent, of course, but Joe couldn't afford to be questioned by the law.

He looked again at the bikini bottoms and formed an idea. "This is for you, Roxy," Joe whispered. "And you, too, Roy – you asshole."

Speaker Gonzalez was in no real hurry to get back to Tallahassee, of course, but he was going through the motions. He caught a commercial flight from Puerto Rico to Miami, then hopped a flight to Orlando. When he got to his car in the general aviation lot, he was perturbed to find his cell phone battery was dead.

Gonzalez found a pay phone and called the office. It was almost six o'clock.

"Mr. Speaker!" It was Clay Chester. "Where are you? Sheriff Tobin is getting pissed that you haven't called him."

"I'm in Orlando, Clay. I just landed, and I'm beat. Call the sheriff and tell him I'll be in Tallahassee tomorrow about noon. That'll have to do."

"Okay. You missed a big day in Tallahassee, Mr. Speaker."

"What happened?"

"A bunch of the blacks marched on the courthouse – hundreds of 'em. They were pissed because a judge dismissed the charges against Carrie Stevens. She's that reporter from the *Suncoast Gazette*."

"Refresh my memory, Clay. I've been in Puerto Rico, remember."

"Oh, right. She's the one who ran over those three black kids last Friday night with Rip Snyder's truck. They said she was drunk, but they screwed up the blood test somehow and the judge tossed it."

"Oh, yeah. Now I remember." So much had happened since then. Gonzalez reminded himself to fire the Ripper Group from his campaign payroll. "I'll see you tomorrow, Clay. I'm going to the house and will hit the bed early. Don't call me."

Joe waited until dark. He said goodbye to his friends, who still had the condo for two more days and were sorry to see him leave early. Then he drove to Tallahassee and found the home of Roy Fercal on Magnolia Drive. He parked a block way and walked quietly to Fercal's driveway. Joe reached into his pants pocket, withdrew the leopard skin bikini bottoms and stuffed them behind the rear license plate on Roy's car. Then he disappeared into the night, something he did often.

36

Sheriff Johnny Tobin was still pissed that Speaker Gonzalez was taking his sweet time getting back from Puerto Rico, but his interest in Gonzalez was on the decline. The manager of Apalachicola's swankiest boutique hotel overlooking the river had identified the mystery man in the photograph supplied by John Billings, the retired postal worker, as Roy Fercal of Tallahassee. He was a regular customer, she said, and he had stayed at the hotel the previous weekend.

"Was he by himself?" the sheriff inquired.

"Yes he was, sheriff. He always is these days, since his wife left him. And she was such a wonderful woman, too."

"What does he do here, just hole up and keep to himself?"

"No, he comes and goes like everyone else. Hits the seafood restaurants, mostly."

"Did he come and go on Sunday night, do you know?"

"As a matter of fact he did go out on Sunday night. I remember because there was a storm building off the coast and I offered him an umbrella, which he thanked me for."

"How long was he gone?"

"I can't tell you that, sheriff. I left shortly after he did, trying to beat the storm, you know."

Tobin thanked her and returned to his patrol car. The name Roy Fercal seemed oddly familiar to him, but he didn't know why. He got on the radio and summoned his best two deputies to the office, where they met and discussed the latest finding.

"Here's what we got," Tobin said. "We know this Fercal fella was in the condo with the victim, thanks to the photograph. The picture was taken just before sunset on Sunday, the night the victim was killed. We know where Fercal lives."

"Do we have enough to arrest him?" one of the deputies wondered.

"I don't think so," Tobin replied. "But we sure as hell ought to go question him. It's getting late, though, so I'll go up by myself. I'll tell you what you boys can do. Get in touch with that jackass lawyer from the casino and tell him to surrender the name of the person who was using the condo last weekend. No more stalling."

It was after ten o'clock when Sheriff Johnny Tobin pulled into Roy Fercal's driveway on Magnolia Drive in Tallahassee. He pulled in behind Fercal's car and frowned at something his headlights caught – there was a string or something hanging out from behind the license plate. He walked up to it and pulled.

Tobin stood in Fercal's driveway and looked with amazement at the leopard skin bikini bottoms, which he instantly recognized as a perfect match for the bikini top in the trash bag that contained the victim's purse.

"You sick bastard," Tobin whispered, and realized he was standing in the driveway of a rapist and a killer. Then he looked down at the bumper of Fercal's car and saw the bumper sticker that read

"Reelect Gore." Suddenly, he remembered where he heard the name Roy Fercal before. He's the head of the Democratic Party!

Johnny Tobin was himself a Democrat, but after seven elections and twenty-eight years of service, he needed the help of the Democratic Party like he needed hemorrhoids.

Still, the man would have powerful political connections. Well, that's just too bad. "I don't give a damn who you are," Tobin said to the night air. "We're gonna fry your ass."

Tobin unsnapped his holster, walked to Fercal's front door and banged on it. There was a doorbell, but Sheriff Tobin felt like banging on the door. So he banged on it again, harder this time.

Fercal peered through the curtains, pissed that someone was banging on his door. The color drained out of his face immediately. He opened the door with a mounting dread.

"Are you Roy Fercal?" Tobin boomed.

Fercal nodded but he couldn't get his mouth to work.

"Roy Fercal, you're under arrest for the rape and murder of Roxanne Jones." Tobin read him his rights and Fercal nodded some more.

When his mouth finally started to work, Fercal's voice came out in a squeak. "I want a lawyer." The way he said it, though, made it sound like he was asking for his mommy.

37

Thursday, September 11

Carl Splighter woke up early with a case of the "zactly's." It's an ailment understood by most of the serious drinkers of the world – when your mouth tastes "zactly" like your ass.

He had been to The Pour House the night before, as he often did on Wednesday nights, trying in vain to chase college-age girls. Now he stumbled into the bathroom to brush his teeth. I should quit drinking, he thought, but knew he wouldn't.

With his mouth and ass now tasting (he assumed) decidedly different, Carl plodded into the kitchen and turned on the radio. The local NPR station was playing Morning Edition, and there was a lot of talk about yet another anniversary of 9/11. Several university professors were complaining that the events of 9/11 had given the Republicans an unfair lock on the White House, since no Democrat had been elected since.

By the time Carl finished brewing his coffee, it was time for the local news. The first item made his mouth turn sour again.

The head of the Florida Democratic Party is waking up in the Franklin County jail this morning. Thirty-five-year-old Roy Fercal of Tallahassee was arrested at his home last night and charged with the brutal rape and murder of Roxanne Jones, the chief of staff to House Speaker Alberto Gonzalez, a Republican. Franklin County Sheriff Johnny Tobin says Fercal is refusing to cooperate...

"He's lawyered up, but the evidence is piling up against him. We know he was at the scene at about the time the victim was killed."

Sheriff Tobin says he is waiting for DNA testing to be completed. Miss Jones, of Tallahassee, was raped and murdered on St. George Island Sunday night. Her nude body was wrapped in a blanket and dumped in Tate's Hell Swamp.

Like all news reporters in Tallahassee, Carl Splighter had been consumed yesterday with the news that the charges against Carrie Stevens had been dropped on a technicality, and the ensuing march on the courthouse. The murder of Roxy Jones had been reported, of course, but the marching blacks had pushed Roxy out of the lead. And there simply wasn't time to do much digging on the Roxy Jones thing. Now some radio announcer had scooped all of them with Fercal's arrest.

Carl would have to get moving – another busy news day. Had Roy Fercal actually killed Roxy Jones? When had he and Roy talked last? It was Monday, wasn't it? Yeah, Labor Day. So that would be the day after Roxy was killed.

Did he sound like someone who had raped and killed a woman the night before? Not really, but how does someone feel the day after something like that? Carl had no idea.

He remembered that Roy wanted to meet with Carrie, and Carl had helped set it up. So he meets with Carrie on Tuesday and the next day her charges are dropped like a rock. Then Roy gets arrested for killing Roxy. Is there a connection there somewhere? Carl couldn't see it.

He had a hard time picturing Roy killing Roxy, but the radio report mentioned DNA. If the DNA matches, Roy is guilty as hell, Carl decided. The DNA is always the clincher.

Charlie Ward, the Chairman of the Florida Democratic Party, was already having a very bad day, and it was early. The first phone call from hell came just after six o'clock from T. Esterman Blankenship, the egotistical bastard who serves as the general counsel of the Florida Democratic Party. Charlie hated him, but Blankenship had been the party's lawyer for more than twenty years and couldn't be fired for the simple reason that he knew too much.

"Good morning, Torrance." Charlie liked calling him by his first name because he knew it irritated him. "Kinda early for a lawyer isn't it?"

"Yes, Mr. Chairman, I must agree with you that it is far too early. But, then again, bad news seldom keeps a handy schedule."

"Bad news, eh?"

"Very bad, I'm afraid. And as the Chairman of the Party, you need to be fully aware of it – hence the phone call."

"Ah, yes, hence the phone call. Well, Torrance, you might as well hit me with it straight up. What's the bad news?"

"Roy Fercal has been arrested for murder."

Charlie Ward sat up abruptly and banged his knee on his nightstand. Mrs. Ward groused and got up to go pee.

"I'm not sure I heard you right. Say it again."

There was a disgusted sigh on the other end. "That bully you insist on having around as your executive director – Roy Fercal – is sitting in the Franklin County Jail. He's charged with raping and killing Roxanne Jones."

There was a loud buzzing in Charlie's head and he couldn't make it go away. "Jesus Christ. How do you know this?"

"The little brute called me from the jail to represent him! I can't, of course. He needs a criminal defense attorney, and I try not to mix with the criminal element, as you know."

Yes, I know, Charlie thought. He could see Blankenship picking some imaginary piece of lint from his suit and looking disgusted.

"We'll need to have a conference call with the executive committee right away this morning," Charlie decided. "I'll need you on the line to answer any legal questions."

"Of course, Mr. Chairman. Always obliged to be of service."

The phone rang again ten seconds later.

"Mr. Chairman! Did you hear about Roy? He's been arrested for murder!" It was a member of the executive committee.

"Yes, Gladys. I just spoke with Mr. Blankenship. We'll have a conference call in a couple of hours."

"It's so awful! The news story starts off with the most terrible sentence, about the head of the Democratic Party waking up in jail!"

And so it went, phone call after phone call, and they were all the same. Radio and television stations across Florida were all reading from the same wire copy. It was a public relations disaster.

But won't the conference call be fun!

38

R ip Snyder couldn't believe his own ears. Roy Fercal had been arrested for raping and killing Roxy! Rip thought of Roy as a weenie. He couldn't imagine the little dweeb had it in him to rape and murder. But, nobody suspected Ted Bundy when they looked at him, either.

Guilty or not, this was an opportunity too golden to pass up. He called the head of the College Republicans at FSU and suggested they organize a protest in front of the Democratic Party headquarters at noon.

"Come up with some clever signs," Rip said. "Tell the media you're demanding the Democrats fire Roy."

The college kid agreed it was a great idea and went straight to work on it.

In his head, Rip was already starting to write the lead story for tomorrow's edition of *The Ripper*. He thought FECAL MATTER

HITS THE FAN might be a good headline. He was grinning so much he could hardly drink his morning coffee without spilling it.

Carrie Stevens didn't know what to think about the Roy Fercal story. This was the man who was blackmailing her with her past, so she absolutely believed he was capable of bigger crimes. But this was also the man with enough clout to bribe a judge and a prosecutor and make her a free woman, albeit for his own ends. Apparently, whatever clout he has in Franklin County isn't enough to trump a murder charge. Or is it?

What bothered Carrie the most was her agreement to rat out on Rip in exchange for the vehicular manslaughter charges going away. Did she still need to uphold her end of the bargain?

If Roy goes away for killing Roxy, what can he possibly do to hurt her? Would Roy still be obsessed with ruining Rip, or would he be too consumed with saving himself?

Carrie didn't have the answers, but she decided to do nothing at all for now. Maybe she won't have to turn on Rip after all. She would like that.

The Roy Fercal story hit Jessie Malloy hard. Jesus! This is the man she sold her soul to for a seat in Congress. Would he even be able to deliver on his end of the promise?

And, my God, what would happen if somehow it gets out that she – Jailhouse Jess – had made a dirty deal with a rapist and a killer? She felt sick.

Jessie Malloy, the pride of Sopchoppy and her father's favorite reason for bragging to his friends, had sold out her own people in a slimy political deal that might not even happen anymore. For the love of Christ!

Jessie sat at her desk and pondered what to do. She had promised Reverend Franklin that she would continue to look for justice for the three little girls he buried yesterday. But would she? And where should she look for justice?

Definitely not in the mirror, that's for sure.

Speaker Alberto Gonzalez was driving on I-75 between Orlando and Gainesville when he heard the Roy Fercal story. The reality of it hit him like a lightening bolt and the hairs on his neck stood straight up. Could it be? Could that bastard Fercal actually take the fall for this?

Of course they'll find out the DNA matches, he realized. He balled her right before I killed her! Another shiver went through him, raising goose bumps on his arms. Could he actually get away with it? And could he handle the guilt?

Gonzalez analyzed what he knew as he drove. The news story said "the evidence is piling up against" Fercal. What evidence?

Well, the DNA will match. But how did they even know to look at Roy Fercal? Did someone see Fercal at the condo? Possibly. What other evidence was there? And what was the motive?

There were too many unknowns for Gonzalez to feel comfortable. And what would Roy do to prove his innocence? Obviously, he'll try to convince the sheriff that someone else did it, and that someone else was Alberto Gonzalez!

Gonzalez realized he was still a long way from being out of the woods on this one. And what about Joe? Gonzalez realized with a sinking stomach that Joe could blow his alibi of flying to Puerto Rico on Sunday right out of the water! They had talked at the condo Sunday afternoon!

By the time Gonzalez reached Interstate 10, he decided he needed a lawyer – a damn good one. He called Bannerman Lux.

Sheriff Johnny Tobin decided Roy Fercal was a very disciplined fellow. He had not spoken one word since his squeaky demand for a lawyer. Yes, a very disciplined fellow, indeed.

About the only new evidence the sheriff had gathered was from a neighbor of Fercal's named Hilda Scranton. The old lady recalled an outburst from Mr. Fercal last Saturday morning in which the accused emerged from his house, looked at the morning paper and said, very loudly, "Now you'll get yours, you slimy bitch!"

It wasn't much, but it was the kind of thing juries paid attention to when placed in the proper context. And the context so far was this: the victim was in possession of Fercal's semen, and Fercal was in possession of the victim's bikini bottoms.

Sheriff Tobin was having trouble understanding why the bikini bottoms were stuffed behind Fercal's license plate, but Tobin had Fercal pegged as a pervert, so who knows?

And there was another piece of evidence Tobin was anxious to check out, but he had to wait for Fercal to start talking. The sheriff wanted to know if it was Roy Fercal who left the threatening message on the victim's answering machine, as he suspected.

Tobin was still musing over all of this and enjoying a cigarette when a nice-looking young lady in her mid-thirties arrived in his office and pronounced herself to be Roy Fercal's attorney. She handed him a card.

"Madeline Esterman," Tobin read from the card, "from Tallahassee. Welcome to Apalachicola, Miss Esterman. It is miss, isn't it?"

"Yes, it is. But please call me Maddie, sheriff. I prefer it."

"Maddie it is, then. And I assume you're here to talk with your client."

"Yes, please."

"Right this way, young lady."

Tobin led her to a small room with a couple of chairs and a table, all bolted to the floor. The sheriff retrieved Roy Fercal from his cell, and Maddie thought he looked very weak and defeated in his bright orange jumpsuit.

Fercal's eyes widened in surprise when he saw her. "Maddie! What a surprise! Did Blankenship send you down?"

"Yeah. I kinda got drafted. Good old Uncle Torrance."

"Well, it's good to see you, Maddie."

She responded with a half-hearted smile and looked at Sheriff Tobin, who was staring at Fercal. "Sheriff?"

Tobin broke his stare. "Oh, sorry. I guess I was having a senior moment. I'll leave you two alone. Just let me know when you're finished."

Sheriff Tobin closed the door behind him. He had heard enough. The threatening voice on the victim's answering machine was Fercal, no question. "We're gonna strap you to a gurney and pump you full of poison, you pervert," he said to the door, and reached for another smoke.

"I didn't do it, Maddie. I'm innocent."

Maddie looked at Fercal for a long moment. She didn't want to be here, but her uncle had insisted. "Do it for the good of the party, Mad," he said, and that was that.

"Can you explain how your semen was found in the – let's see – vagina, anis, throat and right ear of a dead rape victim?"

"We had sex, Maddie. But I didn't rape her. It was consensual!"

"Then how did she end up dead? Was it a semen overdose?"

"I don't know how she ended up dead. When I left her she was very much alive." Roy shot her a smile. "And very appreciative, too."

"Spare me. Ever hear of a great invention called the condom?"

"Roxy doesn't like 'em."

"Didn't like them, you mean. Past tense."

Roy flushed and looked away. "Right. Didn't like them."

"What about the bikini bottoms? Why were they stuffed behind your license plate?"

"How the hell do I know? I haven't the foggiest idea." Actually, Roy figured he knew exactly how they got there. They were a message from Joe, and the message was clear – keep his name out of it at all costs. And Roy would comply, if he could, because Joe could be a very dangerous man.

"Well, Roy, if you wanted them as a trophy, you should have put them in the glove box. That way, you could pull them out and sniff them if the mood was right."

For a moment, Roy felt like reaching across the table and grabbing the bitch by the throat. He resisted, but it was no small effort.

"Fuck you, Maddie. Fuck you! Why can't you let it go? Just let it go, for crying out loud!"

"You hurt my best friend, Roy, and you hurt her bad. And I'll never forgive you for it."

"Then you can't be my attorney."

"Sure I can, Roy. I'm it. Get used to it. I represent lots of people I don't like."

"Whatever."

"You'll be arraigned tomorrow and we'll get you out on bail. Then we'll go over this entire scenario with a fine-toothed comb and find a way to get you off the hook. Until then, say nothing to nobody."

Maddie left him staring at the table. Jesus, she hated that man. Maddie had been best friends with Mrs. Fercal when Roy had his first little dalliance with Roxy Jones. Maddie was the one who hugged her and cried with her and got her through it. And now that Maddie and Roy's ex-wife were lovers, well, she had even less tolerance for Roy Fercal.

The protest at Democratic Party headquarters was a bust by any real standard – just nine kids parading around with signs. But a couple of TV cameras were there and that made it just as good as a Million Man March.

Rip Snyder was there, observing, with a digital camera. Some of the signs were quite good, he thought: DUMP FECAL. FLUSH

FECAL. FECAL MUST GO. FECAL STINKS. WIPE FECAL AWAY. Rip pronounced it good. The TV cameras left, and so did the protestors.

39

Friday, September 12

Roy Fercal woke up for the second consecutive morning in the Franklin County jail. He was sick of it. Today, he hoped, a judge would set bail, and he could get out.

He was determined to continue with his schemes to bring down the Republicans while his attorney worked on getting rid of the rape and murder charges. Surely they wouldn't convict an innocent man, would they?

Sheriff Johnny Tobin arrived just before nine o'clock and escorted him to a courtroom. Fercal's mood brightened as soon as the judge entered the room. It was Twinkie Smith, a man Roy helped get elected years ago. His real name wasn't Twinkie, of course, but it looked like he still favored them. He looked at Roy and offered a small grin.

There were the usual arguments from both sides. Roy was accused of a terrible crime and should stay locked up. He's dangerous. No, Maddie countered, he's a respected citizen of Tallahassee and is no risk to anyone. Besides, the charges are bogus. Let him out.

Finally, Twinkie pronounced bail at $50,000, a ridiculously low amount for a man accused of rape and murder, but ol' Twinkie remembered his friends. Fercal made bail, changed back into his real clothes, and left the courthouse with Maddie Esterman.

"I'm starved, Maddie. I know a place here in Apalachicola with the best fried oysters in the universe. Are you game?"

"Fine. We need to discuss your case, though. Will it be private enough for that?"

"Oh yeah. There's a table on the deck overlooking the bay. It's fantastic."

Once they were seated, Maddie had to admit the view was spectacular. "Apalachicola is a beautiful place. Kind of old looking, in a nice way."

"Had you not been here before yesterday?" Fercal was surprised. "Ellen and I came here a lot, just to get way. In fact, this was kind of our table."

"Ellen doesn't want to come here anymore, she told me," Maddie said. "It's too painful. Anyway, I don't want to talk about your ex."

"I don't either, really."

The fried oysters arrived, along with generous helpings of cole slaw, hush puppies and fries. They were terrific, just as Roy had promised.

"Roy, we need to start from the beginning. And I need to know the absolute truth. No lies. Understood?"

"Understood."

"Why were you staying here in Apalachicola last weekend?"

"It relaxes me." One question, one lie. We're off to a great start, Roy thought.

"Did you know Roxy was going to be staying on St. George Island?"

"No." Two for two.

"Then how did you end up having sex with her?"

"She called me." Strike three, Roy thought, but this ain't baseball. "On my cell. Said she had the use of this great condo for the weekend. Her other friends had left and she wanted some company."

"What other friends?"

"I don't know. Old college friends, I think. They were gone when I got there."

"So the two of you were alone?"

"Yes." Finally, something other than a lie.

"And when you got there, did you have the understanding that Roxy was expecting to have sex with you?"

"I should say so. She was buck naked when I arrived and stayed that way the whole time."

"And the sex was consensual?"

"Very."

"And then you left?"

"Yeah. I went back to the hotel."

"Why didn't you stay the night?"

"She didn't want me to. She said the speaker was coming down later that night for some R & R. Obviously, she wanted me gone before ol' fatso showed up."

"I wonder if ol' fatso, as you call him, ever showed up."

"I think Gonzalez killed her, Maddie. I really do."

"You're accusing the Speaker of the House of Representatives of raping and killing his own chief of staff?"

"Not rape, no. She wasn't raped. That backwoods sheriff has it wrong because they found my semen in her. As I said, the exchange of bodily fluids was consensual."

"Then why would he kill her?"

"I don't know, Maddie. Maybe they had a lover's quarrel."

"So the rumors are true? They were lovers?"

"I'm not sure the term 'lovers' is very accurate," Roy mused. "They were sex partners though. Roxy told me. And she hated it. It was disgusting, she said."

"So she tried to break it off, he got pissed and whacked her with a skillet?"

Roy shrugged. "Could be."

Maddie looked out over the bay for a long moment. "Roy, how did you end up with her bikini bottoms behind your license plate?"

"I've been thinking about that," Roy said, and that was true enough. "I think Roxy put 'em there. As a joke."

"Oh, Roy, don't expect a jury to buy that one. They won't be able to visualize a murder victim playing practical jokes."

Roy shrugged again and looked away. "That's all I can think of."

"And when, exactly, did she stuff her bikini bottoms behind your license plate? You said she was naked the whole time."

Roy shot her an angry look. "What are you doing? Cross examining me now?"

"Settle down, Roy. I'm just telling you the 'Roxy playing a joke' theory won't hold up and it'll make you look guilty."

Thanks a lot, Joe, you prick, Roy said to himself. "Then you better come up with a better theory, Maddie, because I'm fresh out of ideas."

"Maybe the killer planted the bikini bottoms," Maddie theorized out loud. Then, to herself, thought that maybe the killer was her client.

Carrie Stevens was feeling a lot better about things today. A doctor had removed the stupid miniature hockey mask from her face and replaced it with a small bandage. Her facial burns were healing nicely, he said, and she should be as good as new in a few weeks.

She called Carl Splighter and said she would return to work on Monday.

"It'll be great to have you back," Carl lied. "Care to join me at the Downtown Getdown?"

"No thanks, Carl. I'd love to," she lied back, "but no more drinking for me. You have fun, though."

After they hung up, Carl reached into his desk and retrieved Carrie's diary. He read page 58 again, his favorite, even though he had practically memorized it.

"If all this is true," Carl speculated to himself, "you're one helluva roll in the hay, Miss Carrie."

Then he licked his lips and read it again, slowly stroking the leather binding.

40

THE RIPPER

Friday, September 12

Greetings! By any measure, this has been a tough week in the Republican Party. We were stunned and grief-stricken to learn of the senseless and heinous murder of one of our rising stars, Roxy Jones. As you know, Roxy was doing a tremendous job as the chief of staff to House Speaker Alberto Gonzalez before her life was so brutally taken away.

It is not within our power to make sense of it. All we can say is that while she was here, Roxy made us better. And now that she's gone, our lives are lessened.

Our hearts and prayers go out to her parents in Ponte Vedra Beach and to all who knew her and loved her.

FECAL MATTER HITS THE FAN

Our sorrow over Roxy's death turned quickly to anger as we learned of the arrest of her suspected killer – none other than Roy Fecal, the head rat of the Florida Democrat Party. I won't go into all the gory details, but this glob of human waste left a lot of evidence behind. And we need a respectful tip of the hat to the man who directed the investigation that led to Fecal's arrest – Franklin County Sheriff Johnny Tobin. He's a lifelong Democrat, but by God, he did his duty.

Sheriff Tobin – consider this your invitation to come on over to the good side. We love a tough sheriff who won't take any crap from – well – crap.

As of this writing, the state's attorney in Franklin County is still considering whether to go for the death penalty. Pardon the bluntness, but here's what happened to Roxy: She was brutally and forcibly raped several times, clubbed in the head with a cast iron skillet, wrapped in a blanket and dumped like trash in a swamp to be discovered by a man hunting for alligators. Strapping Fecal to a cot and filling his veins with poison sounds too good for him, but it's all we got.

Too bad Old Sparky isn't available.

FLUSH FECAL

News of Fecal's arrest spread quickly through Tallahassee, and a bunch of college Republicans over at FSU decided to show their support of alum Roxy Jones by protesting at Democrat headquarters. *(See attached photo.)*

You should have seen the rats peering out the windows, with their beady eyes, as though they were trapped in a sinking ship. And perhaps they are. After all, the law firm of Blankenship, Cutter and Hyde is representing Fecal. That's the law firm that does all the legal work for the Democrat Party. Are the Democrats helping Fecal avoid the Big Flush?

The protestors demanded just the opposite, and rightly so. How can the Democrats keep Fecal on the payroll when he stands accused of rape and murder? Shame, shame, shame.

HERE WE GO A-MARCHING

An estimated 500 black people got it in their heads this week to march on the Leon County Courthouse in Tallahassee. This would be newsworthy enough, but the interesting twist on this event was their decision to include three dead little girls.

It was a sickening sight as the mob held three little coffins in the air in defiance of police in riot gear. *(See attached photo.)* What's next? Hiding behind infants?

And there was the obligatory rock thrown threw a courthouse window and, of course, it was thrown by a teenager with his pants halfway to his ankles. Don't these kids know it's harder to run away from the cops with your pants falling off?

This ugly moment in Tallahassee history was organized by the Reverend Josiah Franklin of the Bradford Road Baptist Church for the stated purpose of demanding justice for the three dead girls. The sisters were tragically killed in a traffic accident near the church. They were walking in the road when a vehicle veered out of control.

It's a horribly sad event, and it's certainly understandable that it stirs deep emotions. But for those who believe in the rule of law, Reverend, justice is in the hands of the legal system, not an angry mob waving the bodies of dead girls in the air.

CONNER GO BYE-BYE

Congressman Billy Conner is a goner. Or, at least he will be soon. He announced this week that the next term will be his last, and not a moment too soon.

The Democrats made a laughable effort this week trying to reminisce about all the good things Conner has done in Washington. I think his career is best summed up by toenail-gate. Remember that?

There were some people in Congress trying to close a couple of military bases in Conner's district, and he missed the vote. Why? His staff said he was having surgery, but we later discovered he was at the Heaven Scents Spa getting a pedicure. We know this because ol' Conner *actually submitted the bill to the taxpayers for reimbursement.*

Hey, Billy Boy: The next time you stick your foot in your mouth, just go ahead and chew the toenails down. It'll save us all some money.

HUNGRY HUSBAND TOASTED IN BROWARD

A Broward County woman was arrested this week for hitting her husband over the head with a toaster oven. She admits doing it, but tells police the poor schlep had it coming.

Apparently, the woman had pulled a piece of toast out of the toaster oven and was amazed to see an image of Jesus burned into the bread. Before she could find her digital camera, though, her stupid husband had buttered the toast and eaten it.

Just out of curiosity, we took a look at the voter files in Broward County and, sure enough, they're both registered Democrats.

WHY CAN'T WE ALL GET ALONG?

As usual, I have carefully proofread this edition of *The Ripper,* and I can't for the life of me figure out why the Democrats despise me so.

KEEP THE FAITH!

Rip Snyder

41

C arl Splighter was in his office, waiting for the rain to stop so he could hit the Downtown Getdown. The phone rang.

"*Suncoast Gazette*, this is Carl."

"Bring me the fucking diary."

Click.

It was Roy Fercal, of course, the only man Carl knew who could have a complete phone conversation in five words. Why waste time with silly words like "hello," "goodbye" and "how ya doin'?"

When the rain let up, Carl left the office with Carrie's diary in hand and walked up College Avenue, across Monroe Street to Adams Street, where the Downtown Getdown was getting under way. But this was the area dominated by families, where the kids bounced around inside a moonwalk and clowns twisted balloons into alligators and such. It was another block and a half down Adams where Carl knew he would meet Fercal – in front of Klinger's.

Unlike last week, when only a handful of Minnesota fans gawked with amazement and fear at the drunken pep rally, there were several Miami fans in attendance and they weren't the least bit intimidated. Occasionally, when a lone FSU fan wandered too close to a group of Miami fans, the Miami fans would yell, "Wide right!" or "Wide left!" These were cruel reminders of bitter losses FSU had suffered at the hands of the Hurricanes over the years, always ending with a missed field goal that could have won the game.

Carl steered his way down the street, grabbed a beer in front of Klinger's and started looking around for Roy. He was startled when Roy grabbed his shoulder from behind.

"You got it?"

"Jesus! Yeah, I got it, Roy. Right here."

Carl handed it over and wondered if he'd ever see page 58 again.

"Did you read *The Ripper?*" Carl asked. "He was pretty rough on you."

"Yeah, I read it. The bastard is asking for trouble."

Carl pointed to the diary. "Plenty of ammunition in there. What are you going to do with it?"

"You'll see," Roy replied as he turned to leave.

"Check out page 58," Carl advised him. "It makes for a good bedtime story."

"Whatever."

Later, in his dimly lit home office on Magnolia Drive, Roy Fercal was painstakingly scanning every page of the diary into his computer. He was pleased to see that Carrie Stevens had pretty good handwriting. It would be easy for people to read.

Roy wasn't really reading the pages; there would be time enough for that later on. But when he got to page 58, Roy remembered Carl's advice and read it. He was not disappointed.

May 15: I showed Rip my "magic trick" tonight. It's the only good thing my mother ever did for me. When I was real young, she taught me how to exercise my vagina muscles to make them stronger. She called it her "Happy Snappy" and I have to admit, it's pretty cool. Anyway,

Rip and I had our usual good sex and after he came I started gripping and kneading him with my Happy Snappy. He never went soft and we were able to go at it again right away. The second time he came, I thought he was going to have a stroke.

Rip loves it. What man wouldn't? ☺

Wow. I might like a piece of that action myself, Roy thought, and wondered if he could make it happen. Then he remembered it was Rip Snyder who actually *was* getting it, and it pissed him off even more.

42

Saturday, September 13

Speaker Alberto Gonzalez rose early on Saturday morning and was remarkably clear-headed. He had arranged, through Bannerman Lux, to meet Sheriff Johnny Tobin in Apalachicola that morning at nine o'clock. That meant they had to be on the road by 7:30, so he had limited himself to only one glass of Scotch the night before.

Gonzalez had confided to Lux, him being his attorney and all, that he and Roxy had been intimate on several occasions. For this reason, and this reason alone, Gonzalez did not want to provide a DNA sample to Sheriff Tobin if he could avoid it.

"It would ruin me politically," Gonzalez reasoned, "if it gets out that I was having an affair with my chief of staff. So I just want to make it clear that I was in Puerto Rico when Roxy was killed, so I can't possibly be a suspect."

Lux understood and he procured an affidavit from the private flying service pilot who swore under oath that he flew Gonzalez to Ponca, Puerto Rico, last Sunday morning.

"We'll tell Tobin that if your alibi checks out, no DNA," Lux decided, and that was that.

Gonzalez showered and dressed and still had about 30 minutes to kill before Bannerman Lux would pick him up. He remembered the mental note about firing The Ripper Group from his campaign payroll, and wondered if he still needed to given the shenanigans of the week.

Hot coffee in hand, Gonzalez booted up his computer, went to Google and typed in "Rip Snyder." He got more than a thousand hits, but it was the entry at the bottom of the first page that caught his eye:

Rip Snyder is a racist pig. Check out what he tells his girlfriend when it's time for pillow talk, straight from the girlfriend's diary: "When he's pissed, he sometimes says that's why people call them ..."

The link was to a website called All About Rip. Gonzalez followed the link and forgot all about his coffee. The website was anonymous, as far as he could tell, but it was, indeed, all about Rip Snyder. There were several references to Rip's use of the n-word, all linked to scanned images of pages in actual handwriting, identified as the diary of Carrie Stevens.

His first thought was: Rip is sleeping with Carrie? Then: Rip needs to be fired, no question. Gonzalez didn't want the n-word floating around *his* campaign, that's for sure.

It was almost 7:30, but Gonzalez didn't hesitate. He dialed Rip's home number.

"It's Gonzalez."

"Mr. Speaker! Good morning! Hey, sorry about Roxy. She was a dandy."

"Yes, she was. Look, Rip, I've been meaning to call you but I've been in Puerto Rico. I need to let you go as my campaign consultant. You're off the payroll."

"What? Why?"

"You've become too controversial, Rip. When the mud flies, I don't want to get hit with the splatter."

"Mud? What mud? I don't know what you're talking about."

"In fact, mud is too weak of a word. More like shit, Rip, and it's about to hit the fan on you. So you're fired; that's it."

"Okay, so I'm fired. I got it. But when you say the shit is going to hit the fan, what do you mean?"

Gonzalez gave him the website address. "Check it out; it's bad. And do me a favor. When the reporters ask you when I fired you, tell 'em it was last week."

It was not safe to be anything small enough to be picked up and thrown in the household of Rip Snyder. He had never been so angry. He was out of control.

Some sonofabitch had posted pages on the Internet that claimed to be from Carrie's diary, and he believed it. It was her handwriting and he remembered talking to her about things, but she had it wrong. He wasn't a racist and he didn't call black people niggers! But he sometimes pointed out things and said that's why *some people* call them that.

Hell, his best golf buddy is black.

"I'm not a racist!" he screamed, picking up a glass ashtray and hurling it across the room. It shattered. "Stupid son of a shit ass bitch!"

Then he wondered how Carrie's diary pages could end up on the Internet. Did Carrie do it? Did she help? Why? And why was she keeping a diary to begin with? Isn't that what teenagers do?

He picked his phone up off the floor, found it still worked, and dialed Carrie's number. All he got was the answering machine.

"Carrie! Jesus Christ, I can't fucking believe it. Some pages from your diary are posted on the Internet! And it's all about me being a racist! What the fuck were you thinking? Did you do this? Call me."

Then he threw the phone back on the floor.

Carrie stared at the answering machine in shock and disbelief. Her diary? On the Internet? Impossible!

She went to her laptop and did a Google search for "Carrie Stevens diary." Sure enough, there was a link to All About Rip.

And there it was. Her diary. Not the whole thing, just certain pages. But it was her handwriting. Her words. It had to be the work of Roy Fercal, but how?

Carl Splighter. That sonofabitch must have found her diary and given it to Fercal so they could crap on Rip. Stupid slimy bastards!

She practically flew to her rusty old Saab and drove to the office. It took longer than she wanted, but she was being careful to avoid running over anybody.

She had intended to search for her diary and confront Carl at his apartment, but it turned out Carl was there.

"Carrie! I thought you weren't coming in until Monday."

Carrie said nothing. She simply strode across the office and slapped Carl on the left cheek – hard.

"You worthless piece of shit! If I had a gun I'd blow your sorry ass away! You'll pay for this, Carl. You're gonna pay!"

Carl was rubbing his cheek. Jesus, she packs a wallop. "What are you talking about?"

"My diary! You stole my diary! And now it's all over the Internet!"

"I didn't steal your diary," Carl protested. Then, puzzled: "It's on the Internet?"

"Yes! And stop denying it. You gave it to Fercal, didn't you? Or did you sell it? You slimy shit."

"I didn't sell it!" Might as well 'fess up, he thought. "I stumbled across it looking for your notes on Gonzalez. I read what you wrote about me – how you'd rather be dead than go out with me. It pissed me off. So I showed it to Roy and he wanted to read it. I didn't know he would put it on the Internet!"

"Fuck you, Carl. You shouldn't have read it. This is all your fault."

His cheek still smarting, he couldn't resist his own verbal slap back at her. "I read about Happy Snappy," he said, grinning now. "It made me hard just thinking about it."

Carrie wound up and slapped him again, harder this time, and left.

It was the first time Carl had been slapped by a woman, and it felt kind of good. Not as good as Happy Snappy, he was sure, but not bad.

43

Carrie felt good about slapping Carl, too, but for a different reason. She ought to go back and bloody his ugly nose. The man was no better than a bucket of spit.

She pulled over at a nearby pay phone and thumbed through the directory and was pleased to find Roy Fercal listed. She noted the address on Magnolia Drive and headed straight for it.

Like Sheriff Tobin before her, Carrie ignored the doorbell and started beating on the door. She even kicked it a few times.

Roy wasn't surprised; he'd been expecting her.

"Well, good morning, Carrie. Come on in. Can I get you some coffee?"

Carrie stormed in and gave Fercal a slap of his own. Jesus, her hand was starting to hurt from all this smacking around.

Roy hadn't expected the slap and it stung. "Okay, I'll take that as a no." He swung the door shut and the two of them stood in his foyer, with Roy rubbing his face and Carrie standing firm and mean with her hands on her hips.

"How in the hell could you do such a thing?" Carrie started right in on him. "Where do you get off putting my private diary on the Internet? Have you no shame? None at all?"

"We had an agreement."

"No! I never agreed to this. I agreed to *tell* you about Rip. That's all. My diary was never part of the deal."

"Well, it just kind of fell into my lap. And that bastard Snyder is asking for trouble. He flat-out convicted me of Roxy's murder in that stupid rag of his. It's payback time."

Jesus, Carrie thought. In her rage, she had forgotten completely about the rape and murder charges pending against Fercal. And now I'm standing in his house, alone with him! Carrie started to feel frightened; Roy was between her and the door.

"I need to go, Roy."

Roy saw the change in her posture. "What's the matter, Carrie? Am I making you nervous?" He stepped closer. "Don't like being alone with a man accused of rape and murder? Is that it?"

"Let me out, Roy."

"In a minute. But first, I want to make sure you understand the rules of the game now. Before long, the media is going to discover your diary pages on the Internet. They'll ask you if the pages are genuine. You'll say yes."

"And if I don't?"

Roy stepped closer still, just inches away from her face, pinning her against a wall. "Then your sordid past as a hot tub whore goes on the Internet, too. I kept my end of the bargain by getting the judge to drop the manslaughter charges. Now it's your turn."

Carrie was very frightened now. Should she try to run? If she kneed him in the groin, could she get away? Was he really a rapist and a killer?

Suddenly, Roy stepped back and opened the drawer of a mirrored piece of furniture in the foyer. He withdrew Carrie's diary and held it out to her.

"This is yours. I must say, I enjoyed it very much, especially page 58. That was a doozy."

Now Carrie was confused. "Page 58? Why page 58?"

"The part about Happy Snappy. I'd like you to show it to me sometime. It sounds great."

Carrie's face colored. She snatched the diary out of Roy's hand and turned to leave. "Fuck you, Roy." She was at the door. The doorknob was turning. She was almost out.

"Yeah, exactly. Fuck me. You know, with the Happy Snappy."

"Never." She was halfway out the door.

"Either show me the Happy Snappy or I put page 58 on the Internet."

Carrie stopped. She looked longingly at her rusty old Saab. Suddenly, it seemed far away.

"So I either go to bed with you, or you make me world famous?"

"That's right, Carrie. Whaddya say?"

"I'd rather be famous." Carrie slammed the door behind her and ran to her car. She could hear Roy laughing hysterically behind her. Carrie drove off as fast as the rusty old Saab would take her.

Jimmy Flain was in his office on this fine Saturday morning, not because he had any serious work to do, but just because it was the only place he felt he belonged. He was wondering if Roy Fercal was really a murderer and whether he would consent to an interview when an e-mail popped up. It was from somebody identified as Snoopy.

"Check this out. Proof that Rip Snyder is a racist. Click here."

What's this? So, of course, Jimmy clicked the link and was taken to All About Rip. It was pretty convincing, especially if the diary pages are real. But people fake stuff on the Internet all the time. You can't trust anything.

Jimmy thought about it. There was obviously a connection of some kind between Rip Snyder and Carrie Stevens, but were they really lovers? It seemed impossible, yet Carrie was driving Rip's truck last weekend when she – when she – *ran over three black girls!*

Jesus, Jimmy thought, this could explode into something if it turns out the diary pages are real. How did they get on the Internet? Jimmy didn't know, but he aimed to find out.

He called the *Suncoast Gazette* office in Tallahassee and got Carl Splighter.

"Hey, Carl. It's Jimmy Flain. Have you seen Carrie around?"

Carl's hand went involuntarily to his left cheek. "Yeah, I seen her. Why?"

"I need to ask her about something. It's a story I'm working on."

"About her diary being on the Internet?"

"You know about it? Is it true?"

"Yeah, Jimmy, it's true. And she's pretty pissed about it."

"Will she confirm the diary pages are real?"

"I don't know, Jimmy, but they're real alright."

"Well, I kinda need her to confirm it. Can you give me her home number?"

It was against company rules, of course, to give out a reporter's home number. But Carl remembered the slaps and rattled off the number from memory. "And you didn't get it from me."

After he hung up, Carl figured he'd better inform the boss about the latest developments in the soap opera of Carrie Stevens. He called his editor, Jeremiah Bundt, at home.

"This is getting to be a regular thing for you, Carl, bothering me at home on a Saturday morning."

"Sorry, but you need to know this pronto."

Carl filled him in on the facts as he knew them. Carrie was sleeping with Rip Snyder, the Republican operative, and kept a diary. Now parts of the diary are on the Internet making the case that Snyder is a racist. Other news organizations were doing stories about it and would obviously identify Carrie as a reporter for the *Suncoast Gazette*.

"What should I do?" Carl asked.

"Fire the bitch," Bundt answered without hesitation. "And do the biggest damn story you can put together. I'm not gonna tolerate one of my reporters bouncing on the bedsprings of a Republican."

"I don't have the authority to fire her, do I? I'm not her superior."

"You are now. I just promoted you to Tallahassee Bureau Chief. And your first job is to fire that little slut."

44

"That went well," Gonzalez said as he stepped into the warm sun.

The speaker and Bannerman Lux were getting into Lux's car for the return trip to Tallahassee from Apalachicola.

"I agree," Lux said. "Sheriff Tobin is obviously sold on the idea that Fercal killed Roxy. He'll check out your alibi, just to be thorough, but if it checks out, you're in the clear."

"It'll check out."

"Do you think Fercal and Roxy had some kind of history? I mean, what's his motive?"

"Who knows? Maybe he's some kind of psychopath. You know, like he gets his kicks by being rough with women, and it got out of hand."

"But hitting her in the head with a cast iron skillet?" Lux was having a hard time seeing it. "That's not sex play getting out of hand, Mr. Speaker. That's murder."

Gonzalez grunted his agreement. He didn't want to talk about it. "Are you having your usual tailgate party at the game tonight?"

"Oh yeah. And in honor of the opposition, we'll be serving up Hurricanes. I hired Klinger's to cater it."

"Sounds like fun."

"You need to stop by just to see Buffy, if nothing else."

"Buffy? Who's Buffy?"

"She's this girl who works for Uncle Nip's. They catered my party last week. She was serving the hot dogs and, let me tell you, she has this routine she does when she slips the wiener into the bun that is unbelievable. It's like watching a live sex act. She was so popular, I'm bringing her back."

Gonzalez laughed and said, "I'll be there."

"Good. And bring your appetite. You'll want lots of hot dogs."

Exhaustion was setting in on Carrie Stevens. Her right hand hurt, and she thought it might be a little swollen, from whacking that bastard Carl and the slimy Roy Fercal. She was still shaken by her encounter in Roy's home. And when she got back to her apartment and looked in the mirror, the person who looked back was a frightened, disheveled stranger.

Eight days ago she felt like she was on top of the world. Rip and I had a good thing going, she thought, and I was a respected member of the capital press corps. Then I tossed it all into the shitter for a few too many swigs of gin and a chance to catch Speaker Gonzalez on the take.

She wondered what to do about the Gonzalez story. She could try to pick it back up, perhaps, when she started back to work on Monday. But she wasn't that hot for it, frankly. She had other problems.

There was a fresh message on her answering machine. She walked wearily to it and hit play.

"Hi, Carrie. It's Jimmy Flain. Look, I'm sorry about having to do this, but we're doing a story about your diary pages showing up on the Internet. You know, the stuff about Rip Snyder being a racist and all. Can you give me a call please? And, like I said, I'm real sorry about all this..."

Carrie sat heavily on her sofa. The moment of truth had arrived. She could stick it up Fercal's ass, she realized, by telling Jimmy Flain that the diary pages were fake and that Fercal put them on the Internet to get back at Rip. That sounded like a plan. It would save Rip and keep her from being so embarrassed.

But then Fercal would put the Shelby Hoagensteiner story on the Internet and her life would be over. She would lose her job – no question. She had faked her resume. Nobody would hire her. She would be a laughingstock. And the Barboni family might come after her, too.

No. She had no choice but to follow Fercal's plan and confirm the pages were real. Of course, that meant Rip's life in Tallahassee was pretty much over.

"Sorry, Rip," she whispered to the empty room and picked up the phone.

"This is Jimmy Flain."

"Hi, Jimmy. It's Carrie."

"Carrie! God, Carrie, I can't tell you how sorry I am about all this. But it's a story we can't ignore."

"I know, Jimmy. You're just doing your job."

"Yeah, well, I still hate it." Jimmy cleared his throat. "Have you seen the website with your diary pages? All About Rip?"

"Yes."

"Are the diary pages real? Are they really from your diary?"

Carrie hesitated. "Yes."

"And the stuff in there is true? Rip Snyder really said all that stuff?"

More hesitation. "Yes." Carrie's voice was very small.

"Do you have any idea how your diary pages ended up on the Internet?"

Carrie thought about this one. Should she give Roy up? "No, Jimmy. I have no idea."

"One other thing, Carrie. Uh, the diary pages insinuate – but don't come right out and say – that you and Rip are lovers. Are you? Lovers, I mean?"

Carrie's eyes blurred. "Not anymore, Jimmy. Not after this." And she hung up.

The room closed in on her, collapsing like a house of cards. She managed to get to the bathroom before throwing up.

Rip Snyder didn't recognize the number on the Caller ID screen, so he let the machine answer. When Jimmy Flain started leaving his message, Rip snatched up the phone.

"Jimmy! It's Rip! I'm not gonna comment on your stupid story about some website claiming I'm a racist. It's bullshit, Jimmy, and you should know better. If you want a comment, call my lawyer, because I'm gonna sue the bastard who did this."

"I just talked to Carrie. She says it's all true."

This threw Rip for a loop. Carrie said that?

"Well, I'm telling you it's bullshit. I am not a racist! I don't run around calling people niggers. Look, Jimmy, I'm not commenting. Call my lawyer. His name is Bannerman Lux."

"So are you saying that Carrie is lying?"

"I'm not saying anything, but that website is a crock of shit."

"So is the website also wrong about claiming you and Carrie are lovers?"

"What kind of question is that, Jimmy? What are you now – a gossip columnist? It's none of your damn business. My private life is nobody else's business. You got that? Now bug off, Jimmy. I'm not commenting."

Jimmy hung up the phone thinking that for a man who wasn't commenting, Rip sure provided him with plenty of quotes.

45

It was Game Day, and Bulldog was in his element. The weather was perfect. A cold front had swept through and the temperature was only in the eighties. Hell, it might dip into the seventies by the time the game ended tonight.

Bulldog was walking the parking lots around Doak Campbell Stadium, making sure people weren't getting out of hand. He had already graciously accepted offers of three cheeseburgers, a bratwurst and one unbelievable homemade brownie. They offered beer and bourbon, too, but Bulldog stuck with Coca-Cola. He wasn't much of a drinker.

He was strolling along the south end of the stadium, using his toothpick to find every last morsel of the brownie, when he spotted her. She was hard to miss.

She was exceptionally tall, Bulldog thought, or maybe it was just that her legs seemed to go all the way from her ankles to her neck. She was dressed in the provocative Uncle Nip's uniform. The pink shorts looked like they were painted on. The shirt was pulled up and tied in a knot right beneath her breasts. It was clear to God and everyone why they call it "Uncle Nip's."

She was serving hot dogs, but that description was inadequate. The man standing in front of her watched transfixed as the girl picked up the hot dog and gave it a playful wiggle. She giggled, ran her tongue all the way around her lips and stared at the man's crotch. Then she used the pinkie finger of the hand holding the hot dog to slowly open a bun. Smiling coyly at the man in front of her, she slipped the hot dog part-way into the bun from the bottom, slid it almost all the way back out, then slid it in further, then partially out, and finally all the way in. The look on her face went from coy to ecstasy as she held the hot dog out in front of her. As the man took it, she caressed his hand and formed her lips into a brief kiss.

"Good God almighty!" Bulldog said to no one in particular. He just stood there, staring, as the girl started over for another customer.

"Pretty amazing, isn't it?"

Bulldog looked over with disgust at the small, balding man who interrupted him.

"Her name is Buffy." He stuck out his hand. "And I'm Bannerman Lux. Welcome to my tailgate party. Can I interest you in a hot dog?"

"Jesus," Bulldog snickered. "You could charge admission for that. But I'd have to bust ya for operating a porno shop."

They both got a good laugh at that one, and Bulldog got in line for a hot dog of his own.

Later, when the game was about to start and the hot dogs were all gone, Speaker Alberto Gonzalez – who had consumed two of them – cornered Buffy.

"That was quite a show," Gonzalez said, offering her his best smile. "I was looking for a tip jar but didn't see one. I'd like to leave you something."

"Oh, that's okay. My tip is included, and Lucky takes care of me."

"Really, I insist."

Buffy looked down and saw the man was holding a hundred dollar bill, folded in half. Her eyes met his and that coy, sexy smile returned. And she somehow managed to pull her skin-tight shorts away from her, just a smidgeon.

"Just slip it right in there, Big Boy." Her voice was breathy, sexy.

Gonzalez slipped the bill into her shorts, just a little, and was pulling away when she grabbed his hand. "Don't be shy. Go for the gusto."

Gonzalez looked around; no one seemed to be watching them. He slipped the bill down further, waiting for her to stop him. Finally, his fingertips felt the gentle brush of pubic hair and he withdrew his hand.

"A little bashful, are we?"

Gonzalez smiled nervously. "We're right out here in the open. You know, people can see."

Buffy laughed. "It turns me on, doing things like this in public. I like showing off. And pretending to have sex with a bunch of hot dogs doesn't exactly finish the job, know what I mean?" As she said this, her right hand gently brushed his crotch, as if by accident.

Gonzalez swallowed hard. "Are you going in to see the game? I'm sure I could get you in. It's a suite."

"A private suite? Just the two of us?"

"No, not private."

She looked disappointed. Buffy gently laid a hand behind his neck. "I'd rather go someplace where it can be just the two of us. I mean, since you're too bashful to have sex in public."

Gonzalez couldn't believe his luck. He was almost giddy. "Let's go to my place. And, by the way, my name is Al."

Buffy laughed. "I know who you are. Lead the way, Al. I'm starting to drip on that money you put down my pants."

As they were leaving, Buffy could feel the hundred dollar bill brushing against her and she thought: I'll bet there's plenty more where that came from.

The game itself would go down as an instant ESPN Classic. Two top-rated college teams moving up and down the field with magnificent catches and brutal hits. It was 21-21 at the half, and tied again at 35-35 after three quarters. The fans were delirious, and full of bourbon, when Florida State forced Miami to punt with two minutes to play and the Hurricanes leading 45-43.

The Seminoles took the ball on their own 14 yard line and managed to drive to the Miami 35 yard line and get out of bounds to stop the clock with three seconds to play. Miami fans started chanting "Wide right!" The FSU fans, during the timeout, recalled where they were for Wide Right One and Wide Right Two, and then Wide Left One. Surely it wouldn't happen again!

Doak Campbell Stadium was shaking with noise and excitement as the Seminoles lined up for the kick. It was no easy task – a field goal from 52 yards away – but the kicker had made one from 50 yards away in an earlier game. Could he do it?

The kicker put all he had into it, and the ball sailed high and true. It started losing steam, though, as it got near the goal line. Finally, with the entire stadium in breathless anticipation, the ball hit the crossbar and bounced away.

"Doink!" the ESPN announcer shouted. "This time it's a doink!" And a new chapter in FSU frustration against Miami was written.

46

Sunday, September 14

Another Sunday morning. But this time, Tallahassee was in a sour mood. Church attendance was down.

The same scene was replayed over and over all over Tallahassee – the man of the house would walk outside to retrieve the paper, remove the plastic lining, open it up and grunt in disgust. Some of them would swear out loud. A few of them threw the paper in the trash.

The top of the front page was consumed by the one-word headline: "DOINK!" Most of the bottom of the page was taken up by a remarkable picture showing the football striking the crossbar. Beneath the photo was a sub-headline: "Same song, different verse."

Most folks didn't really want to read about the game – they already knew the outcome, for crying out loud – but they couldn't help themselves. It was like staring at a multi-car pileup on the freeway.

The article that had most people talking all day was a sidebar about a football player at Tallahassee's other, mostly black university – Florida A & M. He had wanted to go to Florida State, but the coach said he wasn't good enough for a scholarship. So he signed up with FAMU and yesterday, by God, he kicked a 55-yard field goal to beat Grambling.

So it was in this darkened condition that folks in Tallahassee read Jimmy Flain's story about Rip Snyder and racism. The headline was simple enough: "WEBSITE CLAIMS GOP LEADER RACIST." Nothing unusual about that. Heck, Republicans are always being accused of racism. But the sub-headline hinted at something juicier: "Lover's diary spills the beans."

> *Republican operative Rip Snyder is a racist. That's the damning conclusion of a website called All About Rip. The evidence? The private diary pages of a Tallahassee woman who admits to being Snyder's secret lover. The pages are full of racial epithets spewing from Snyder's mouth and dutifully recorded in the diary of Carrie Stevens, a reporter for the Suncoast Gazette.*

> *Stevens denies any knowledge as to how her private diary ended up on the Internet, but she admits the pages are real and the incidents described actually happened. She also claims her love affair with Snyder is over.*

> *Stevens is the same woman who was charged a week ago with three counts of vehicular manslaughter in the tragic accident on Lake Bradford Road that killed three African-American children. The charges were dismissed on a technicality, however, after it was learned hospital employees made a mistake with her blood test. The incident led to the dramatic march on the Leon County Courthouse last week by an estimated 500 African-Americans demanding justice.*

> *Stevens, 25, was driving Snyder's truck at the time of the deadly crash, a detail that has still not been explained. In one incendiary quote, the diary talks about running over black kids and wondering if the world would be "a better place."*

> *Snyder, 40, of Tallahassee, denies the claims of racism.*

> *"I am not a racist! I don't run around calling people niggers," Snyder claimed to a reporter. "My private life is nobody else's business. You got that?"*

The article went on with more vivid quotes from the website and concluded by giving out the website address. This, of course, prompted many people to go online and see for themselves. It was all there.

What people also discovered was a link to page 58 of Carrie's diary, the graphic description of her Happy Snappy, which Roy Fercal had posted the night before. By the end of the day, page 58 was e-mailed around the world and back again. When Carrie chose fame over going to bed with Fercal, she got her wish. She was famous indeed.

The Reverend Josiah Franklin made a habit of reading the Sunday paper before church, in case he wanted to include some of the latest news in his sermon. He skipped right over all the football coverage, but he read the story about Rip Snyder very carefully. Then he read it again and steam started coming out of his ears.

Then his computer chirped at him, telling him he had an e-mail message that was marked urgent. Probably somebody telling him about the article. He checked the computer. Actually, someone had e-mailed him Snyder's newsletter from Friday. It pushed him over the edge.

Franklin called a friend of his who operated an old school bus for one of the larger Baptist churches in town. They arranged to have the bus at the Bradford Road Baptist Church later that morning.

The atmosphere in Franklin's church that morning was one of pure anger. Many of the people in attendance had also read the Jimmy Flain article. When the Reverend Franklin stepped in, his stern face only added to the tension.

He wasted no time. Josiah picked up on the mood of his congregation instantly; they were ready for action. He read the most inflammatory stuff from the All About Rip website for those who didn't know and he could feel the rage building. Then he added stuff from Snyder's newsletter, about how stupid they all looked marching on the courthouse, and how racist it was to tell black kids it would be easier to run away from the cops if they dressed better.

They had all seen the bus outside. So when the Reverend Franklin suggested they get on the bus and pay Mr. Snyder a visit, the congregation rose as one.

They packed as many as they could into the bus. Others piled into cars and followed. It was a convoy headed for Killearn Estates.

It was a typical Sunday morning in Killearn. Folks were pissed about the football game, but they carried on. There was jogging to do, church to attend, dogs to walk, flowers to look after, and golf to play. It was a glorious morning, cooler than it had been, and all was right with the world on the north side of Tallahassee. That is, until the convoy arrived.

The joggers, dog-walkers and gardeners looked on curiously. A busload of blacks in Killearn was certainly an oddity, but they could see it was a church bus and the folks inside were impeccably dressed, so there was little reason to be alarmed. Maybe it was some kind of field trip.

But then the cars followed – about a dozen of them. The blacks in the cars looked angry. The joggers picked up the pace; the gardeners went inside. Clearly, something was amiss.

By the time the convoy turned down Langford Drive, everyone knew there was trouble ahead. The ordinarily peaceful quiet of Langford Drive had been broken.

The bus stopped in front of Rip Snyder's home and the people started piling out. The Reverend Franklin handed out some small, hastily-made signs decrying racism and demanding justice. They formed a small mob in front of Snyder's home, blocking the street, and started chanting "No justice, no peace!"

The ruckus had attracted the attention of the entire street, and they went out in their yards to see what was up. The women and children scurried quickly back inside, while the men kept watch.

Judge Busby Brown was running a little late for his tee time and was doubly alarmed when he found his usual route to the Killearn Country Club blocked by a mob of blacks. He quickly turned around and headed for the back entrance, hoping like hell nobody in the mob recognized him.

The chanting continued and the mob closed in ever tighter to Snyder's house. They expected the curtains to move, but nothing happened. After a time, Franklin walked up to Snyder's front door and rang the bell. No response. Rip Snyder wasn't home.

47

By any measure, Rip Snyder was having a lousy weekend. When the shit hit the fan – as Speaker Gonzalez predicted – about the website accusing him of racism, Rip lost three political clients and roughly $7,000 a month in reliable income.

It was all so frustrating, Rip thought, because he wasn't a racist. Sure, the diary pages were real but Carrie had twisted his words or didn't fully understand what he was saying. If a person observes certain behaviors and expresses an opinion that the behaviors are the reason *some people* use the n-word, does that make the person a racist?

He needed guidance, so on Saturday night he called Big Daddy Malloy in Sopchoppy. They agreed to get together for a round of golf on Sunday morning, and that's where Rip was headed.

Of course, Rip lived on a golf course – one of the best in the area – and paid some pretty hefty fees to belong to the private club. But he wanted to get away, and Rip really liked Wildwood Country Club, where he was meeting Big Daddy.

Wildwood was less than an hour's drive from Rip's home in Killearn Estates, but it felt like a world away. The Killearn Country Club is an old course. They used to play a PGA Tour event there. The topography, soil and trees greatly resemble southern Georgia. Wildwood, on the other hand, was fairly new and felt more like a Florida course – flat, sandy soil, with plenty of palmetto trees to set the mood.

It was a truly sparkling September morning in North Florida. Rip parked his truck and was getting his bag out from behind the seats when a young man pulled up in a cart.

"Good morning, Mr. Snyder," the young man said as he took Rip's bag. "It's good to see you again. Mr. Malloy is already here. I'll get your clubs loaded up."

"Thank you," Rip acknowledged and tipped him five bucks. He didn't remember seeing the kid before, but it was nice to feel welcome.

Rip strolled into the pro shop to pay his greens fee and was greeted by the local pro.

"Hey, Rip. Have you been thinking about our conversation the other day?"

"Yeah, Arnie, I have, especially this morning. Sure is nice out here today." The pro's real name was Roger Willoughby, but everyone called him Arnie because the guy enjoyed it.

"Well, we'd love to have you, Rip. You know that. Just say the word."

"Thanks, Arnie. I'll think about it."

Willoughby had been campaigning to get Rip to join the Wildwood Country Club. The only thing that stopped him was the long drive from his house to the course. But, after losing $7,000 a month, who knows what's coming next?

Big Daddy Malloy was on the putting green, and he was hard to miss. At 6'5" and 275 pounds, it was easy to see where he got the name Big Daddy. Rip thought his real name was Michael, but nobody ever called him that. He wouldn't even answer to it anymore.

Big Daddy played college football at FAMU and tried out for a couple of NFL teams but never made it. He was retired now, after a brilliant high school coaching career and raising a large family with his wife, Mabel. But the real pride of his life was his daughter, Jessie – the Leon County state's attorney.

"Good morning, Big Daddy," Rip called over to him. "Did you bring your wallet today?"

Big Daddy looked up slowly from a practice putt. "Hello, Rip. Yeah, I brought my wallet, and a bank bag, too. I wanted to make sure I could carry home my winnings." Then he calmly stroked the putt into the dead center of the cup.

"Ha! That'll be the day. How's Big Momma?"

Big Daddy flashed a big smile. Only Rip was allowed to call Mabel Big Momma. "Getting bigger every day – and sassy, too. I can't believe I stayed with that woman for almost 40 years now."

"She give you grief about playing golf today?"

"Yeah, Jessie was down visiting. But I told Mabel that under the circumstances, you needed to have your ass whipped by the biggest, baddest, blackest man available. And that would be me."

Rip swallowed. "So the Malloy family read the paper this morning?"

"Yes we did, Rip. Yes we did. And I'll bet Mabel is still laughing her ass off." Big Daddy was chuckling himself.

"Really? I don't think it's funny."

"You will, Rip. One of these days, after it all blows over. We'll talk about it," Big Daddy said as he stroked another practice putt into the hole, "while I'm whipping your ass."

They walked together to the first hole where their clubs were polished and waiting on the golf cart. The starter, a perky retired woman named Betty something, greeted them warmly.

"Good morning, fellas!" Then she looked at Rip. "Ooh! Mr. Snyder! We have a celebrity in the house! Can I have your autograph?" Then she cackled, and Big Daddy was laughing, too.

"Jesus, is this the way it's going to be today?" Even Rip had the beginnings of a grin. He couldn't help it. This was good medicine.

"Nah. It could get worse," Big Daddy said in a dour voice, and he and Betty shared another laugh.

"What'll it be today, Rip? The usual?" Big Daddy inquired.

"Yeah, I guess. Five dollars a bet, automatic press on 8 and 17. I'll give you two a side to make it fair, like always." Rip walked onto the first tee. He was just about to start his swing when Big Daddy spoke up.

"I think we should double it."

Rip backed off. "Double it? You mean ten bucks a bet?"

"Yeah. And keep your strokes. I don't want 'em."

"But you can't beat me straight up, Big Daddy. You know that."

"Bullshit. Watch me."

Rip shrugged his shoulders. "Okay, it's your money. And soon it'll be my money."

The first hole at Wildwood is a par five with a severe dogleg left. It's reachable if you cut the corner, which is guarded by a grove of trees. The entire right side at the corner is bordered by a large waste bunker. Rip usually teed off with a three wood on number one to avoid the bunker. But he changed his mind after Big Daddy doubled the bet. Rip took out his driver and tried to cut the corner.

Rip heard Betty cackling again as his ball sliced into the bunker. "Sorry, Mr. Snyder. I don't want your autograph no more." More cackling.

Big Daddy was fighting the urge to laugh as he stepped up on the tee. He, too, had his driver, except his tee shot went high and long and with a slight draw. It landed in the middle of the fairway, no more than an eight iron from the green.

"Let the whipping begin," Big Daddy announced.

"One good shot does not a whipping make, Big Daddy."

"True enough," he agreed as they got into the cart. "But 75 of 'em ought to leave a mark."

Rip agreed that 75 shots would leave a helluva mark.

The Reverend Josiah Franklin was a little embarrassed that he had bused his congregation to Snyder's home only to find it empty. So they left their homemade signs propped up in some of the bushes and slipped them into the cracks around the front door and departed. Damn, he thought. Not even a news camera.

At the Killearn Country Club, Judge Busby Brown was getting ready to tee off with his foursome.

"What's the deal with all the blacks?" Judge Brown asked his colleagues. "Fuckers were blocking the street."

"Didn't you read the paper this morning?" one of them responded. "They were storming Snyder's place, on account of he's some kind of racist."

"Rip Snyder? That Republican jerk?"

"Yeah, that's him."

Judge Brown grinned with satisfaction. "Good! Maybe they'll burn his fucking house down."

Riley Sorenson, who owned every Mexican fast food joint within 50 miles of Tallahassee, felt the need to speak up.

"Jesus, Judge. You Democrats are all alike. You start out complaining about them blocking the street, and then you cheer them on to burn down a man's house because he's a Republican. It's no wonder you can't win an election anymore."

"And this comes from the lily-white Swede who peddles Mexican food? Tell me something, Riley. How many Mexicans you got working for you?"

"Mexicans? None. I don't trust 'em."

They all had a good laugh at that one and got the golf game started.

By the time Rip and Big Daddy stepped up on the 18th tee, Rip was indeed feeling the effects of a whipping. He had lost the front nine and the first press and the back nine was already gone. If he didn't win 18 outright, Rip would lose all five bets -- $50. The best Rip could hope for was to win 18 and keep the loss to $40.

Eighteen at Wildwood is a dead straight par four, longer than most, guarded on the front by water. Big Daddy hit his tee shot into the left rough.

"You brought the water into play, Big Daddy. Too bad." It was Rip's attempt to get his opponent thinking about the water.

"I'm not thinking about the water, Rip. I'm thinking about all the beer I can buy with your money."

"We'll see." Rip hit his tee shot down the right side of the fairway, in perfect position. "I'm getting a bit thirsty myself."

Rip's tee shot was shorter than Big Daddy's, even though it was straighter. Rip selected a five iron and pulled it to the far left side of the green – with the pin tucked way on the back right.

"Looks like three-putt territory to me," Big Daddy said. "Maybe even four, the way you've been kicking it around."

"Yeah, and maybe I'll just drain it, too."

Big Daddy's lie was bad in the rough. He was indeed thinking about the water; Rip could tell. "Maybe you should lay up short of the water."

Big Daddy looked at Rip with disdain. "Big Daddy never lays up." He selected a seven iron and promptly flew it into the water.

"God damn it!" Big Daddy's voice bellowed down the fairway.

Rip didn't laugh, though he wanted to. Big Daddy dropped behind the water and lofted a perfect lob wedge to within two feet of the hole.

"Nice shot, Big Daddy. Pick it up. Helluva bogie."

All Rip needed was a two-putt to win the hole and save himself ten dollars. His first putt lost steam and ended up on the lower side of the hole, about four feet away.

As Rip was lining it up, Big Daddy spoke up.

"You know, Rip, I've been laughing about the racism stuff in the paper all day but you've got a serious problem. I mean, I understand what you're saying about simply trying to point out what other people think, but it's too fine a point on a very blunt problem. The word 'nigger' is like a bomb. When it goes off, it doesn't matter if it was planted on purpose or left behind by accident. The shrapnel is real.

"And that crap you wrote about black kids running away from the cops, that was over the line. You need to apologize for that in your next newsletter. A heartfelt *mea culpa* would be a good start."

Rip looked at Big Daddy carefully. The air hung heavy and still between them. "Do you think I'm a racist, Big Daddy? Do you think that?"

Big Daddy broke into a grin. "Hell, no, Rip. I know you better than that. You're not a racist. You're a pain in the ass sometimes, but not a racist. And I'll say so – publicly, if you want. You're my friend, man. I'm here for you."

Rip looked quickly at his golf ball. His eyes were tearing up and a lump was forming in his throat. He stroked the putter, but couldn't see the hole. He listened for the familiar sound of the ball dropping into the cup, but it never came.

"Jesus Christ, you're a lousy putter." Big Daddy put one of his massive arms around Rip's shoulders and squeezed. "C'mon, let's go drink some beer."

48

I t had been a long nine years for Ricky "The Boner" Barboni. That lousy bitch Shelby Hoagensteiner had ratted him out after he was kind enough to give her a job at the Pecker Palace. Sure, he knew she wasn't eighteen, but who cares? She was good-looking, not the least bit bashful, and she knew her way around the south forty of a paying customer.

"Paradise," as she was known, made him a lot of money. Then she tattles to the feds and gets him busted for trafficking in underage prostitutes. On top of that, his beloved Pecker Palace was seized and sold to a bunch of preachers who donated it to the local fire department who burned it down just for practice. Bastards!

Ricky had been thinking about all of this every day for his nine-year stint in the federal prison at Tallahassee, Florida. For nine long years he had fantasized about getting revenge, always ending up the same way: Ricky would rape her in exchange for sparing her life. In the end, he always killed her anyway.

He had masturbated to this fantasy countless times. Now, as he waited for the guard to come for him and set him free, Ricky made himself a promise. "The next time I get a boner for you, Shelby, it'll be for real."

O utside the federal prison, Louie "The Rock" Barboni was getting impatient. Is Ricky ever coming out?

Louie didn't like sitting in the parking lot of a federal pen one bit. He wondered if the tower guards were watching him with binoculars, running the tags on his custom van with the blackened windows and the mattress in the back, looking for an excuse to bust his ass.

He took another hit from the bottle of Fighting Cock bourbon in the brown paper sack and flipped the bird to no one in particular, just in case the bastards were looking.

Truth be told, Louie didn't want to be in Tallahassee at all at that moment. The old man had ordered him to drive down from Chicago to pick up The Boner when the feds let him go. This really pissed Louie off, because when HE got out of the federal prison in Springfield, Missouri – sick with hepatitis – Louie was on his own.

"Take the fucking bus," the old man had told him. The bus! Take the fucking bus! Jesus!

As it happened, Louie stole a cherry red mustang convertible and made it to Chicago without any help from the family, thank you very much.

That was pretty much the story of his life. Louie was "The Rock" because he did all the hard stuff. He broke the knees that needed breaking, cut off thumbs when necessary, and killed the dirty bastards who had it coming. His younger brother, The Boner, sat around all day dreaming up ways to make money selling sex. And for some reason the old man liked The Boner the best.

"Well, it's about fucking time," Louie blurted when he saw The Boner stroll into the parking lot. He took another hit of Fighting Cock and emerged from the van.

"Ricky! How ya doin'?"

"Hey, Louie. Thanks for comin'." They embraced, briefly, before Ricky pulled away. "What the hell have you been drinking? Bourbon?"

"Damn right, Ricky! It's called Fighting Cock! How 'bout that?"

Ricky laughed. "Fighting Cock, huh? Sounds perverted. I like it! Let's have some."

They climbed into the van and Louie handed the bottle to Ricky. He took a long pull.

"Hey, be careful with that stuff," Louie said. "It's 103 proof! It'll knock you on your ass!"

"Shut up and drive, Rock. This is good shit. Puts me in the mood to find some fighting pussy!"

They laughed as Louie guided the van out of the parking lot, moving south on Capital Circle. Ricky looked around the inside of the van.

"Nice wheels, Rock. You always wanted a van with a bed. We need to put it to use."

"No need, Ricky. I got us into a Nodaway Inn not far from here. Two beds. We can trade off, like old times." He grabbed the bottle and took a hit.

"Gimme that," Ricky protested as he snatched the bottle back. "You drive. I'll drink."

Louie grunted his disapproval and drove to the Nodaway Inn.

"I got an idea, Rock," Ricky yelled from the shower. "I think the old man will go for it, too."

Louie was watching a football game and thumbing through the Yellow Pages, looking for easy pussy. "Does it involve fucking? And making money?"

"Of course."

Figures, Louie thought. It's all The Boner thinks about.

"Well, I'll be go to hell!" A news promo was on, and there was a picture of Carrie Stevens on the screen. Louie cranked up the volume.

"...*the buzz is all about a website called All About Rip.*"

"Ricky! Come see! It's that bitch who ratted us out! On the TV!"

"...*a diary that has tongues wagging in Tallahassee. Racist allegations and steamy sex. Tonight at eleven.*"

Ricky emerged from the shower, naked and dripping wet, but the promo was over. "What the fuck are you talking about, Rock?"

"She was on the TV! That stripper you hired! The one who ratted us out to the feds! What was her name?"

"You mean Paradise?" Ricky was fully alert now.

"That's it! Paradise!" Louie was pointing at the TV with the remote. "That little teenybopper who sent us to prison. She's in the news! Right here in Tallahassee! Can you believe it?"

"What do you mean, 'she's in the news'? How do you know it was her?"

"Oh, it was her, Ricky. No question. There was some kind of news promo about a website and sex. Film at eleven."

"And you're sure it was her?"

"Damn it, Ricky, it was her! We'll watch the news at eleven o'clock and you'll see for yourself!"

Ricky considered this. "No. If the stupid TV news people know about it, they must have read it in the paper. Go out and buy some papers. If that little bitch is living in Tallahassee, we'll find her."

"And then what?"

Ricky reached down and stroked himself. "Well, The Boner has a little gift for Paradise," he said wistfully.

Louie looked on and saw Ricky was getting aroused. "Shit, Ricky, if you're gonna whack off, at least wait 'till I'm out the door."

"And get some more of that Fighting Cock, will ya? With the papers?"

"Yeah, sure, Ricky. Like you need it." The door closed and Louie was gone, leaving Ricky alone with his fantasy.

C arrie Stevens was holed up in her apartment, the shades drawn. A bottle of gin was slowly disappearing. She had run out of tonic, and the gin-on-the-rocks thing tasted like lighter fluid, but she didn't care. Her computer was turned off. Somehow, her private e-mail address had been found out and was plastered all over the Internet. Her mailbox was overflowing with messages begging her to demonstrate the "Happy Snappy."

"Fuckin' perverts," she slurred again and took another hit of gin.

Her life was officially in the toilet. She had been shocked to see her story spread all over the front page of her very own *Suncoast Gazette*. Even worse was the quote from that bastard Jeremiah Bundt, who indicated her "employment status was being evaluated."

"I'm fucked," Carrie said to the walls. "I'm totally fucked."

The phone rang again; she ignored it again. It was either a pervert or a reporter, or both. She wanted neither.

Could her life be over at age 25? Should she go ahead and end it, officially? She pondered this, but rejected it. Suicide just wasn't in her.

"Must be time to run and hide again," she offered to the walls, but got no response. She drained the rest of her gin and reached for the phone. He had helped her disappear once; would he help her again?

49

L ouie "The Rock" Barboni returned to the Nodaway Inn with the promised Fighting Cock, a stack of Sunday papers and a bucket of chicken.

"Gotta eat," he explained.

Ricky grabbed a leg and started munching. "Jesus Christ!" he exclaimed, his mouth full of chicken. "It IS her! Right here on the front page!"

"Told ya, asshole," Louie replied, cracking open the Fighting Cock. "The bitch is right here under our noses."

"It's unbelievable! What are the odds?" Ricky washed the chicken down with a hit of bourbon. "So she changes her name and moves to Tallahassee. Smart move. Then she starts banging some guy with political connections and keeps a diary! Stupid move! Now her diary is on the Internet and her picture is plastered all over the news. Jesus!"

"Says here she's a reporter with the *Suncoast Gazette,* in the Tallahassee Bureau," Louie noted as he munched on a thigh. "I wonder where the office is?"

Ricky grabbed the phone book and looked it up. "Right here," he said, a greasy finger touching the page. "On College Avenue." Ricky grinned so hard his hit of Fighting Cock dribbled down his shirt. "I've got a plan."

Louie looked expectantly at his younger brother. "Does it involve fucking?"

"Of course!"

"Of course," Louie echoed, shaking his head. Christ, what a horny bastard.

H e thought about not answering. The number on the caller ID was unfamiliar to him and the area code indicated it was from Tallahassee or maybe the Panhandle. But there was the tingling of a possibility in the back of his brain, and not that many people had the number of his private cell phone, so he picked it up.

"This is Brad."

There was a sharp intake of breath on the other end; then, crying. And he knew.

Brad left his wife knitting in the family room, walked into his home office and shut the door.

"Carrie," he began, "I know all about it. It's all over the news. I'm sorry."

There was more crying on the other end as Carrie tried desperately to compose herself. It wasn't working.

"Listen, Carrie, if you called to ask for help again, the answer is yes. Hell, it'll always be yes."

This caused more crying, and Brad just sat there and let it happen. His own eyes grew moist as he waited. Then, the crying abated. He heard her blow her nose.

"Thank you." It was breathy and thick with emotion.

"What do you need, Carrie? Anything; just say the word."

"I need to get out. To disappear again. Like before."

Brad thought about his wife knitting in the family room and thought, hmmm, probably not *exactly* like before.

"Okay, Carrie," he said carefully. "Let's get you out of Tallahassee, so you can hide from the reporters while we figure this out. Let me make some arrangements and I'll call you back."

"I'm not answering my phone."

"Okay. Call me back in 15 minutes. And don't worry. It'll be okay. I promise."

Later, Carrie scribbled "noon, Delta" on a notepad, along with "Maisson Hotel, Westshore." She planned to go to the office in the morning, slap the shit out of Carl Splighter one more time and quit the *Suncoast Gazette*. Then she would return home, throw some clothes together and get to the airport in time for her flight.

She stumbled off to the bedroom and plopped face down on the bed, finally giving in to the gin.

The Rock and The Boner polished off the bucket of chicken and made a dent in the Fighting Cock. They were hugely disappointed to discover that Tallahassee had no tittie bars.

"That just ain't natural," Ricky opined, and Louie agreed. They did, however, locate an escort service with the ability to send over two fairly attractive college girls who actually seemed to enjoy the idea of being passed back and forth between a couple of mobsters.

Ricky thoroughly enjoyed his first taste of freedom after nine years. In the back of his mind, though, was the persistent idea that tomorrow would be even better.

50

Monday, September 15

The Barboni brothers were up early on Monday morning, despite the dull ache of too much bourbon. There was business to attend to.

"No more Fighting Cock for me today," Ricky announced. "Shit, that stuff is wicked."

"Told ya," Louie responded. "We'd better get going."

"Yeah. Did you rip the map out of the phone book?"

"I looked at it. College Avenue is easy to find from here. Leave it to me."

With that, the two most dangerous men in Tallahassee packed up their stuff and strolled out of the Nodaway Inn.

"Jesus. Is it always this hot in the morning?" Louie wondered.

"Hotter, usually. You get used to it. Do we have time for breakfast?"

"A drive-thru, maybe. We can eat while we watch for her."

This got Ricky grinning. "We're coming for you, Paradise, and we've got a big ol' boner!"

Louie just rolled his eyes and drove.

A cross town, Carrie Stevens was waking up in a fog. Jesus, she hadn't been that drunk in a long time. How do alcoholics put up with this shit every day?

She forced herself into the shower, as hot as she could stand it. She let the water cascade down her body while she waited for the queasiness to go away. Cleaning up helped a little. Then she remembered her scheduled flight to Tampa and the possibility of another new life ahead. This perked her up even more. Then she remembered her plan to slap the piss out of Carl Splighter and she actually left the apartment with a spring in her step.

Here I come, Carl, you bastard.

R ip Snyder was worried sick about Carrie. She was ignoring the phone; that was obvious. And he couldn't really blame her, either. My God, the whole thing was out of control.

Carrie would be fired by the *Suncoast Gazette*; that was obvious. What would she do? For that matter, what in the hell was HE going to do? The whole thing had already cost him more money than most people make in a year. If his subscribers started dumping him, well, then what?

And his talk with Big Daddy Malloy was still on his mind. Big Daddy made clear that he needed to publicly apologize. The sooner the better. People like to forgive, the big fella said, but only if they think the person is truly sorry.

Rip had given the idea a lot of thought and decided Big Daddy was right. A special Monday edition of *The Ripper* was called for. A heartfelt apology would be issued and perhaps the storm clouds would start to clear.

Perhaps.

On his way to the office, Rip detoured past Carrie's apartment. Her car was gone. Would she be going to work after all this? It'll take some balls to walk into the press center, that's for sure.

Rip felt a rumble in his stomach and realized he hadn't eaten last night, so he decided to swing through Whataburger. As he was pulling in, a van with darkened windows that was pulling out sped in front and cut him off.

"Hey!" Rip shouted, laying on his horn. "Stupid jackass!"

The driver's side window lowered and a black-haired man calmly looked at Rip, smiled, and flipped him the bird. The window went back up.

"What an asshole!" Rip growled. Illinois plates, he saw. "A damn Yankee."

"Should've shot the fucker," Ricky advised as he bit into a breakfast sandwich.

"Two reasons why not," Louie said. "One, I don't have a gun. Two, I don't go around shooting people in broad daylight with a dozen witnesses."

Ricky looked on in disbelief. "What do you mean you don't have a gun?"

"My only mission was to pick up my little brother at the prison! Why would I need a gun?"

"You always need a gun! Jesus! I've never known you to be without a gun."

"Ricky, I'm on parole. I'm not supposed to have a gun and I'm sure as hell not gonna carry one across state lines and keep it in my FUCKING VAN while I'm sitting in the FUCKING PARKING LOT of the FUCKING FEDERAL PRISON!"

"Okay, okay, calm down," Ricky said. "You've got a vein bulging on your forehead. Don't have a stroke."

Louie drove in silence.

"Okay, so we don't have a gun," Ricky reasoned. "Do we have a club or something? In case we need it?"

"Need it? For what?"

Ricky rolled his eyes in disgust. "Jesus Christ, Rock, you're slippin'. What are we gonna do? Snatch that little bitch off the streets of Tallahassee with our bare hands?"

"Oh, that. Well, I got a knife."

"A knife? Where? How big?"

"Big enough," Louie said quietly as he slid the knife out of a sheath attached to his seat next to the door.

"Jesus Christ!" Ricky took it from his older brother and hefted it. "It's huge!"

Ricky admired it. The blade was about a foot long and three inches wide. He scraped his thumb across the blade. It was deadly sharp.

"Where did you get it?"

"Off e-Bay," Louie replied as he parked across the street from the press center. "Here we are."

Ricky handed the knife back to Louie and eyed the press center with concern. "I don't like it. Too many people."

"Let's see if she shows up; maybe watch the traffic pattern a little."

"Good idea, Rock."

51

The Rock and The Boner kept vigil over the press center. They made crude comments about the people who went inside.

"They're all a bunch of slobs," Ricky observed. "Who dresses them anyway?"

Then: a rusty old Saab pulled into the parking lot.

"Here comes another slob," Ricky predicted. "A fat tree-hugger, maybe."

But this was no slob. Except for the bandage on her nose, this woman was drop-dead gorgeous. And Ricky had the added advantage of already seeing her naked.

"There she is!" Ricky exclaimed. "Paradise!"

"Looks like somebody busted her upside the head," Louie noticed. "What's with the bandage on her nose?"

"I don't know, Rock, but look at her walk! Feisty, spirited. Jesus, what a turn-on!"

"Shit, Boner, what *doesn't* turn you on? I gotta admit, though, she looks good. Even the bandage gives her a sense of...I don't know...something..."

"Mystery?" Ricky offered.

"That's it! Mystery! Like maybe she enjoys getting knocked around a bit, you know? Some women like that."

Ricky stared while the door closed behind her. "Well, she's about to get knocked around whether she likes it or not. The question is, how? I didn't count on so many witnesses."

"Well, Ricky, let's think it through. There's got to be a way."

C arrie was focused on Carl Splighter. His beat-up old Plymouth was in the parking lot. Time to kick some ass.

There was a gathering of four or five reporters from other papers near the door. They stopped talking immediately. Obviously, she was the topic de jour.

Carrie ignored them and walked straight up to Carl's desk. He was on the phone. Carrie picked up the phone book and whacked Carl hard across the top of the head.

The phone dropped out of his hand and clattered to the floor. "What the fuck!"

Carrie dropped the phone book, went around the desk and slapped Carl hard on the cheek. "This is what the fuck, you asshole! Thanks for ruining my life!"

Carrie reared back for another slap, but Carl rose from his chair and caught her wrist.

"Stop it! Stop it! You can't come in here and smack me around! You're fired!"

Carrie kicked up with every ounce of her strength, catching Carl square in the balls. A loud "OOOOF!" emerged from his mouth as he fell to his knees.

"Fired, my ass! I quit! You can shove this fucking job!" Carrie picked up the phone book again and served up another whack on Carl's head. He went prone on the floor.

Carrie kicked him in the ribs for good measure and headed for the door. She saw the reporters gathered at the window, looking on in horror.

"Ya'll can report that Carrie Stevens turned in her notice at the *Suncoast Gazette.* And here's my quote: fuck off."

With that, Carrie emerged from the building and surprised her suitors across the street.

The Rock and The Boner had just about decided to call the *Suncoast Gazette,* provide a hot tip on a story and snatch Paradise on her way to cover it when they saw her leave the building.

"Jesus, she looks pissed," Louie observed.

"Follow her," Ricky ordered. "And don't lose her."

Louie laughed. "I've tailed people halfway across Chicago. I think I can handle Tallahassee."

A few blocks later, Louie was cussing. "The traffic in this town is ridiculous!"

"Probably because there aren't any tittie bars," Ricky reasoned. "People have nothing to do but drive around."

"It's nine o'clock in the morning! Who goes to a tittie bar at nine in the morning?"

"Nobody. They're not open, but they oughta be. You know, for the people who work odd hours. They need their jollies, too."

"Is that your big idea? You know, from the shower yesterday? You gonna open up a chain of 24/7 tittie bars?"

"No," Ricky said dismissively. "I'm gonna sell condoms."

"Condoms! You can buy condoms in gas stations, for crying out loud. I thought you said fucking was involved and making money, too. How do you make money selling condoms?"

"By charging two hundred bucks apiece."

Louie gave Ricky a queer look. "Two hundred bucks! For a condom? Nobody will pay it. It's stupid!"

"Oh, they'll pay it, alright, if it gets delivered by an 18-year-old who's willing to teach them how to use it properly."

Louie laughed out loud. "Jesus, Ricky! It's prostitution. You'll get busted again!"

"No it ain't! We're selling the condom! The safe sex lesson is free!"

Louie laughed some more. "Tell it to the judge!"

"I'm serious! A guy I met in the joint thought I could even get a federal grant. You know, for AIDS prevention."

"Aw, Jesus, Ricky, stop it." Louie was laughing so hard he was crying. "Honest to God, nine years in the hole was too much for you. We need to find you some more pussy!"

"All the pussy I need is in that Saab up there," Ricky said, pointing at Carrie's car. "And she doesn't even know it yet."

52

C arrie understood how some people lose control and turn into killers. If she'd had a gun or a knife or even a baseball bat, she might have gone over the edge and killed that slimy Carl Splighter. It felt good to hurt him – really good.

She wondered if he'd call the cops on her. Probably not. He'd hate to admit to a beating at the hands of a woman.

Carrie was anxious to get the hell out of Dodge, at any rate. She cursed the traffic and made a mental list of what she needed to take before disappearing. As little as possible, she reminded herself. You can't travel fast unless you travel light.

Then she thought about Rip. God, he didn't deserve being in the middle of this. And she couldn't just disappear without saying goodbye. It wouldn't be right.

Carrie picked up her cell phone and pressed speed dial number one: Rip.

He recognized the number immediately. "Carrie! My God, I've been trying to call you! I want to help, if I can. Where are you?"

"Aw, Rip. I'm so sorry about everything." Her voice was shaky. "Look, Rip, I'm leaving Tallahassee. For good. I've got a noon flight. I wanted to say goodbye."

Rip stood up from his chair. "You called to say goodbye? Over the phone? After everything we've been through? You can't do it. I want to see you."

Carrie sighed heavily. "I don't know, Rip. I don't have much time. I need to pack and everything...."

"I'm on my way." Rip snapped his cell phone shut and tore out of the office. Jesus. Was Carrie really leaving? Just like that?

Carrie dropped her cell phone into her purse. Well, crap. She was hoping she wouldn't have to face Rip. She knew it was cheesy of her, but she just wanted to get the hell out of town and start over. No complications.

She wheeled into the parking lot of her apartment building and checked her watch: almost 9:30. Tick, tock.

"Make sure we see what door she goes into." It was Ricky Barboni, stating the obvious.

"Gee, I never would have thought of that," Louie said.

"Shut up. Get the knife."

Louie pulled the van into an empty spot. He handed the knife to Ricky. "What's the plan?"

"You stay here," Ricky ordered. "Keep the van running. I'll walk her out and force her in the back. When we're both in, start driving. I don't care where; out in the country someplace. Don't stop for anything."

"Roger that."

Ricky got out of the van and looked around. The coast was clear. He walked toward Carrie's apartment door, holding the knife stiffly to one side.

"Jesus, that doesn't look the least bit suspicious," Louie said to himself. He fished around and found a half-empty bottle of Fighting Cock and took a hit, then another.

Ricky was wondering if he should ring the doorbell, knock, or kick the door down. He decided to try the doorknob first. It was unlocked! He simply swung the door open and stepped in.

R ip was doing his best impression of Jeff Gordon as he fought the traffic and ran stop lights on his way to Carrie's apartment. He was out of control – panicky – and he knew it. He didn't want to lose Carrie. It had been a rough ten days, for sure, with more tough times ahead. But, Jesus, the thought of her disappearing from his life was unbearable.

He floored it.

" R ip, is that you?" Carrie called. She was already tossing stuff into a suitcase in her bedroom. "Rip?"

She walked into the living room and stared straight into the eyes of hell itself.

"Hello, Paradise." Ricky was grinning.

Carrie screamed and headed for the kitchen and the back door. Ricky was laughing now as he caught her from behind. His left hand went over her mouth as he brought Carrie to a stop. He stepped on her right foot and brought the knife up to her eyes. She could see her panicked reflection in the blade.

Carrie tried to bite down on Ricky's hand, but he jerked her head up and brought the knife to her neck.

"I'll slit your throat, baby, don't think I won't." His breath was hot on her ear. "Just relax. I'm not here to kill you, though I will if I have to."

Carrie could feel his sweat.

"Here's what we're gonna do, sweetheart. We're gonna walk out of this apartment together holding hands, like two lovers. If you try to get away, I'll kill you on the spot. We're gonna go for a ride and have a little fun. If you're a good girl, I'll let you go. Okay?"

Carrie had no faith whatsoever that being a "good girl" would set her free. But there was a knife being held to her neck and she was certain Ricky would use it. So she nodded.

"Okay," Ricky said softly. "I'm gonna take my hand off your mouth now. If you scream, you're dead."

Ricky took his hand away from her mouth. Carrie stayed silent.

"It's been a long time, Paradise," Ricky whispered. She could feel him getting aroused as he pressed against her. "For nine long years I have thought about this moment. Time for some fun."

Carrie thought she might vomit. "Don't do it, Ricky. Let me go, please."

"I'll let you go, Paradise. But not yet. After."

Carrie's knees grew weak.

"Now, we're gonna walk out holding hands, like I said. No trouble, okay?" Ricky waved the knife in front of her, as if she needed a reminder.

"Okay."

53

R ip tried to get himself to calm down. He didn't want Carrie to leave, but he couldn't just storm into her apartment and demand that she stay. He took some deep breaths. He slowed down a little.

"Calm down, Ripper," he said quietly between breaths. "Calm down."

He was only a block away now and could see Carrie's car in the parking lot. What would he tell her?

"Start with 'I love you'," he said out loud. "That would be…"

Rip stopped talking to himself in mid-sentence. Carrie was walking out of her apartment with a strange man, holding hands! What the hell?

Rip pulled over about half a block away to watch. What was going on?

He watched as Carrie and the man walked their way to a van in the parking lot. The van! Jesus! It's the asshole from the Whataburger! What the hell is going on?

The side door of the van slid open and he saw Carrie flinch. She tried to pull away from the man, but he slapped her and shoved her into the van. Rip caught a glimpse of the knife as the man jumped in behind Carrie and slid the door shut.

"Holy Christ!" Rip jerked his truck into gear and took off. The van lurched out of the driveway just ahead of him. "God damn it! No!"

There was no calming down now. Rip gunned the truck and bumped the back of the van. The van took off faster.

Inside the van, Ricky had Carrie pinned to the mattress in the back and was slapping her repeatedly. He felt the bump from Rip's truck.

"What the fuck was that?" he demanded.

"Some sonofabitch rammed the back of the van!" Louie shouted. "He must have seen you!"

"Drive faster! Head for the country and don't stop for anything!" Ricky grabbed Carrie's blouse and ripped it open. She was struggling, but Ricky was too strong for her. "Fight all you want, Paradise! I like it better that way!"

"You promised to let me go!" Carrie was sobbing and she thought her nose might be bleeding.

Ricky laughed. "What a stupid thing to say! It's time you know the truth! After we have our way with you, we're going to cut off your head and give it to the old man! Like a present!"

Ricky smacked her backhanded, hard, and she lost consciousness.

Rip gunned the truck again and tapped the back of the van, trying to push it out of control.

"Damn it, Rock! Lose him!" Ricky was removing his pants.

"I'm trying! The guy is crazy!"

There was an intersection up ahead, and Louie saw the light turn yellow. He floored the van and turned right. Rip gunned the truck and drove straight into the back right side of the van. The van swerved and skidded into the concrete median before tipping over. A retired couple traveling in the other lane hit the tipped-over van head on.

Louie was partially ejected. He ended up with his head protruding from the van's windshield up to his shoulders. His face was bleeding. Ricky was tossed into the side of the van. A tire iron that was lying on the floor hit him hard on the head. The half-empty bottle of Fighting Cock burst into shards.

Carrie was tossed into the side of the van, too, but her fall was broken by Ricky. She was unhurt, except for the beating Ricky had inflicted earlier. She regained consciousness but was confused. For a moment, she was back in Rip's truck after running over the poor black girls.

The back doors of the van creaked open, and a man looked inside. Dear God, it was Rip!

"Carrie! My God!" Rip's voice caught at the sight of her bloodied face and ripped clothing. He scrambled into the van and took her hand. "Are you hurt? I mean, can you walk? Can you get out of the van?"

She nodded weakly and allowed Rip to lead her into the street. "Who the hell are these people, Carrie? What were they doing to you?"

Carrie just wrapped her arms around Rip and held on. "They're from my past, Rip, the past you know nothing about. They came to kill me."

"Kill you? Why?"

Carrie just shook her head. "Get me out of here, Rip."

The sound of the siren interrupted them. A Leon County Sheriff's vehicle pulled alongside the wreckage and a huge man in a green uniform huffed his way out. It was Bulldog.

He took one look at the wreckage and rested his eyes on Rip and Carrie. He pulled the toothpick out of his mouth, pointed it at the two of them and said, "Christ almighty. Not you two again!"

54

"Well, at least you didn't kill anybody this time." Bulldog had looked the scene over and tended to the retired couple, who were remarkably unhurt. Less could be said for the Barboni brothers, who were whisked away to a hospital.

Bulldog sucked hard on his toothpick. "What the hell happened here?"

Rip and Carrie looked at each other, unsure how to proceed.

"Oh, don't tell me," Bulldog said, holding up a hand like he was stopping traffic. "Your memory is failing you again, is that it? Christ almighty."

"Back off, Deputy," Rip responded hotly. "She wasn't driving; I was."

"Okay. That's a start. So tell me. Why is your truck – a brand new truck I might add – sitting cockeyed out here with dents in the front, the van is tipped over, and that poor older couple is without a ride?"

"It's a long story."

"Yeah, well, let's hear it."

"Not right now," Carrie interjected. "I'm standing out here with my clothes ripped open and a bloody lip. Can't we do this later? I'd like to change clothes and take care of my face."

"I don't know. It might be better if it's fresh in your memory."

"Don't worry, Deputy. It's as clear as a bell, believe me. But can't we please do this later?" Carrie pulled at her torn clothes in a useless attempt to cover herself.

Bulldog sucked on his toothpick.

"C'mon, Deputy," Rip joined in. "Let me take her home to straighten up. We'll meet you at the courthouse in, say, two hours?"

Bulldog checked his watch. "That'd be during lunch. How about one o'clock? Will that work?"

"Thank you, Deputy," Carrie offered. "I'll see you then and tell you all about it."

Rip led Carrie to his dented truck – it was just a few days old – and they drove off in the direction of Carrie's apartment.

"Do you want to tell me why those two assholes in the van were trying to kill you?" Rip was looking straight ahead as he drove. The sight of Carrie in her ripped-up condition was hard to take.

Carrie just shook her head. "There are things about me you don't know, Rip. Things you'll never know."

"But I want to know!" Rip protested. "I want to know everything about you! Maybe I can help! I'm crazy in love with you, Carrie!"

This caused Carrie's breathing to catch and she looked at Rip hard.

"Yes, that's right, Carrie. I said it. I love you. And I mean it. I know it wasn't supposed to happen. It was only supposed to be about the sex. But somewhere along the way, I don't know, I fell in love. There it is."

"Don't do this, Rip."

"Don't do what? Tell you how I feel? Well, I'm sorry, but I love you and I want us to be together."

"Dammit, Rip, I don't have time for this."

They arrived at her apartment. She looked at him and her heart skipped. "Come in, Rip. We need to talk."

In they went, with Rip looking around nervously, wondering if the neighbors were watching him walk her to the door with her clothes all torn up.

Inside, Carrie started scurrying around, tossing off her torn clothes and throwing on a tee shirt and a pair of shorts.

"I don't have much time, Rip, so you're just going to have to listen. No questions."

"But, what...."

"No questions! It's a matter of life and death. Life and death, Rip, got it?"

Rip nodded.

"Good. Those guys are from a crime family in Chicago. I used to work for them – as a stripper," Carrie looked away as she said this. "They were into some bad stuff and I testified against them. Now they're here to kill me. I don't know how they found me, but here they are. And they won't stop until I'm dead."

She let the reality of what she said sink in.

"That's why I'm leaving, Rip. I have no choice but to disappear. I'm on the run."

"But they'll be back in jail after this," Rip protested. "I saw the knife! I'll testify to it!"

Carrie shook her head sadly. "These guys play for keeps, Rip. I need to leave. And I need you to help."

"Help you leave? I don't want you to leave! I want you to stay! I'll help you somehow!"

"No, Rip. My mind is made up. I have no choice." She was standing by the door with an overnight bag. "I'm asking you to do a very hard thing, Rip, I know. But, please, if you love me, let me go. Help me go."

Rip's vision was blurring. "Oh, God, Carrie."

"Rip, please. I need you right now. I need you to take me to the airport. Right now."

"Now? The airport? What about Bulldog?"

"Forget Bulldog, Rip. I'm leaving. C'mon! If you can't drive me, I'll drive myself. But I don't want my car at the airport. I don't want any clues."

"You're serious?"

"As a heart attack."

So Rip gave in against his better judgment. They drove in silence past the Lake Bradford Road Baptist Church and the still-visible spot where Carrie ran his old truck off the road. Rip pulled into short-term parking and grabbed Carrie's suitcase.

"Rip, you don't need to walk me in. You shouldn't. You can't know where I'm going."

He just turned and walked toward the terminal. She scurried along behind him.

"I assume you'll carry this on?" Rip asked.

Carrie nodded.

"Okay. Go get your ticket. I'll wait for you at the security checkpoint. That way, I won't know where you're going." He hurried on and didn't look back.

It was getting close to noon when Carrie walked up to Rip at the security checkpoint. He handed her the carry-on.

"Rip, I want you to know I love you, too. And I'm so very sorry for everything that happened. I'd take it back in a heartbeat. But I can't. I'm living on borrowed time here, Rip, and it's about up. I hope you can forgive me someday."

Rip wrapped his arms around her and buried his face in her hair. He breathed deeply of her scent and memorized the way his arms felt on her back. He closed his eyes and tried to make them both disappear. It didn't work.

The loudspeaker announced the final boarding call for a Delta flight to Tampa. Carrie pulled away. Her voice caught.

"Goodbye, Rip."

Rip's eyes flooded as he watched Carrie go through security and hurry off to her plane. She never looked back.

Eventually, Rip meandered out of the terminal and walked toward his car. Behind him, he heard a plane take off and looked up. It was Delta.

He checked his watch – ten minutes after twelve. "Your flight to Tampa was ten minutes late, Carrie," he said to the air, "or should I say forty years too early?"

55

Ricky "The Boner" Barboni was the first of the Barboni brothers to arrive at his senses in the hospital. His head was banging away like there was a woodpecker sitting on it. There was activity nearby. He was in the emergency room; that much was clear.

What happened?

Slowly, his mind rearranged the pieces until they fit. He needed to find The Rock and get the hell out of the hospital before some federal marshals showed up.

Gingerly, Ricky got himself out of bed and peered out from behind a curtain. He could see his brother across the hall with his head bandaged. He snuck across the hall and shook his brother awake.

"Rock! Wake up! Wake up!"

Louie groaned and struggled to come awake. "Ricky? Is that you?"

"Listen, Rock, we have to get the hell out of here. Now!"

"Where are we?"

"We're in a hospital. But we need to go. They'll arrest us!"

"I'm tired, Ricky. I need to sleep."

"No! Get up! We're leaving!" Ricky was pulling his brother up. "C'mon!"

Louie was stumbling, but they managed to careen down the hall together. A nurse arrived.

"What are you doing? Back in bed with you! Right now!"

Ricky mustered all of his strength and hit the nurse flat on the nose, which broke with an audible *crack!* A piece of the bone jammed up into her brain. She went down hard.

Louie snapped to attention as the nurse went down. His head was clearing. "Jesus, Ricky! I think you killed her!"

"Forget about her. Let's go."

Bulldog was halfway through his second Whataburger when he overheard the request for assistance at the hospital. Two patients had assaulted a nurse and run off. Ordinarily he would've ignored it, since it was a city police matter. But he put two and two together and figured the guys from the van were causing trouble.

"Christ almighty."

He set the rest of the burger aside and took off. The hospital emergency room was already cordoned off when he got there, right behind reporter Jimmy Flain.

"Hey, Bulldog. What are you doing here?"

"Shit, Jimmy. I'm sure you know more than I do."

Jimmy beamed at this. "Well, it seems two guys who were brought in from a traffic accident didn't like the service, so they left. Problem is, they whacked a nurse on the way out."

"When you say they 'whacked a nurse,' Jimmy, do you mean...?"

"Yep," Jimmy nodded. "Killed her. Bare handed."

"Christ al-fuckin-mighty," Bulldog was sucking on his toothpick like it was a lifeline. "Ain't this a pile of shit?"

"What's your involvement, Bulldog? You know something. What is it?"

"Later, Jimmy."

Bulldog was already inside his cruiser. Snyder and that Stevens woman had better lay it all out for him, chapter and verse. No more stalling.

56

Bulldog was sitting behind his desk, sucking on a toothpick and looking agitated when Rip shuffled in. Rip didn't want to be there, but figured he had to.

"Where's the Stevens woman?"

"Atlanta."

"Atlanta!" Bulldog turned and spit the toothpick into a distant trash can. "I don't have time for jokes. Where is she?"

"Atlanta."

"Christ almighty! Are you serious?"

"As a heart attack." Rip felt like he was having one, too. God, he missed her.

Bulldog pointed to a chair. "Sit your ass down and spill your guts. And it better be good."

"The two bastards in the van abducted her at knifepoint. I saw it. That's why I was chasing them. Carrie said they came here from

Chicago to kill her and she had no choice but to run. So I took her to the airport and she hopped a flight to Atlanta."

"Jesus Christ." Bulldog rubbed his face. "So she never had any intention of coming here to clue me in."

"No."

"Did she tell you what happened in that van?"

"No, but it was pretty obvious, don't you think?"

Bulldog grunted. "So tell me what you know."

Rip went through it, as truthfully as he dared.

"You could have killed somebody," Bulldog admonished. "You should've called the police."

"And she'd be dead by now," Rip responded, his voice rising. "I know what I did was dangerous, but I saved her life. It's too bad I didn't kill the two bastards in the van. How are they, by the way?"

"They're on the loose, last I heard."

"What?"

"They ran out of the hospital. Killed a nurse, too."

"Jesus. Carrie was right. They play for keeps."

"Dammit. We need her here. She knows stuff about these guys that could be useful! Does she have a cell phone?"

Rip shook his head. "She's gone, Deputy. Forget about it."

"Dammit!" Bulldog punctuated it by slamming his enormous fist down on the desk. He pointed at Rip. "Have you told me everything you know about this?"

"Yes."

"Then get the hell out of my office. I've got work to do."

"You're not giving me a ticket or anything for the accident?"

"Do you want one?"

"No."

"Okay, then. I'm convinced you saved that lady's life, and that counts for something. Now beat it."

57

They were nervous.

The Barboni brothers had managed to steal a car from the hospital parking lot – the keys were in it – but they were on pins and needles as they drove deeper into the countryside to the south of Tallahassee.

"Why are we going south anyway?" Louie wanted to know. "Chicago is north."

"We can't drive all the way to Chicago in a stolen car, Rock. They gotta be looking for us hot and heavy by now."

"So what's the plan, Ricky?"

"Find a place to hide, I guess. Call the old man. He'll know what to do."

"Jesus, he'll be pissed."

"Yeah."

"What about the girl? You still want to kill her, don't you?"

Ricky grunted. "More than ever. But things are too hot right now. I don't want to get caught."

"Yeah, me neither."

They rode in silence for awhile.

"Kinda spooky out here," Louie said. "I didn't know Florida looked so much like Deliverance with all these big trees and shit. I thought it was all beach and palm trees."

"Well, you thought wrong, Rock."

They were cruising south through the Apalachicola National Forest and there wasn't much to look at – except trees.

"Was that a town?" Louie wondered. "Didn't look like much. Spring Hill, I think it said. Is there a map in this stupid car?"

He started rummaging through the glove box and produced a ratty old map of Florida.

"What road are we on?" Louie asked as he unfolded the map and found Tallahassee.

"Hell if I know. Wait – there's a sign up ahead. 373. Highway 373."

Louie traced the map with his finger. "Jesus! We're in the middle of nowhere!"

Ricky grinned. "Good! I like the middle of nowhere. I got a plan."

"Good, Ricky, because my head hurts. I need some pain pills or something."

"Here comes another town," Ricky said. "This is where we do it."

Louie looked at the sign. "Helen. What a name for a town. Helen, Florida. I don't know, Ricky. There's nothing here."

Ricky pulled into the sandy driveway of a shabby old house with a small, falling-down detached garage. The shrubs around the house were overgrown. It might have been abandoned, but a thin old man in a ratty pair of overalls was chugging through the tall grass with an old Snapper riding mower.

Ricky jumped out of the car in a frenzy, waving his arms at the old man and pointing at his brother. "Help! We need some help here! Help!"

The old man killed the engine, but kept sitting on the mower. He figured the young whippersnapper could walk over.

"It's my brother! We were driving a four-wheeler through the woods and he whacked his head! He needs a doctor!"

The old man spit. ""You ain't from around here, are ya?"

"No. We're on vacation. You know, in the woods."

"Yankees, by the sound of it."

"Yeah. Chicago. Look, buddy, my brother needs a doctor. Is there one close by?"

"Closest doctor is in Tallahassee. They got lots of doctors. Of course, ain't none of 'em worth a shit." He spit again. "Looks like somebody already bandaged him up good. And he's awake. What do ya need a doctor for?"

"He's in bad pain. And he ain't right. You know, in the head."

The old man nodded, and spit. "Knocked him loopy, huh? Yeah, better have a doctor look at him. Even if they are a bunch of idiots."

"You got a phone? Maybe I should call ahead."

"Yeah, I got a phone. Long distance, though."

"We'll pay," Ricky said with his best smile, "and I can't thank you enough."

The old man dismounted from the mower and spit again. "Right this way, Yankee. And I might have some whiskey, too. You know," he said with a wink, "for the pain."

Louie watched them enter the old house and knew what was coming. Ricky emerged in less than two minutes with blood on his shirt. He hopped in the car.

"Pretty nice for an old fart," Ricky said dismissively as he hid the car behind the house, out of sight from the road. "Let's hang out here for awhile."

"Another chapter for my memoirs," Louie noted. "I think I'll call it 'I Went Through Helen, Florida'. Get it?"

"Yeah, I get it, Rock. Now help me stash the body in a closet or something."

58

Madeline Esterman punched Roy Fercal's cell phone number and waited for him to pick up. She knew better than to wait for an answer.

"Hey, Roy, it's Maddie," she began briskly. "I have some news about your case."

"Shoot." Roy could tell she had no interest in small talk.

"I don't know what strings got pulled or who pulled them, but Judge Smith has been assigned to preside over your case. I think you called him Twinkie."

Roy felt a flood of relief wash over him. "Twinkie! That's fantastic!"

Roy was pacing now, running his right hand through his hair. He couldn't stop grinning. Jesus – he was home free!

"I thought you might like that," Maddie said. "Now we have a decision to make."

"Decision? What decision?"

"Do you want to go ahead with a trial by jury, or would you rather waive it and let this Twinkie fellow render judgment?"

"Let Twinkie do it!" Roy was practically jumping for joy. "Waive the jury trial. Jesus! What a stroke of luck!"

"Luck?" Maddie responded sarcastically. "Is that what it was – luck?"

"I swear to God, Maddie, I had nothing to do with it. But I'll take it! You bet your ass I'll take it!"

"Okay. I'll take care of waiving the jury trial, if you're sure."

"Do it! And let's get this over with as soon as possible. Good old Twinkie!"

Yeah, good old Twinkie, Maddie thought as she hung up. She decided that whoever is looking out for Roy Fercal has got some serious juice.

She was wrong about that.

59

Tuesday, September 16

"How long are we gonna stay here, Ricky?" Louie was squirming in his seat, and he had soggy corn flakes trying to escape his mouth. "The old fart is starting to stink."

"You heard the old man, Rock," Ricky reminded him. "We sit tight until the phone rings."

They had talked to the head of the Barboni family last night, through a secure channel. They used the dead guy's phone to call the cell phone of "The Beef," a huge bodyguard who was at the old man's side at all times. The Beef immediately took the old man to a nearby park, where he handed the phone to him and listened with some enjoyment to the ass-chewing that followed.

"Listen, you clumsy bastards," the old man had said. "Your stupid-ass plan to play kissy face with that fucking stripper has put the whole family in jeopardy! Now, Ricky, keep that goddamn prick of yours in your pants and the both of you sit tight until Beef calls you back with directions."

The old man had handed the cell phone back to his bodyguard and said, "Maybe their mother was right. They should have been aborted."

The Tallahassee area was alive with police activity. The nurse Ricky Barboni killed was somewhat of a local hero. She had raised more than $30,000 last year alone for cancer research. She was an emergency foster mom for kids who were taken away from abusive families in the middle of the night. And she volunteered 20 hours a week at a local hospice.

The people wanted justice.

By morning, the news was out that the alleged killers were from a crime family in Chicago. Details of the attempted kidnapping and assault of the now-famous Carrie Stevens were emerging. Reporters were desperate to talk to her but, of course, she was "unavailable for comment."

The talk in the coffee shops had turned against Carrie. "Wasn't she the one who ran over those little colored girls?" "Where's she from anyway, up north?" "She's the reason those damn mobsters came to town, I'll bet." "The town's going to hell, that's for sure." And, of course, "Do you think the Seminoles can beat Clemson on Saturday?"

The car the Barboni brothers stole belonged to a patient who was getting a mammogram and she was highly pissed to discover her vehicle missing after enduring an especially painful procedure at the hands of a doctor who could care less. A description of the vehicle had gone out over the media and was reported in the newspaper the following morning, which is where Norma Spatzke read it before heading out to the Publix store to buy peaches.

Norma was positive she had seen that very car the day before go speeding past her house while she was planting mums.

She called 911 from her house, which was a modest rancher between two dirt roads south of the airport. Thirty years earlier her husband, Fred, had bought the lot for next to nothing because of its proximity to the airport on one side and the Munson Slough on the other, which constantly flooded and bred mosquitoes the size of coconuts. Norma had never forgiven him, but she couldn't bring herself to move away, even ten years after he fell out of his bass boat on Munson Lake, stinking drunk, and drowned in two feet of water and three feet of grass.

Her little slice of God's green earth was just south of the Tallahassee city limits, so her call was routed to the Leon County Sheriff's Office, which took the information and alerted one Deputy Bowser, interrupting him in mid-doughnut at the Krispy Kreme.

Bulldog was mildly irritated at having his late-morning, post-breakfast, pre-lunch snack interrupted, but he wanted very badly to put a bullet between the eyes of both Barboni brothers, so he stuffed the rest of his raspberry-filled cruller into his mouth and headed for the squad car.

The Beef called the Barboni brothers shortly before noon. He was pleased to learn that the old fart the brothers had killed left behind a plain-looking Ford pick-up with the required number of dents, scratches and rust spots to look normal.

"Drive the truck to a little town southeast of you called St. Mark's," Beef instructed. "At the end of the road, park in front of a bar called Shuck Me. Sit on the dock in the back and have lunch or something. A guy in a boat will pull up and ask about a couple of fellas looking to go deep-sea fishing. That would be you. Get on the boat and disappear."

"Where are we disappearing to?" Louie wanted to know. In his line of work, sending people off to disappear on a boat was a bad sign.

The Beef grunted. "Don't worry. The old man still has a little patience left. The boater will take you to a place called Cedar Key for a few days, then on to Tampa. Lay low for awhile. Really low."

"I was out here planting my mums, see," Norma was telling Bulldog, pointing with her hands. "And this car goes whizzing by, real fast, going that way." She was pointing south, into the national forest.

"Did you get a look at the guys that were in it?"

"Not really," Norma admitted. "They were going pretty fast. But there were two of them. That I'm sure of."

Bulldog looked off in the direction of the forest and sucked on his toothpick. The forest might look pretty good to a couple of killers looking to hide, he realized.

"Thank you, ma'am," he said with a tip of his cap. "You did the right thing." Then he waddled off to the cruiser and headed south.

60

Ricky and Louie Barboni wasted no time getting themselves out of Helen, Florida. They backed the pick-up out of the shed, replaced it with the car they had stolen in Tallahassee, and headed off to St. Mark's.

It started raining.

"Fucking wipers ain't worth a damn," Ricky complained as he squinted to see through the greasy mess on the windshield.

Louie was busy with the map. "Should be a little town up ahead called Hilliardville. When we get there, turn left on 267."

"Whatever."

Sure enough, Hilliardville came and went.

"Ain't nothing here," Ricky observed. "Middle of nowhere."

The rain was coming down in sheets now, and Ricky had slowed the old truck to a crawl. Louie looked nervously behind them.

"Stay on this road all the way to another one called 363. Then turn right, Ricky."

"Maybe I should pull over 'till it quits raining so damn hard. I can't see shit."

"You pull over now and I'll kick your horny little ass," Louie said. "We need to get the hell out of Dodge."

"Hilliardville," Ricky corrected. "We need to get the hell out of Hilliardville."

This got Louie laughing. "We went through Helen, Florida, to get to Hilliardville!" Louie was singing, making it up as he went. "Then off we went, hell-bent, to celebrate the kill!"

Now Ricky was laughing, too. They used to make up songs like this as kids. "Hi ho, hi ho, it's off to work we go! We'll find us a bitch, a cute little bitch, and teach her how to blow!"

The laughter continued, and before long the rain let up, and then stopped.

"Here it is," Louie announced. "Shuck Me."

"Good thing, Rock, 'cuz there ain't no more road."

Ricky parked the truck in the gravel lot next to a couple of motorcycles. He eyed the worn building and announced, "Looks like my kind of place."

And in they went.

O ver the years, Bulldog had driven every inch of every road in Leon County, but it had been awhile since he'd had a reason to venture into the Apalachicola National Forest. Folks out here didn't have much use for law enforcement. He knew a few people who owned wooden signs in the shape of a pistol that read, "We don't call the sheriff."

He got to Helen when it started raining. It was time to turn around. The Wakulla County line was just ahead.

Bulldog pulled into the driveway of an old friend and noticed a riding lawnmower sitting out in the rain. Hmmm. He'd never known old Joe to leave his Snapper out in the rain.

Bulldog pulled his cruiser up close to the house and killed the engine. Then he honked the horn. Nothing. Maybe the old fart went to town or something.

Bulldog struggled out of the cruiser and listened. Nothing but rain. He knocked on the front door. He knocked harder. He tried the door. It was unlocked.

The smell of death was unmistakable. Jesus. "Joe? Are you in here? Joe?"

Bulldog covered his nose as best he could and walked to where the smell seemed the strongest – a closet – and swung the door open.

"Christ almighty!" Bulldog looked down at old Joe. His throat was cut. "Poor bastard."

Bulldog went to his cruiser and called it in. Then he got to looking around and found the stolen car in the old garage. He got back on the radio.

"Find out what kind of vehicle Joe Stanker of Helen owned and put out an APB on it," Bulldog barked. "The bastards are probably driving it." He wanted to find the little bastards and shoot 'em both, right then, but he knew it was his job to secure the scene. And he didn't know which way they went. All he could do was swear, and he proceeded to do so.

61

S huck Me was a long, long way from Chicago, in more ways than one. The first thing Ricky noticed was the pile of fresh oysters in front of a bored looking old man who was busy prying them open. He looked up as Ricky and Louie passed and, with a nearly toothless grin, said, "Can't get no fresher than these! Just pulled 'em out this morning!"

They nodded and continued on toward the back. They found a large room with wooden tables, a long bar and several open-air windows to a body of water beyond.

"Sit wherever you like," invited the bartender, who looked like he couldn't escape the 1960s and didn't want to. "Get ya something?"

"You got Fighting Cock?" Ricky inquired.

The bartender broke into a grin. "Are you kidding? I got the champion!" Then he made like he was about to unzip his shorts.

"Promises, promises." It was a waitress who was zipping by with a platter of oysters on the half shell. "All talk, no action."

"Open wide enough and you'll see some action!" The bartender was grabbing his crotch, but by now the waitress was ignoring him. He turned back to Ricky. "How do you take your Cock?"

"On the rocks."

"Both of ya?" They nodded. "Two Cocks on the rocks!" He said it loudly, like he was barking out an order at a Waffle House. The other customers either ignored him or smirked.

"Yep," Ricky remarked, "my kind of place."

Louie threw down a twenty and told the bartender to keep the change. He looked up appreciatively and stuck the bill in his shirt. The waitress returned.

"You fellas hungry?"

"Starving," Louie said at once. He was damn hungry and his head was throbbing.

"Grab a seat someplace and I'll get you some menus." She scurried off as Ricky and Louie found a table outside overlooking the water.

Louie enjoyed the burn of the whiskey as he looked out over the water. "Ya reckon that's the Gulf of Mexico?"

"That ain't the Gulf, you dumbass! Whaddya think those trees are over there? Cuba?" Ricky downed half his drink in one gulp.

"Oh, yeah." Louie took another sip. "So what is it?"

"That's the St. Mark's River." It was the waitress. "It empties into Appalachee Bay, which empties into the Gulf. It's a real pretty boat ride."

"You like boats?" Ricky was looking closely at her. She was young, built pretty good and had just a hint of skanky slut about her, which he liked.

· "I practically live on one when I'm not working," she confided. "My name is Hannah." She stuck out her hand. "And you are?"

"Boner," he responded immediately as he took her hand. "My friends call me Boner."

Hannah laughed and shook her head, but made no effort to withdraw her hand. She turned to Louie. "How about your friend here? Do you really call him Boner?"

"He doesn't have any friends," Louie groused while he kicked Ricky under the table. "C'mon, Boner, let's order some food before the boat gets here."

"Boat? What boat?" Hannah was really curious now.

"Yeah, we're going fishing," Ricky said. "The boat is going to meet us here. You should come with us." Ricky winked at her. Louie kicked him again.

"Down boy," Louie was losing patience. "Can we get some food here?"

"Sure," Hannah replied. "Our lunch special is smoked mullet."

"Mullet? What the fuck is mullet?"

"It's a fish," Hannah informed Louie. "And we smoke it right here. But if you're real hungry, you'd better get some oysters, too. Mullets are kind of small."

"Mullet and oysters it is!" Ricky decided and held up his glass. "And I need more Cock!"

"Don't we all," Hannah tossed back at him as she departed.

Ricky turned to Louie and said, "I'm in love."

Louie rolled his eyes and sipped his whiskey. How long before the boat arrived?

The boat arrived about an hour later, just as the Leon County Coroner was driving away from Helen with the body of Joe Stanker. The All Points Bulletin on Stanker's truck had gone out, with the search focused primarily on southern Leon County and parts of Wakulla County. The prevailing theory was that the Barboni brothers would most likely try to hole up in the woods and that, being from Chicago, they wouldn't be worth a damn at it.

Ricky and Hannah, the waitress, had been flirting with each other all through lunch. When the boat pulled up, Ricky renewed his invitation for Hannah to join them. Louie was inside, negotiating with the hippy bartender for the purchase of the rest of the bottle of Fighting Cock. The bartender, feeling greedy, suggested fifty bucks. Louie tossed him a hundred and said, "Keep the change."

The bartender couldn't believe his luck. He looked around the nearly empty bar and stuffed the c-note into his shirt pocket, alongside the twenty. "Ya'll have a good time."

Hannah, uncertain at first, finally gave in and made the biggest mistake of her young life. She got on the boat. Ricky's grin was almost sickening.

A Wakulla County deputy spotted Stanker's truck in St. Mark's a couple of hours later. When he went into Shuck Me and described the Barboni brothers to the bartender, the deputy was disappointed to learn they hadn't been there.

"Nobody come in here today I didn't already know," the bartender assured him. "Just the locals today. That's about all we get during the week anymore."

The deputy nodded and left. He did his duty, checking with the few other bars and restaurants in the area, but he came up empty. The Barboni brothers, it seemed, had disappeared into thin air.

62

Wednesday, September 17

"This is the craziest damn thing I've ever done! I could lose my job!"

Hannah, the waitress from Shuck Me, was twirling Ricky Barboni's chest hairs around a finger as they lay naked on the most gorgeous canopy bed she had ever seen. The windows of the luxury bedroom were open, allowing a gentle breeze to wander in from the Gulf of Mexico.

Ricky snorted. "How much do you make with that lousy job anyway? Three hundred a week? Why bother?"

"It pays the bills. And I like living on the water."

"So come work for me."

Hannah laughed. "I don't even know who you are or what you do! All I know is your friends call you Boner." She reached down and touched him softly. "And for good reason."

Ricky could feel himself responding to her gentle touch. "I run tittie bars and sex clubs, stuff like that. It's good money. Fun, too."

"Tittie bars? It figures. I don't think I'm cut out for the sex business."

Ricky reached between her legs and found her wet. "On the contrary, I think you're a natural."

Downstairs, Louie and the boat captain heard the canopy bed tapping against the wall and eyed each other over their coffee cups.

"Jesus Christ!" the captain said. "They're at it again!"

Louie could only grin. "He's making up for lost time. I swear to God; he's the horniest sonofabitch on the planet. It gets him in more trouble, that pecker of his."

The captain scowled. "That reminds me. The boss gave me very clear instructions. I was to pick you two up, bring you to this private vacation house on Cedar Key for a few days, and then drop you off in Tampa. He said to make sure you aren't seen by anybody." He pointed upstairs with his right thumb. "That whore up there makes me nervous."

Louie leaned in and lowered his voice. "Me, too. But I reckon Ricky is smart enough to realize we can't let her leave. Besides, he'll get tired of her; always does. I suspect she'll fall overboard or something."

The captain nodded. "It's a shame, really. The poor bitch has no idea what's coming."

"They never do, my friend. They never do."

The *tap, tap, tap* of the canopy bed increased in intensity. The captain took his coffee outside on the wraparound porch and busied himself by watching a pelican catch fish.

B ack in Chicago, the Beef reported to the old man that his wayward sons, Louie and Ricky, had indeed been picked up by boat and were currently safe and sound at a vacation home the family controlled in Cedar Key, Florida. He did not say anything about the complication of the waitress, because the boat captain had discreetly neglected to mention it in his phone call.

"Good," the old man grunted. "Let's hope the little bastards keep their zippers up for a change."

63

Thursday, September 18

Rip Snyder was miserable.

In all the excitement surrounding Carrie's abduction, the car chase, and all the rest, he had forgotten all about the special Monday edition of *The Ripper* in which he was going to follow Big Daddy Malloy's advice and apologize for his insensitivities. He was sitting in his home office, trying to come up with the right words in advance of his usual Friday publication.

Rip was avoiding his downtown office because to get there, he would have to drive by Carrie's old office, and he couldn't face it.

God, he missed Carrie. He feared for her safety and wondered what would happen to her. The thought of never seeing her again tore at his insides.

He pictured her inside that awful van, beaten and torn, being raped. He remembered how she looked when he forced open the van door, how she hugged him like there was no tomorrow. He remembered, and for the umpteenth time he started to weep.

The loud banging on his front door shocked him back to the present. He quickly wiped his eyes and made his way to the door. Rip swung it open without thinking and stood face to face with the Reverend Josiah Franklin.

Behind the reverend, on the sidewalk, were about a dozen black women with protest signs and a young, white woman with a television camera. Ah, Jesus.

While Rip looked at Franklin through eyes red with grief, Josiah's eyes were gleaming. A slight grin teased his mouth, though he was trying to suppress it.

"Ah, Mr. Snyder. We meet at last."

"What do you want?"

"Where's your Southern hospitality, Mr. Snyder? Aren't you going to invite me in?"

"You show up at my door with a TV camera in tow and you want me to invite you in? Forget it. Now beat it."

Rip started to close the door, but Josiah reached out his hand and held it open. "Not so fast, Mr. Snyder. I have something for you."

Then Josiah stepped back on the porch, reached inside his jacket and produced a piece of paper. "This is for you." He held it out, but not far enough so Rip could reach it.

Rip stepped onto the porch and snatched it out of Franklin's hand. "What is it?"

"It's a lawsuit. The mother of those three kids you helped slaughter is suing you for wrongful death. I told her I would deliver the lawsuit personally."

Rip looked at the paper but was too confused to read it. "Suing me? Why me? I didn't do anything!"

"Oh, but you did, Mr. Snyder. You gave your truck keys to that little slut of yours when she was drunk. The blood of those kids is on your hands."

Rip felt the anger boil over inside. "What did you call her?" He stepped forward, right into Josiah's face.

"I called her your little slut. You got a problem with that? Do you?"

Rip could feel the spittle from Franklin's lips as he spoke. He snapped. Rip grabbed Franklin's jacket and shoved him backwards, hard enough that Franklin stumbled backwards down the porch steps. He landed clumsily on his backside and bounced on the sidewalk. Rip threw the lawsuit at Franklin. "Get the hell out of here and go back where you belong!"

Then he looked at the shocked faces of the black women. "All of ya! Get the hell off my property!"

Rip took one last look at Franklin as the reverend gathered himself. Funny, Rip thought. He's still grinning. Rip went inside, slamming the door behind him.

The local news that night was ugly. Rip had called Bannerman Lux after the altercation and they watched it together in Lucky's office.

Rip recognized the young female reporter. The story began with her talking directly into the camera with the front porch of Rip's house behind her.

"Racial tensions between a local African-American minister and a leading member of the Florida Republican Party bubbled over into violence today in this normally quiet Tallahassee neighborhood. The Reverend Josiah Franklin says he was trying to help the grieving mother of three slaughtered children find justice when he personally delivered notice of a wrongful death lawsuit to Rip Snyder. As you can see, all hell broke loose."

The story cut to the video of Rip shoving Franklin down the porch steps and throwing the paper at him. Rip could be heard shouting, "Go back where you belong! All of ya!" Then the TV screen filled with the face of Reverend Josiah Franklin, who was sporting a scratch on his forehead.

"How did he get that?" Rip wondered. "I shoved him on his ass, not his head!"

"Shhh!"

"I guess he was trying to tell me this boy doesn't belong way up here in Killearn," Franklin said, looking at the reporter. "So he assaulted me. You saw it. I'll heal, but when are we going to heal the racial divide in this city? How long before black folks are free to walk the streets without fearing a beating from another white Republican?"

"Jesus! How do they let him get away with that?"

"Quiet!" Lux admonished again.

"The mother of the three little children killed in a wreck involving Snyder's truck witnessed the assault on Reverend Franklin, but was too shocked to comment. As for Mr. Snyder..."

There was a quick video clip of Rip slamming the door shut behind him.

"...Perhaps he figured he'd said enough already."

"I think I'm going to be sick," Rip offered, weakly. "It was a setup. Had to be."

"Yeah, and you fell for it, Rip. Nice going."

"Jesus, Lucky. What next?"

"Well, I suspect you'll be arrested for assaulting a man of the cloth. That'll play well. Plus you'll need to defend yourself against a lawsuit filed by the grieving mother of three dead little girls. Your clients are dropping you like a rock. On top of that, you'll be in serious hock to your lawyer. Can I get you a drink?"

64

Friday, September 19

THE RIPPER

Greetings. Please forgive me, but this will be the last edition of *The Ripper* for awhile. You'll need to keep the faith without me. Oh – and pray for me, too. I might need it.

MEA CULPA

In the last edition, I rather callously dealt with the remarkable scene of 500 marching black people, three tiny coffins hoisted into the air, and one kid who threw a rock through a courthouse window.

It has been pointed out to me by someone I deeply trust that my comments in that regard were insensitive. I agree. I apologize.

But let me add a few more thoughts.

Just the other day I was playing golf across the street from a playground. Several young children – toddlers, mostly – were swinging and sliding and generally having a great time. A young black man drove up with his stereo blaring loud enough to drown out a jet engine. I didn't recognize the song, of course, but the n-word and a slew of obscenities were being repeated over and over. The kids noticed and so did the parents.

A lot of us white folks are confused about this n-word business. We know it's a bad word and we try hard not to use it. We try to hang out with people who don't. So why is it okay for black folks to drive around with it blasting out of their stereo speakers? Forgive us for being confused, because we really want to do the correct thing. But, darn it, some people are making it difficult.

The law requires that we treat each other equally regardless of race and sex and all that stuff. Heck, it's basic decency. But it seems ridiculous to think that all this equality stuff is going to come naturally. It takes work.

White people and black people are not universally alike. When white folks who pay attention to the way they dress see a group of black kids with their pants drooping down below their butts, it takes a lot of work to treat those kids equally. We don't need to dress alike or talk alike or act alike to get along, but a person shouldn't be surprised at being treated differently *when they deliberately dress offensively, talk offensively, or act offensively.*

We're way ahead of where we used to be regarding racial tensions in America, but we're a long way off from our ultimate destination of pure equality.

In the meantime, please understand that most of us white folks are working hard at it. But at times we wonder: are both sides working equally as hard?

Keep the faith.

Rip Snyder

It was only six o'clock in the morning and Rip was already on the road. He feared Franklin would actually press assault charges. He couldn't face being arrested, so he got up early, wrote and published *The Ripper*, and hit the highway.

I'm on the run, he thought gravely. *Just like Carrie.*

Rip was on Interstate 10, heading east. He would take I-75 south to Tampa; to Carrie.

It was stupid, maybe, he realized. Tampa is a big place. How would he find someone who didn't want to be found? And for that matter, he couldn't be sure she was actually in Tampa. She could have switched planes and flown someplace else. But he had to try. His heart was in charge now, and his heart was demanding that he find Carrie.

I'm on the run.

Roy Fercal wasn't sleeping all that well, either. He was confident that Twinkie Smith would do the right thing and find him not guilty of the murder of Roxy Jones. But being an accused murderer does not do good things to the mind.

He had been burning up the phone lines last night after watching the altercation between Rip Snyder and Josiah Franklin on the local news. What a blessing! Roy finally hit pay dirt with a producer at CNN who promised to get a copy of the news report and evaluate it. Roy was pushing to get it on *Inside Politics*.

Roy fired up the computer at mid-morning and checked on *The Ripper*, just out of curiosity. He read Rip's backhanded apology with even more glee. He jumped on the phone again.

He needed the Reverend Franklin to throw another punch – a big one.

Jimmy Flain hung up the phone and hollered across the news room at his editor.

"Reverend Franklin has called a press conference! He says he has more to say about this Snyder business. I'm headed over there right now."

"So beat it already."

The press conference was incredibly well-attended; all the local television and radio folks were there, along with most of the statewide papers. Rip Snyder and Josiah Franklin were hot copy.

It was being held on the sidewalk in front of the federal courthouse. Roy Fercal stood to the side and watched.

"Thank you for taking time out of your busy day," Franklin began. He was wearing a bandage on his forehead, even though he didn't need it.

"As you know, I was assaulted yesterday by Republican operative Rip Snyder in a racist incident that still troubles my heart this morning. The whole black community is suffering today. The oppression is real. The pain is real. And the anger is real.

"Then we awoke this morning to learn even more about the dark nature of Rip Snyder's racial bias. On his weekly blog this morning are spewed references to the way black folks dress, talk and act. He says we're *offensive*. That's the word he used. *Offensive.*

"Essentially, Rip Snyder is accusing the black community of standing in the way of racial harmony and equality. This kind of nonsense cannot go unchallenged.

"Rip Snyder is one of the most recognized leaders of the Florida Republican Party. His words are the words of the party. His bigotry is their bigotry.

"Rip Snyder is also a paid consultant to the Republican National Committee. His bigotry is their bigotry, too.

"Today, on behalf of African-Americans across this country, I call on President Waddell to condemn Rip Snyder, condemn his conduct, and cancel his contract with the RNC.

"If not, we can only assume the President and his cohorts in the Republican Party subscribe to the same racist attitudes spewed forth by Mr. Snyder."

Roy Fercal was trying hard not to grin. It was perfect! The Reverend Franklin was a natural.

Jimmy Flain had noticed Fercal was there, so when Franklin finished up Jimmy walked over for a quote. The television crews noticed and followed, just to make sure they didn't miss anything. Roy was surprised; he wasn't expecting it.

"What's your interest here, Roy? Are you representing the Democratic Party?" Jimmy was scribbling notes.

"No, uh, I just found out about it and wanted to watch."

"Do you agree with Reverend Franklin? Should the President condemn Rip Snyder?"

"Absolutely. The man is garbage."

"Are you still working at the Party, Roy? I mean, with your murder case and all?"

"There's no reason for me to quit the Party, Jimmy. I'm innocent."

CNN bit, chewed and swallowed the story – hook, line and sinker. Their White House correspondent ended the daily press briefing by asking the President's press secretary if President Waddell was going to publicly condemn Rip Snyder.

"You got me there, Judy. Who is Rip Snyder?"

"A Republican operative in Florida. He uses the n-word a lot. He says blacks are offensive and should go back where they belong. Stuff like that."

"Well, I can assure you President Waddell in no way supports that kind of talk, or hate speech of any kind."

"But will he condemn it?"

"Of course."

"And what about Snyder's contract with the RNC? Will it be cancelled?"

"What contract, Judy?"

"He's under contract as a consultant. Will the contract be cancelled?"

"I'm sure the President will see to it personally. Thank you all very much."

I t was the lead story that afternoon on CNN's *Inside Politics*, watched by every political junkie from coast to coast, including a stunned Carrie Stevens from her room at the Maisson Hotel Westshore in Tampa.

"What started as a feud between a local Republican operative and a minister in Tallahassee, Florida, has reached all the way to the White House today. Judy Cleaver has the story…

"This is Reverend Josiah Franklin, pastor of a Baptist church in Tallahassee, Florida, and a noted leader in the civil rights movement. The bandage on his head is from an assault at the hands of Republican operative Rip Snyder.

The scene from Rip's home was played out, except CNN showed it in slow motion, which made it look far worse. And when Rip was seen yelling at everyone to "go back where you belong," CNN zoomed in on his snarling face, making him look like a crazed madman.

"Reverend Franklin was delivering a copy of a lawsuit to Rip Snyder when he was assaulted. The lawsuit accuses Snyder of the wrongful death of these three black children, who were run over and pushed into a sewer by Snyder's allegedly drunken girlfriend in Snyder's borrowed truck.

"Snyder is the author of The Ripper, a Republican blog widely known in Florida and despised by Democrats for what they say is hate speech.

"At a Tallahassee news conference this morning, Reverend Franklin referred to passages from The Ripper accusing blacks of being offensive and obstructing racial harmony. He called on President Waddell to condemn Snyder and cancel his consulting contract with the Republican National Committee. A White House spokesman assured CNN that President

Waddell would see to it personally. Judy Cleaver, CNN, at the White House."

The anchor just had to ask a question.

"Judy, are there concerns at the White House that Rip Snyder could become a liability in the re-election campaign?"

"They're not saying so publicly, Sam, but privately, yes, they're worried that the footage of a Republican operative assaulting a black minister could be very damaging. As for the Democrats, they think the 'Snyder Factor,' as they're calling it, could turn Florida, at the very least, into a blue state this year. The head of the Florida Democratic Party – his name is Roy Fercal and, yes, that's his picture there on the screen – is openly calling Rip Snyder 'garbage.' That's his word – garbage."

"Thank you, Judy. Up next, a call for impeachment from a Democratic senator who says he's tired of low standardized test scores in his home state. Is President Waddell responsible for stupidity? We'll find out when Inside Politics *returns."*

Carrie turned it off and sat in silence. Jesus. Rip is hosed.

65

At 26 Ocean Drive in Ponte Vedra Beach, Richard Jones could have gone across the street and played golf with his buddies at the Sawgrass Country Club. Or he could have strolled onto his magnificent veranda off the great room and enjoyed the sea breeze while looking over the Atlantic Ocean. Or he could have been at the office, barking orders to underlings who were feverishly trying to keep up with his growing chain of Tuscan-inspired restaurants.

Instead, he was holed up in his den, puffing on a huge Cuban cigar without really enjoying it like he used to. Almost absentmindedly he was flipping through satellite channels and staring at a plasma television that cost him ten grand. The channel surfing stopped when he got to CNN. It was time for *Inside Politics*. Richard Jones was a political player. He paid attention.

Richard watched Judy Cleaver's report on the Snyder business and knew it was mostly bullshit. The Democrats are playing the race card again. Since when is that news?

But he gasped out loud when the picture of Roy Fercal was put on the screen. He hit the pause button on the digital video recorder and studied the face carefully.

So this is the man the police arrested for raping and killing my baby girl. "You fucking bastard," he said out loud; then, louder. "You fucking bastard! Why are you alive and my daughter dead! You bastard!"

Thanks in large part to his money, Richard Jones had all kinds of connections. He played golf with the governor. He had dined with President Waddell in the White House residence. He had connections all over the place – savory and unsavory.

With Fercal's picture still frozen in front of him, Richard picked up the phone and reached out to one of his most unsavory connections.

After arranging to meet on his veranda, Richard hung up and stared at the television screen. And for the zillionth time he wished Roxy had agreed to stay home and work in the restaurant business instead of insisting on making her own way in the world.

His money couldn't keep Roxy home and it won't bring her back. But it could, perhaps, move the process of justice forward just a tad.

Richard turned off the television, stubbed out the cigar, and wept one more time for his baby girl.

Rip Snyder had driven into Tampa before noon, blissfully unaware of the hot poker Roy Fercal and CNN were planning to stick up his backside. He had followed the signs to the airport because he didn't know where else to start. After finding a relatively inexpensive hotel, Rip had collapsed on the bed for a much-needed nap.

His cell phone rattled him awake just after 4:30. It was Dan Wolfner, Rip's contact at the Republican National Committee.

"Hey, Rip, I'm sorry, man.   But I wanted to tell you personally."

"Tell me what?"

"Chairman Bailey is sending you a letter canceling your contract. You're out, man. Sorry."

"Just like that?"

"Yeah, just like that."

"Well, Dan, that sucks a big one. What's the reason?"

"What, you don't know? It's all over CNN, for God's sake!"

"What's all over CNN?"

"Rip! You whipped up on a black preacher on the national news, man! President Waddell got boxed in and had no choice but to put your head on a platter. Man, when you step in the shit you step in deep!"

"It's all bullshit, Dan. You know that."

"It doesn't matter, man. And I know it sucks. Shit, if you were a Democrat who got this famous this fast, you'd get a raise. But around here, you're fired. And that's it."

"Well, thanks for the call, Dan. And it's been good working with you."

"Same here. Down the road, man. Down the road."

Rip put the cell phone down and realized he didn't have a single client left. He looked at the clock; it was just before five. Exactly two weeks ago he was on top of the world. How can one man's life evaporate so quickly?

66

"I thought you said Ricky would get tired of that whore and she'd fall overboard or something." The captain was chewing on a cigar stub, steering his boat along the coast of St. Petersburg.

Louie Barboni shrugged. "Like I said, he's making up for lost time. And I think he actually likes her."

The captain spit. "Shit. I'm sure she's figured out by now that we're not on our way back to St. Mark's."

"Oh, hell yes. But Ricky convinced her to hang around awhile, maybe go into the tittie bar business with him."

"The tittie bar business! Christ! You guys are on the run for murder! There'll be no more tittie bars for you fellas."

Louie eyed the St. Pete skyline. "Any idea what the old man plans to do with us?" There was a touch of nervousness in his voice.

The captain threw the cigar butt overboard. "Don't be so nervous. If he wanted you dead, you'd be dead already. Plus, you're family. That counts for something."

"That's what Uncle Benny thought."

"Benny was disloyal. He deserved what he got."

The boat splashed ahead for several minutes before the captain pulled back on the throttle and turned toward the coast.

"What's up?" Louie inquired.

"We're gonna pull around the southern tip of St. Pete and make our way to a place called Davis Islands. There's a small airport there. We'll dock and wait for a plane to take you away."

"Away? Away where?"

"Hell if I know. My job was to do what I've done. But I want to make one thing clear. The old man doesn't know about Ricky's little whore and she wasn't part of the deal. He should have gotten rid of her out in the Gulf. Now it's more complicated, but he needs to do it. She won't be allowed on the plane. I know that for sure."

Louie nodded. "Understood."

The meeting on the veranda at the home of Richard Jones didn't take long. A couple of Scotches were poured. Seats were taken overlooking the ocean. Richard took a serious gulp of Scotch to settle his nerves. Inviting a hired killer into his home was serious business.

"I've got a job for you."

The killer laughed. "Jesus, Richard. This isn't a gangster movie. You want me to whack someone, just say it."

"Okay."

"Okay, what? You want me to whack someone or not?"

"Yes, I want you to whack someone." Richard felt sick just saying it. He took another gulp of Scotch.

The killer took his own sip. "Relax, Richard. You've already done the hard part, except for the money. You've decided to have someone killed. You wanted it bad enough that you called me. So let's do it. Give me a name."

Richard nodded, but he kept his eyes on the ocean. "Roy Fercal, in Tallahassee. He's the head of the fucking Democrats."

The killer burst into laughter. "Is that why you want him dead? Cuz he's a Democrat?"

"No." The humor was lost on Richard. He looked the killer in the eye and held his gaze. "He's my daughter's killer. I want the fucker dead."

The killer nodded. "That's a good reason." He took a sip of Scotch. "You want it to look like an accident?"

"No!" Now Richard was animated. "I want everyone to know the bastard got whacked. I want it to hurt. I want people to shiver when they read about it. Make him beg for his life; shit like that."

"Understood."

They made the financial arrangements, which were considerable, and the killer departed. Richard managed to pour himself another Scotch, though his hands were shaking.

Rip Snyder was drinking Scotch, too, but it was rot gut. Two weeks ago, if he found himself sitting in the bar of a seafood joint in the Tampa Bay area, he wouldn't have settled for anything less than single malt. Today, though, he was suffering through well Scotch.

He was in a daze. The past two weeks were like a nightmare. What next?

Rip had left the hotel after his phone call from the RNC and driven aimlessly for a time, finally crossing the 22nd Street Causeway and finding a non-descript seafood bar overlooking an island in the middle of what he assumed was Tampa Bay.

He felt the burn of the cheap Scotch as he watched a small plane land on a runway on the island. He envied the person in the plane. He obviously had something to do; places to go; people to see; a purpose in life.

Rip Snyder had nothing.

Below and to his right was a small private marina. One of the larger boats had people on it. From his table on the outside deck he could hear the laughter and music. He hated them.

Rip ordered another round of rot gut and watched as a pretty good-sized boat approached the marina. The captain obviously knew what he was doing as he maneuvered the boat toward a slip near where Rip was sitting. It was fascinating to watch. The boat slid easily into the marina and the captain killed the motor.

The second glass of cheap Scotch arrived, and then a third. A beautiful sunset was under way – the kind of sunset lovers should share. Rip's heart ached. He wanted to reach across the table and wrap Carrie's hand in his own. Instead, he picked up his cell phone and dialed her number.

Roy Fercal was pacing his living room floor with anticipation. He had received a call late that afternoon from someone claiming to represent "a very wealthy industrialist" who was "sick and tired of the Republicans" and wanted to donate a "huge sum of money under the table."

They arranged to meet at Roy's Tallahassee home to avoid being seen together in public.

Roy loved raking in big bundles of political money. The doorbell rang promptly at the appointed hour. He looked outside to see a tall, dark-haired man with deadly cold eyes. He was lugging a black satchel.

Jesus! Was he bringing the money in cash?

Roy opened the door and let him in.

Amazingly, in such a quiet neighborhood, nobody heard the screams.

67

Rip was disappointed when Carrie didn't answer, but he rambled right into a long message.

"Carrie, hi, it's me. I'm in Tampa. I know I wasn't supposed to know where you went but I kind of noticed which plane you got on and there's nothing really left for me in Tallahassee anymore either, so I'm trying to find you.

"I've been thinking about what you said, you know, that you're living on borrowed time and all. I understand now. Hell, we all are. Stuff can change so fast. And I'm sitting here watching the sunset and I miss you so much I could die. So please forgive me for running after you like this but I love you."

He picked up a book of matches and recited the name of the bar and the address.

"If you're still in Tampa, please, call me back and come over. Please. I love you and I need you in my life. If we're gonna live on borrowed time, we might as well do it together. Call me, Carrie. Bye."

Rip flipped the phone closed and took a gulp of Scotch.

"Hannah tells me Tampa has the best tittie bars in America, maybe the world!" Ricky Barboni had emerged from below the deck of the boat with Hannah in tow. "We're gonna check a few of 'em out. Catch a cab or something."

"Out of the question," the captain groused. "Not a chance."

"Fuck you! You're not the boss of me. If I want to go to a tittie bar, then I'll just by God go!"

Louie stepped in. "Hey, Ricky, cool it, man. You guys going to a tittie bar don't really fit in with our schedule."

"Well, then, fuck the schedule and fuck you, too. We're going to some tittie bars, and that's that."

"You can't do it, Ricky. You know that."

"Get the fuck out of my way, Rock. You can't stop me and you damn well know it."

Louie held his ground, or tried to. Ricky shoved him hard and Louie lost his balance, falling clumsily on his backside.

"C'mon, Hannah," Ricky said as they departed the boat. "Let's go find us some tittie bars."

The captain helped Louie up, who looked away, embarrassed. "That little bastard has been kicking my ass his whole life," Louie mumbled. "Never changes."

"Well, it's about to change pretty damn quick," the captain assured him. "Got no choice."

The captain reached into a box and withdrew a pistol, sticking it in his pocket. "You stay with the boat, Louie. I'll be back directly."

Rip heard the commotion on the boat below and craned his neck to see what was going on. Some guy and a girl were walking away. The guy looked familiar. The captain of the boat was helping some guy up, and he looked familiar, too.

Jesus Christ! It's the Barboni guys! Both of 'em! Right here in Tampa!

Rip grabbed for his cell phone, but in his haste he actually knocked it off the table and it clattered to the floor. He reached down to pick it up and smacked his head on the table.

"Fuck!"

Rubbing his head, Rip hit the speed dial button for Carrie. He had to warn her! She had to stay away!

Rip turned to look back at the boat. It was empty.

L ouie Barboni watched the captain leave and wondered if he was headed out to kill just the woman or his little brother, too. What a mess.

He heard a commotion above him and turned to look. Shit! Some sonofabitch had spotted him and was going for his cell phone to call the cops!

Louie moved quickly, hopping off the boat and bounding up the back steps of the ramshackle bar. He came up from behind as the guy turned to look back at the boat.

Louie didn't hesitate. He reached up, grabbed the cell phone and closed it.

"You don't have to call me, man, I'm already here!" Then Louie slapped him on the back like there were old friends. When Rip turned, startled, Louie's eyes went wide. "You! You're the bastard who wrecked my van!"

Louie was talking in a coarse whisper, but the deck was empty except for the two of them. "The big hero, riding to the rescue of that little whore in Tallahassee!"

Rip started to yell for help, but Louie stepped on a foot and silenced him. "One fucking word and I'll snap your neck like a twig. We're gonna take a little walk to the boat, like old friends."

Louie led Rip down the back steps, with an arm wrapped around his neck like friends, but just a split second away from a choke hold. They got on the boat and went below deck. Rip felt a sudden chop on the back of his neck and a shooting pain down his arms as he collapsed and lost consciousness.

68

The captain slid into the backseat of a cab and said, "If a person wanted you to take him to the very best tittie bar in town, where would you go?"

"That depends," the cabbie responded. "Would this person want the classiest place, or the sleaziest?"

"The sleaziest."

"Well, that would be the Pinky Ring, no question. Nude wrestling. For a fee, customers get to be a coach and rub the women all over with oil. Quite a turn-on."

"Take me there."

"Yes sir. Hope you got plenty of twenties."

Carrie Stevens was listening to the voice mail message from Rip for the second time. It touched her heart when he said they should spend their "borrowed time" together. She could tell Rip really meant it when he said, "I love you." But would he still love her if he knew the truth about her past?

It was a question without an answer, and there was only one way to get the answer. She looked out her hotel window at the final rays of the sunset and made her decision.

Rip Snyder fought his way back to consciousness. His neck felt like it was on fire. He was sitting in a chair, but he wasn't tied up or anything. He looked up and saw Louie Barboni sitting in another chair next to the doorway that led up to the main deck. Louie was holding a lead pipe.

"Welcome back," Louie said, and he started tapping the pipe against his left hand. "You and me need to have a discussion."

"I got nothing to say to you."

Louie stood and swung the pipe hard. Rip moved his head back and the pipe whizzed by just inches from his nose.

"Next time I won't miss," Louie assured him, and Rip believed it.

"What's your connection to Shelby Hoagensteiner?" Louie demanded.

Rip looked bewildered. "I don't know anybody by that name."

Louie thumped Rip in the chest with one end of the pipe. "How stupid are you? The next wrong answer means I start breaking bones. Nod your head if you understand. Good."

Rip was trying to get his breath.

"Shelby is that little whore you rescued up in Tallahassee. What's your connection?"

"Friend. She's a friend."

Louie nodded. "What are you doing in Tampa?"

"I'm on vacation."

"Alone?"

"Yeah. Alone."

"Why isn't Shelby with you? She owes you. You saved her life."

Rip shook his head. "She ran off."

"Where to?"

"She didn't say."

The pipe found Rip's groin this time. There was a loud *whoof* as Rip exhaled in pain and doubled over onto the floor.

"Bullshit." Louie grabbed Rip's cell phone and hit redial. "Let's see who you were calling when you were so rudely interrupted."

Rip could hear the phone ringing. He figured she wouldn't answer, but she did.

"Rip! I got your message. I'm on the way over. I love you, too, and I…"

Louie flipped the phone closed and tossed it aside. "So she's on the way over, huh? Won't this be a fun little rendezvous?"

Carrie stared at her cell phone with disgust. The damn things never work when you really need them. She had lost Rip in mid-sentence.

"How much further?" she asked the cabbie.

"Not far. Don't worry, miss. I'll get you there."

Carrie stared out the window at the gathering darkness and prayed she was doing the right thing.

The cabbie pulled up in front of the Pinky Ring and handed the captain a business card. "When you get ready to leave, call me from inside and stay inside. It's a bad neighborhood. You understand?"

The captain took the card and slipped it in his pocket. "Thanks."

The cabbie sped away quickly. The captain looked around and decided the cabbie was right. Most of the buildings were boarded up or burned out.

The front door to the Pinky Ring was, not surprisingly, pink. He pulled it open and stepped into a brightly lit foyer. Ahead of him was another pink door with a mirror to one side. He pulled on the door, but it was locked. There was a buzzer. The captain pushed it.

A disembodied male voice told him to slip twenty dollars into a slot above the buzzer. He did so and the door opened.

"Welcome to the Pinky Ring." The man was obviously a bouncer. He was impossibly big. The captain stepped in and the bouncer pulled the door shut behind him.

The captain could see the brightly lit stage, but it was almost completely dark everywhere else. He waited for his eyes to adjust.

"Hi, sweetie." It was a tall, black woman who approached him. She pressed her ample breasts against him. She smelled like Crisco.

"My name is Magic. What's yours?"

"Crisco."

She laughed. "Okay, Crisco. Have you been here before, baby?"

"No."

"Let's find a table and I'll tell you how it works." Her hand brushed his crotch ever so lightly.

"I can't see anything."

She laughed again. "Don't worry, Crisco. Just hold my hand and follow me."

Captain Crisco did as he was told.

The cabbie that picked up Ricky and Hannah was describing his favorite tittie bars in great detail, of which there were many. He brought up the Pinky Ring, but when he said it was in a very bad part of town, Hannah suggested they try someplace else first.

"Yeah, the Pinky Ring is only for guys who think it's neat to rub a naked woman all over with oil – and I do mean all over – and then watch her rut around with another naked woman," the cabbie acknowledged. "It's not for everybody."

Ricky looked hopefully at Hannah, but she shook her head. "That's not for us."

Ricky's heart sank. For the first time since their little affair started, he found himself wishing Hannah wasn't around.

"How about Nuts & Bolts?" the cabbie offered. "It's a co-ed club."

"What's a co-ed club?" Hannah wondered.

"They have both male and female dancers. All nude, too. Plus a couples lounge. I hear it gets pretty wild."

"Take us there," Ricky ordered. He offered a big smile to Hannah. "Good choice, girlfriend." Then he thought to himself: Once I dump your ass, I'm headed straight for the Pinky Ring.

69

"Tell ya what we're gonna do," Louie said as he stood over Rip. "You'll sit on the top deck and keep an eye out for Shelby. When you see her, wave her over to the boat. If you don't, you're a dead man. I'll kill you right in front of her. Cooperate and I'll let you go. It's her I want."

Rip nodded, knowing full well he was a dead man no matter what.

"Good. You know, it's amazing how much more cooperative people are after they get a good knock in the nuts."

The captain's eyes were starting to adjust. He thought somebody a couple of tables over was getting a blowjob, but he couldn't be sure. On stage, two shiny women were locked in what appeared to be simulated sex – or maybe the real thing. Magic was seated close to him, rubbing the inside of his leg.

"Here's how it works, sugar," Magic said in a low whisper. "For a hundred bucks, you get to be my coach and rub me all over with oil. I'll be naked, of course."

The captain ran his hand up her thigh until it touched her thong. "Do I get to rub you anywhere I want?"

"Anywhere," Magic whispered, giving his crotch a squeeze.

The captain nodded his head to a glass-enclosed shower in the corner. It was big enough for two. "What's that for?"

Magic smiled. "For another hundred, you can help me lather up and shower off the oil."

By the smell of things, the captain guessed there weren't many coaches who popped for the extra hundred. "Anything else?"

Magic nodded in the direction of the table where it appeared a blowjob was under way. "Well, that's up to you, Mr. Crisco."

Hannah said they should sit in a dark corner instead of the stage and Ricky agreed with her. He usually liked to sit front and center and be close to the action, but he certainly had no business being the center of attention.

Like the Pinky Ring, the Nuts and Bolts was awash in almost total darkness except for the stage. A nude woman was onstage, picking up cash and her thong. A few other dancers were wandering around topless, soliciting lap dances.

"Get yourself a good seat, ladies!" It was the phony-sounding voice of the deejay. "Things are so hot in here, somebody called the fire department! And guess who's here to hose you down! Here he is, ladies, Peter Treasure!"

There were about a half-dozen women seated near the stage who started squealing as a handsome hunk emerged from behind a screen wearing a fireman's hat and a thong, grinding to the upbeat music. They stuffed cash into his thong, most of them reaching in low for a cheap feel.

The music switched to something slower and sexier, and the thong came off. More cash was offered up. By the time the song was over, the ladies were delirious.

Ricky noticed that Hannah was breathing heavily and rubbing him. He saw a sign in the back that read "Pleasure Lounge -- Couples Only." There was a male attendant watching the entrance.

"Let's go in there," Ricky whispered to Hannah, and she readily agreed.

The attendant stopped them. "It's fifty dollars."

"Here's a hundred," Ricky said, "and you never saw me."

"I'm as blind as a bat," the attendant said, stuffing the c-note in his shirt pocket and holding a heavy curtain aside. "You've got the place to yourselves."

"Can I buy you a drink?"

"Sure, Crisco." Magic signaled the bartender, and a waitress came over.

"Got any Sam Adams?"

"Sure thing, honey. You want the usual, Magic?"

"Please."

The waitress turned to the captain. "That'll be twenty-eight dollars." She pulled her thong open and waited.

"Jesus Christ!" The captain looked at Magic. "What are you drinking, champagne?"

"I'm worth it, honey." He could feel her rubbing his crotch again.

The captain stuck two twenties into the open thong of the waitress. "Keep the change."

The captain got his Sam Adams, and it was ice cold. Magic's drink looked like a small glass of Seven Up, but he held his tongue.

"I'm looking for a couple of friends of mine," he said. "A man in his thirties and a young woman about twenty. I was hoping they might be here."

"You're not a cop, are you?" Magic's warm demeanor disappeared. "Please tell me you're not a cop."

"I'm not a cop, Magic. Just looking for some friends. It's cool."

Magic relaxed. "Ain't no women here, except for the dancers. Never is."

Damn it, the captain thought, I was sure the sleaziest joint was the best place to look. "I gotta go," he said, and started to get up.

Magic reached for him. "Don't rush off, baby. I thought we could have some fun tonight, you know, get it on."

"Maybe next time, Magic. Maybe next time." He tossed a hundred dollar bill on the table. "Here. Take a shower."

Ricky emerged from the couples lounge in such a short time that the attendant was surprised.

"I left my rubbers in the car," Ricky explained. "I'll be right back." He slipped the attendant a twenty.

"Shall I keep her busy until you get back?" the attendant joked.

"If I'm not back in five minutes, she's all yours."

The attendant grinned and stuffed the bill in his shirt. He wondered if the generous man would tip him again when he came back.

Five minutes went by; then ten. Nervously, the attendant went behind the curtain.

"Hello? Hello? Are you there?"

Hearing nothing, not even breathing, he fumbled around and hit the light. He gasped. There, on the mattress, was the woman. Her head was bent around like a rag doll.

70

R ip Snyder sat in the gathering darkness of the boat's top deck and prepared himself to die. There was no way he was going to "wave her over" as that monster down below had instructed. He prayed that Carrie would run when he hollered at her to run for her life. He prayed some more that she would make it. And he prayed for a quick and painless death.

He marveled again at how quickly his life had gone from the penthouse to the outhouse. That night two weeks ago at The Tapper, when he was drinking with his buddies and looking forward to a night of sex with Carrie seemed years away now. Was it ever real?

Rip remembered watching some goofy television show years earlier. The good guys were pinned down against impossible odds. The leader told everyone to prepare to die and come to peace with it. That way, he said, you'll act with bravery instead of cowardice when the battle rages. That's the best way to win, he said.

But that was a TV show. This was real, and Rip held no illusions about winning. Death was at hand and Rip was ready.

He heard a car door slam from the parking lot. He squinted into the lights and realized it was Carrie. Rip stood, his legs shaky.

"Carrie! It's a trap! Run for your life! Run!"

Louie Barboni sprung to his feet, cursing. He grabbed the lead pipe and hurried to the upper deck.

"You stupid motherfucker! You're a dead man!"

"Bring it on, asshole," Rip responded, bracing himself for the attack. "Bring it the fuck on."

Louie swung the pipe hard, directly at Rip's head. Rip ducked and raised an arm in self defense. The pipe cracked against the upper part of the arm. The pain was incredible.

Rip pushed forward into Louie's midsection and they both went tumbling onto the deck floor. The pipe skittered away.

They rolled around on the deck, each of them trying to throw a punch but unable to land anything serious. Eventually, Louie got the best of Rip and pinned him down with his legs. Louie wrapped his hands around Rip's neck and started to squeeze.

This is it, Rip realized. I'm dying. He used his mind to send Carrie a final "I love you" and let himself go limp.

By the time Hannah's twisted body was discovered, Ricky Barboni was in a cab halfway to the Pinky Ring. He dismissed the cabbie's warnings about the bad neighborhood and tossed him a hundred dollar bill.

"All I want you to do is forget you ever saw me, Habib," Ricky said, deliberately using the name listed on the taxi license.

The cabbie grabbed the bill. "You don't exist, my friend. And this trip never happened." Then he sped away.

Ricky was met at the door by the same tall, black woman. "Hi, sugar. My name is Magic. What's yours?"

"Boner," Ricky said, enjoying the feel of her breasts against him. "My friends call me Boner."

Magic smiled. "Well, Boner, you've come to the right place. Let's get comfortable."

When the captain's taxi arrived at the Nuts & Bolts, he was alarmed to find an ambulance and police cars at the entrance. He gawked, trying to see what was going on, but eventually ordered the cabbie to drive on.

"What do you suppose happened in there?" he asked the cabbie.

"Let me find out. The dispatcher usually listens to the police radio."

The cabbie radioed in. Somebody had found the body of a young woman in the couple's lounge. Her neck was broken. And nobody saw anything.

The captain huffed. "I wonder what that cost him?"

"Pardon me?" the cabbie asked.

"Oh, nothing. Take me back to the marina."

Rip's world was spinning into blackness. He refused to fight it.

Suddenly, Louie loosened his grip.

Carrie, after hearing Rip's shouted warning, had run *toward* the boat. She watched in horror as Louie choked the life out of Rip. She jumped on the boat with both feet. Louie, startled, let go.

"What the fuck?"

Carrie was acting on pure adrenalin. She picked up the lead pipe and smashed it into Louie's skull in one smooth motion. He collapsed. She kept beating him, over and over, every blow finding his head. Blood spattered and oozed.

Rip started moving and groaning. Carrie dropped the pipe and went to him.

"Rip! Rip, darling, please be okay. Please. My God, Rip, please."

She held his head and Rip's eyes fluttered open. His vision was blurry at first, but it cleared enough for him to see Carrie.

"Carrie! My love! How?"

"Shhh, Rip. Don't talk. Just breathe. Just breathe, baby." She stroked his hair.

"Where is he? Where's Barboni?"

"He's dead, Rip. It's okay."

"Dead? How?" Rip looked around and saw Louie's body, his head oozing blood.

"I hit him over the head with a pipe."

"You saved my life."

"So we're even."

Rip nodded and smiled. "I love you, Carrie."

"I love you too, Rip." Carrie looked around. "We need to get out of here. Now."

Rip agreed and Carrie helped him up. "I told you to run away, Carrie."

"You don't run my life, Rip. Don't you know that by now?"

"I reckon."

71

The captain couldn't believe his eyes. Right there, on the deck of his boat, was Louie "The Rock" Barboni, dead as a hammer. It was obvious somebody had beaten him to death with the blood-covered lead pipe lying nearby. But who?

Was it Ricky? Did the brothers get into a nasty fight that turned deadly?

The blood was still fresh. He looked around. Nobody was paying him or his boat any attention. Time to move.

He fired up the boat, backed it out of the slip and headed for the open waters of the Gulf of Mexico. Louie Barboni would be buried at sea, and the captain would do his best to disappear.

Ricky Barboni and Magic had one helluva good time. He oiled her up – every crack and crevice – and watched with glee as she "wrestled" with a stunning Oriental woman. Then he popped for the shower and lathered her up.

They found a dark corner and engaged in most of Ricky's sexual fantasies until the Pinky Ring closed. Between Magic and the cocktail waitress, Ricky left behind almost eight hundred dollars. But he was dizzy with ideas for new tittie bars, and he had Magic's private phone number for future use.

By the time the cabbie dropped Ricky at the marina, it was almost five o'clock in the morning. He was exhausted and desperately needed some sleep. When he got to the boat slip, however, the boat was gone.

What in the hell?

He found a pay phone and called Magic.

"My friends left me high and dry," he said. "I need a place to crash for a few hours."

"Bring it on, Boner. Bring it on home to mama."

Rip and Carrie were dozing in the comfort of her bed at the Maisson Westshore Hotel. They had made love, frantically at first, then more slowly.

Rip had a huge ugly bruise on his left arm and you could see where Louie had choked him. He got up for a drink of water and Carrie stirred.

"Where you going, loverboy?"

"I need some water. Want some?"

"No. Just hurry back."

Rip returned with his water, set it on the end table and slid back into bed just as the first rays of sunlight were streaming through the windows.

"I still can't believe it, the way you went after that monster," Rip whispered. "And then you just calmly tell me, 'Oh, I hit him over the head with a pipe.' Like it was nothing."

Carrie pulled him close and put her lips next to Rip's ear. "Listen to me, Rip. This is very important. If you ever stop making the earth move for me, I'll hit you over the head with a pipe, too."

Rip pulled back and looked into her eyes. He expected them to be dancing with the joke, but they looked dead serious. Afraid she might not be kidding, Rip erred on the side of caution.

Slowly, carefully, tenderly, like she was made of blown glass, Rip made the earth move for her.

Epilogue

C arrie was initially hesitant to introduce Rip to Brad, the magazine owner who had saved her twice, but she had spilled her life story to Rip and he was still around, so she decided there wouldn't be any more secrets.

Brad was thrilled. It turned out he had been a subscriber to *The Ripper* and was on cloud nine to actually meet Rip Snyder. He went on and on about Rip's writing abilities. Before the evening was done, Brad had decided to start another lifestyle magazine on Marco Island and, by golly, Rip and Carrie could run it together.

Brad bought them a three-bedroom rancher with a private pool right on one of the canals on Marco Island. He rented office space and *The Marco Life* was launched.

Speaker Alberto Gonzalez promoted Clay Chester to chief of staff and hired him to run his congressional campaign on the side. Much to Clay's dismay, Gonzalez also hired Buffy to raise money for the campaign on a commission basis.

"She knows nothing about it!" Clay protested, but to no avail.

"Just watch her produce, and you'll thank me," Gonzalez assured him, and he was right. Buffy started hauling in $50,000 a week right away. What Clay didn't know was that the money was being laundered from the speaker's bribery account in Ponca, Puerto Rico. Buffy got to keep twenty percent. And all she had to do was suffer through the occasional intimate moments with Alberto.

Roy Fercal's body was discovered by a cleaning lady. The coroner arrived just after Jimmy Flain and announced the probable cause of death was a heart attack, brought on in all likelihood by the 58 holes in his body that had been inflicted by some kind of drill. "HEAD DEM DRILLED TO DEATH" was the headline, but the paper refused to run Jimmy's picture.

The Reverend Josiah Franklin was hired by CNN to host a weekly talk show on the intersection of race and politics in America today. He taped it in Washington on Fridays and it aired on Sunday mornings, usually at the same time he was ministering to his flock at the Bradford Road Baptist Church. He hired Belinda to serve as his traveling secretary.

By the way, the "lawsuit" Franklin waved in Rip's face that day back in September was phony. There never was a lawsuit. As hard as it is to believe, it was nothing but a publicity stunt.

Bannerman Lux wanted Rip to sue Franklin for harassment, but Rip was enjoying life on Marco Island and he told Lucky to forget it. "Come down and see us, Lucky. You'd like it here."

Leon County State's Attorney Jessie Malloy announced her intention to run for Congress the same day the cleaning lady found Roy Fercal's body. She didn't want Congressman Billy Conner getting any wise ideas about retracting his retirement.

Big Daddy Malloy was so proud he was crossing over two fairways at the Wildwood Country Club just to tell people about it.

Deputy Sheriff Bill "Bulldog" Bowser was put on notice by the sheriff that he was too fat and if he didn't lose weight he would be fired. So Bulldog quit stopping at Krispy Kreme. It was like losing a friend.

For a while he kept looking at strangers like they might be the Barboni brothers, but they never were and eventually he forgot all about it.

Ricky Barboni holed up with Magic for several days. Eventually, he shaved his head completely bald and grew a beard to conceal his identity. He made contact with the old man, who informed him that Louie was dead and the captain of the boat who allowed it to happen had been "taken care of."

"You're on your own, Ricky," the old man growled. "Don't do anything stupid."

As far as anyone knows, Ricky "The Boner" Barboni is still on the loose. Most likely, he's doing something stupid.

The Florida State Seminoles finished the season 11-1, the only blot on their record being the famous "DOINK" game against Miami. They were paired for a rematch in the Rose Bowl, and Florida State won the national championship going away.

It was a glorious moment, and everyone in Tallahassee decided life was very, very good.

THE END

About the author

Daryl Duwe is himself a veteran of the political wars. He lived in Tallahassee, Florida, for two years while working in Republican politics. Prior to that, he was a well-known Republican spokesman in Missouri and the state's first "blogger." Of course, that was before anyone knew what a "blog" was. His Internet newsletter, the *Missouri Grapevine*, was considered groundbreaking at the time it debuted in 1996.

He also has two decades of experience in radio journalism. Born, raised, and educated in Iowa, Daryl currently resides in Missouri with his wife, Yolanda, and their cats, Birdie and Bogey.